Addy of the
DOOR
ISLANDS

Leigha,
Know His grace —
Judy DuCharme
2 Cor. 9:8

"Between 1854 and 1929, 'Orphan Trains' ran regularly from the cities of the East Coast to the farmlands of the Midwest, carrying thousands of abandoned children whose fates were unknown. *Addy of the Door Islands* is a story of two such sisters, who through a series of unfortunate events become orphan children during one of the most challenging eras of history.

"This book is a delightful story of hope and the enduring faithfulness of God. The author, Judy DuCharme, combines the history of Door County with her knowledge of the area and accounts of the hardships of the early settlers to give us a story so believable that you feel you know the characters of the book, the struggles that they faced, their belief in the power of love and forgiveness, and the deep, abiding power of faith which sets them all on the path that is God's plan for their lives."

—MICHELLE KEMP
Master Gardener, Vice President of Friends of Peninsula State Park, Door County, Chairperson of Ellison Bay Service Club Flower Project

"Addy of the Door Islands is such a lovely fictional story that includes so much actual fact. My own mother-in-law came from out East to Chicago on the Orphan Train at age nine to her new family to be a helper for the sickly mother. She arrived on the steamer in Ephraim just like Addy.

"I'm an eighteen-year docent for the Ephraim Historical Foundation, founded in 1853 by a Moravian mission-oriented minister in northern Door County, Wisconsin. I continue to love the facts and endurance these people have been through, and I so enjoyed this heart-warming story of Addy and her love for the Door County Islands."

—KAREN SOHNS EKBERG
Ephraim Historian Docent,
Volunteer for the Ephraim Historical Foundation

"Spunky and prone to getting herself into trouble, Addy takes her place in the tradition of such heroines as Caddie Woodlawn and Anne Shirley.

With an atmosphere as fresh as a breeze off the water, DuCharme draws readers into a tale of adventures and tenderhearted family life. Charming characters and evocative settings support a delicate handling of weighty themes like grief, loss, and trauma. Even when the story deals with sadness and difficult questions, threads of hope and joy buoy it up."

—KIRSTEN PANACHYDA

Author of *Among Lions: Fighting for Faith and Finding your Rest while Parenting a Child with Mental Illness* and *Kneeling Among Lions: Praying when your Child has a Mental Illness*

"In *Addy of the Door Islands,* Judy DuCharme has crafted a delightful story reminiscent of Anne of Green Gables but tells the story of Orphan Train sisters, Addy and Molly. The sisters have fun, and sometimes scary, adventures, all while learning to trust God's plan and their new family. I fell in love with Addy and Molly, just like their adoptive parents did. I think you will, too!"

—PAM HALTER

Author of the award-winning picture book series, *Willoughby and Friends*

"Heartwarming, evocative, touching. Take a trip back in time in *Addy of the Door Islands* to discover what happened to two Orphan Train girls and how they not only survived but thrived."

—RICK HAMLIN

Author of *Even Silence Is Praise, Ten Prayers You Can't Live Without* and *Pray for Me.* Contributing Editor and Retired Executive Editor of *Guideposts* Magazine

"For those who have read *Lainey of the Door Islands,* you will really like this read, too. Judy combines the maritime history of the Door Peninsula through the nautical community of boats, islands, and towns with an intriguing story. Door County was settled by these mariners, and in reading this, you feel like you are there. Her historical accuracy using actual names, geographical descriptions, and the challenges of navigating these waters adds to the enjoyment. The descriptions of the shipwrecks and accidents bring to life the dangers of navigating Death's Door and the waters around the Peninsula and in the Great Lakes. Get ready because the first few pages of *Addy of the Door Islands* will seem like the next chapter of Lainey of the Door Islands, and you will not be able to stop as it takes right off and does not stop."

—CAPTAIN JIM ROBINSON
U.S. Coast Guard Licensed Master, Shoreline Scenic Cruises & Charters,
Gills Rock, Door County, WI

"Judy DuCharme has followed up her popular first book, set in the water-encircled beauty of Door County, Wisconsin, with a charming continuation of the story of the characters we grew to love and admire in *Lainey of the Door Islands*. In *Addy of the Door Islands*, DuCharme relates the story of a young orphan who finds love and acceptance as she grows in wisdom and faith to temper her high spirit and determination. Among a group of hardy people steeped in the knowledge that God guides their paths if they take the time to listen and follow, Addy and her sister Molly find love and acceptance and learn to love the wilds of the rocky islands of northern Door County. DuCharme has drawn delightful characters, and the reader is richer for knowing them."

—JILL VANANTWERP
Emeritus Professor of English, Grand Valley State University,
Grand Rapids, Michigan

"Whether yours is that of a young mother's tender heart or more like the heart of an adventurer awaiting the next surprise, *Addy of the Door Islands* will draw you in and keep you! And just when you think you've got the story's rhythm, she catches you off guard. A laugh or a tear is likely. As someone who has generally preferred a biography to a novel, Judy's books are reconstructing my preferences!"

—SARA STOPHEL HECKER
Wife, Mother, Author of *Trumped by Sovereignty*

"Judy DuCharme does it again! Another gripping page-turner of life in nineteenth century Door County that continues the story of Lainey and spotlights another spunky young girl. Intertwined within the story of *Addy of the Door Islands* come raging storms, endangered lives, new life, lost and reclaimed love, impetuous decisions, fulfilled dreams, and much more. And through it all, author DuCharme masterfully weaves in God's promise from Isaiah 43:2—"When you pass through the waters, I will be with you." You'll laugh; you'll cry; you'll cheer. But you won't want it to end!"

—JULIE LAVENDER
Author of *365 Ways to Love Your Child: Turning Little Moments into Lasting Memories* (Revell) and *Children's Bible Stories for Bedtime* (ZKids/Penguin Random House)

"If you need a book to lift your spirits, *Addy of the Door Islands* is for you. This second book set in the Door Islands does not disappoint. Though Addy faces great difficulty, she is determined to carry on for herself and her little sister, Molly. Readers will find themselves lifted by her courage and resiliency, heartened by the surprises her new life brings, and wanting to visit the Door Islands to experience the places she lived."

—DENA DOUGLAS HOBBS
Campus minister in Middle Georgia
Co-author of *When Anxiety Strikes: Help and Healing for Your Storms*
Mother-by-adoption to a spunky, hard-working girl and bio-mom to a funny, caring boy

"*Addy of the Door Islands* by Judy DuCharme transported me into the unique life of an island community of faith a century ago. The time, the struggles, the close-knit community, and the faith reminded me a bit of *Little House on the Prairie*. I can picture it being read by parents to their children and both enjoying it. It's a picture of true religion—caring for widows and orphans in their distress."

—DEE BRESTIN
Author of *The Friendships of Women* and *Falling in Love with Jesus*
National Speaker and Bible Study Teacher, Resident of Door County

"Green Bay on the north shore of Door County, Wisconsin, provides the setting where the winds and currents of Death's Door have bedeviled ship captains for centuries. And while this book plies the waters of history, including what was once known as Orphan Trains, history simply doesn't do justice to the concept. The cast of characters and twists which attend the lives of two sisters, ostensibly orphans, is masterful. This episode tells of Addy and Molly, growing up in exigent circumstances, which by turns will make you laugh and cry. Judy DuCharme has a knack for telling a story and weaving the narrative, but this one might be the best."

—GILBERT C. POTTER
Attorney, JD MSU School of Law, Broker Agent, Hillman, MI

"In this compelling sequel to *Lainey of the Door Islands*, Judy DuCharme presents a beautiful narrative of the reality of two girls who have been abandoned as young children and the emotional ramifications of that abandonment. She seamlessly weaves this together with the wonderful history and constancy of a community willing to accept and help these two sisters from a family whose foundation is irrevocably cracked.

"As a licensed clinical Christian psychotherapist with twenty-five years of experience of helping many who struggle with feelings of rejection and self-worth after abandonment, I have seen firsthand the far-reaching effects of this devastation and its root functioning as a type of trauma that is exceedingly challenging for a human being to overcome. However, our Father God, Who "never leave[s] . . . or forsake[s us]" (Deut. 31:6), is at the very heart of this moving novel. It depicts the multi-faceted elements of coming to terms with figuring out how to live life on one's own. Simultaneously, it demonstrates how a loving and powerful God can begin to knit hearts together to form a new family that learns how to grow together and, in the process, bring Him glory.

"In this thoughtfully rendered sequel, the reader is pulled deeper into the lives of Lainey, Addy, Molly, and their family and walks with them through the adjustments and learning processes of how to connect with each other and with their God.

"*Addy of the Door Islands* is presented within the context of the beautiful backdrop of stunning Door County and is filled with rich history. Readers will be treated to an unforgettable journey as they join Addy and Molly on their God-ordained paths toward acceptance and wholeness."

—SUSAN C. BROZEK, M.S.W., L.C.S.W.
Director, Founder, and Licensed Clinical Psychotherapist of Healing Word Psychotherapy Services, LLC,
#1 Bestselling Author of *The Identity Effect, A Few Words of Comfort for the Grieving, A Few Words on Your Identity in Christ, and A Few Words on Becoming Holy, Whole, and Fit* and *Healing Words*
TV Broadcast Show Host at The NOW Network
International Radio Broadcast Host of *The Way of Healing* at Reaching Out Radio
Co-Owner of Resthaven Retreat House in Door County

"*Addy of the Door Islands* is a sweet love story—love between sisters who refuse to be separated; love between a husband and wife who have more than enough love to share; and a tight-knit community, whose love and support of each other is still operating in Door County today. Most of all, it is a story of the love of God, Who takes what the enemy meant for evil, and causes it to turn to good."

—HEIDI PENCHOFF
Owner Simple Solutions Estate Sales and Services, Ephraim, Wisconsin
Granddaughter of an Orphan Train child, Door County native

"Judy DuCharme has done it again. Her writing style and attention to detail captivates readers and quickly places them into the story. I love how with one mention of a town, a harbor, a building, or a name, I feel connected to the story. This is a fantastic read and one I didn't want to put down. As its prequel did, *Addy of the Door Islands* left me wanting more and put my thinking and imagination into overdrive as to what is next."

—SARAII R. GIBSON
Rasmus Hanson's Great-granddaughter
Co-Owner of Jackson Harbor Soup, Washington Island

Addy of the
DOOR
ISLANDS

JUDY DuCHARME

AMBASSADOR INTERNATIONAL
GREENVILLE, SOUTH CAROLINA & BELFAST, NORTHERN IRELAND

www.ambassador-international.com

Addy of the Door Islands

ISBN: 978-1-64960-303-6
eISBN: 978-1-64960-325-8

Cover Design by Hannah Linder Designs
Interior Typesetting by Dentelle Design
Edited by Katie Cruice Smith

Scriptures taken from The Holy Bible, English Standard Version. ESV® Text Edition: 2016. Copyright © 2001 by Crossway Bibles, a publishing ministry of Good News Publishers.

AMBASSADOR INTERNATIONAL
Emerald House
411 University Ridge, Suite B14
Greenville, SC 29601
United States
www.ambassador-international.com

AMBASSADOR BOOKS
The Mount
2 Woodstock Link
Belfast, BT6 8DD
Northern Ireland, United Kingdom
www.ambassadormedia.co.uk

The colophon is a trademark of Ambassador, a Christian publishing company.

DEDICATION

If you love the Great Lakes or the history that envelops these wondrous waters, this story is for you. If you have ever dealt with abandonment or hopelessness, this story is for you. It is also for all those who have triumphed over loss and confusion. Whatever your situation, this story provides and celebrates the hope and humor that can be found in facing life. May all who read enjoy.

AUTHOR NOTE

Like *Lainey of the Door Islands*, this book mirrors much of the history and life in Door County and its islands in the late-1800s. Names common to the time have been used, adjusted, and changed. Descriptions of the people are meant to reflect the hardiness and the heart of the islanders. Many children were placed on the Orphan Train and subsequently arrived on the steamer in Ephraim. Descendants of those individuals still reside in Door County. Some had a pleasant life, others not so much. The picnics and the name for the Otters are my design as the author, but it may be that kind souls watched out for those mistreated at that time. Door County is where I live now, and Harrisville is where I grew up. The Great Lakes provide delightful places to live. May you enjoy the places you know and explore those you don't.

Along with the many sources used for Lainey, I want to thank prayerful friends who sowed the seed for this book. Many thanks go to Karen Ekberg for sharing her historical expertise as well as providing three books that provided extra background and insights. They are *From Trails to Rails* by Paul Burton (Stonehill Publishing, 2012), *Ephraim Stories* by Paul and Frances Burton (Stonehill Publishing, 1999), and *Door County's Islands* by Paul and Frances Burton with a chapter on Washington Island by Bill Olson (Stonehill Publishing, 2009).

CHAPTER ONE

CLIFFORD MANEUVERED THE LARGE STEAMER vessel, the *Carolina*, alongside Anderson Dock. The tiny village of Ephraim sat quietly along the crystal waters of Eagle Harbor in northeastern Wisconsin. He was late. Several people stood waiting for his precious cargo.

Cargo—what a terrible word for these children, abandoned and orphaned, and now being delivered to families. *Dear God, may they be loved.* They were already frightened, not to mention lonely, heartbroken, and hungry. The waters were rough, the waves assaulting the steamer all the way from Milwaukee. It had been a while since he'd helmed the *Michigan Queen*, the passenger ship from Sturgeon Bay to Chicago. This steamer measured a bit longer. Most recently, he ferried people from Sturgeon Bay to Washington Island and a few villages in between—Fish Creek, Ephraim, Sister Bay, and Ellison Bay. He mostly traveled between Ephraim and Washington Island. It was what he loved. It satisfied his heart and paid well. And most nights, he spent at home with Lainey, the woman he loved with all his heart, at Sunset Resort on Washington Island.

But this voyage. It tore his heart. These were children of the Orphan Train. From across the nation they came, lost and left behind by parents who couldn't afford them, were too sick to care for them, who had died, or who just didn't want them. He couldn't comprehend it in his heart of hearts. He could feel their anger and fear and see it in their eyes. Would they be mistreated; would they encounter kindness; would they be slaves? Most knew they would have to work for the family who took them in. It was only right, wasn't it? They would be fed and clothed and sheltered, but would they be loved?

Lainey had shared with him that she'd lived with that same fear when her parents died in a shipwreck not far from where he now docked the ship. She'd been with her aunt and uncle on tiny Pilot Island. Soon after, her uncle broke his leg and could no longer be the lighthouse keeper. Her aunt and uncle feared they couldn't afford to keep Lainey and briefly considered sending her on the Orphan Train. Amazingly, the Engelsons, lighthouse keepers on Rock Island, took her in. They had traveled with her parents on the ship that went down, and Lainey's parents had saved their son from drowning before they themselves were swept under. Lainey knew they were grateful but soon learned she was loved.

Clifford shook himself from his thoughts. He'd been asked to take this trip and deliver the children to Door County since he'd traveled the seas himself so many times. He found himself almost in tears every time he looked at these dear ones. He allowed two at a time to come into the steering room with him for a few minutes. But then, the seas turned angry with a big blow. The nurses who traveled with the children got sick, as did many of the children. But now they were here, and families had waited two hours past the expected time.

The children all had tags with the name and address of the family taking them in. Clifford decided to embrace each one as they left the ship. He stood at the base of the plank, placed his arm around each child, and then called out the name of the family. As he hugged each child, he asked God to take care of them. A few clung to him, fearful of what was ahead. Two pushed him away. He understood their anger. It was the hurt that dwelt deep within them. A few giggled. They were ready. *Thank you, God.*

The greetings were awkward for most families. Clifford's heart warmed at the two families that quickly embraced the youngsters and offered cookies and cheese before lifting them into their carriages to convey them to new homes. A few just pointed to their wagons, offering barely a hand to help them into the wagon. The tears he saw running down those young faces as they pulled away from the dock haunted his soul. Could he say something? Could he help? *Lord, help them, please.*

One family still had not arrived. All the children except two little girls were gone.

"So, nobody's coming. It's okay. We've taken care of each other for a while. We'll be fine." The young lady, perhaps eleven years of age, grabbed the other. "Come on, Sissy; we'll find some food. You and I, we'll take care of each other." She started toward the road.

"Whoa, young lady." Clifford trotted after them and took the younger girl's hand in his. She was slight, perhaps malnourished, with wispy, blonde hair that went every direction on her head.

She looked up at him with big, brown eyes. "Mr. Captain, where are the people for us? Don't they want us anymore already?" A tear slid down her cheek.

The older girl put her hands on her hip. "Sissy, we talked about this. We can take care of ourselves. We did it already. We can do it again. I didn't want to go on that Orphan Train, anyway. The time on the ship was better, even when everybody got sick." She chuckled. "That was the best part—up and down, up and down. We might just like it here. Maybe I'll get a job on one of these ships."

Clifford smiled. He dropped down on one knee. "Well, young lady, we need to wait for your people. Let me read your tag. And what is your name?"

"It's Adeline, but everyone calls me Addy. My sister is Amolia, but nobody calls her that. It's either Molly or Sissy."

"Well, Addy and Molly, I'm Clifford. I'm pleased to meet you. May I read your tag?"

Addy sighed and lifted her wrist for Clifford to read. "'Gyda and Charles Bergman—one child—preferable a boy or possibly a strong girl.' Addy, I think you probably are a strong girl. But it says 'one child.' Molly, let me see your tag."

Addy raised her chin and pulled her sister close. "It's gone. I pulled it off and ripped it up."

Clifford raised his eyebrows and looked at both girls. "But . . . "

"They were going to split us in Milwaukee, and Sissy had a fit." She pushed out her chest. "I did, too. We're family—the only family we got—so if they don't want both of us, well, we're not going."

"How did you get her on the ship without a tag?"

Addy rolled her eyes. "Mr. Captain, we just did it."

"Okay, let me look at the back of the tag to see if their address is there."

"I can read, Mr. Captain. I already memorized it. It says Chambers Island. Why would they name a town with the word *island* in it? I mean, I get Fish Creek. They obviously have a creek there. Baileys Harbor must be on a harbor, and Sister Bay is next to a bay. I saw all those names on other kids' tags. But *island*. What's that about?"

Clifford wiped his hand over his forehead. "It is an island." He turned and faced the bay. "Look, girls, see that island way out there?

That's Chambers Island. That's why they're not here. It's too rough for them to come in today. I can take you out there tomorrow before I go home. I live on an island as well. Washington Island."

"Are there a lot of people out there?"

"There are on Washington Island. Not so many on Chambers."

"Well, I guess we can explore a lot, Sissy." She placed her arm around Molly. "But doesn't look like we could run away if we don't like it. I was counting on that." She puffed her cheeks and blew out a big breath.

Molly whimpered. "I'm hungry, Addy."

Clifford took her hand. "You two come with me. There's a store just a short walk from here. They serve sandwiches. We can eat there. I'm hungry, too."

"So, Mr. Captain, where do we sleep tonight? We've slept on the ground before, so where do you think we should go?" Addy had her hands on her hips again.

"You can stay on the ship tonight again. I think the nurses are doing that."

"Nope. I watched them leave. They didn't like the ship; they got sick. I heard them say they'd find a hotel and then, even if the waters weren't rough tomorrow, they'd hire a wagon to take them back. They're gone, Mr. Captain."

Clifford nodded his head and forced a smile. "Well, I have a smaller boat than the steamer. I'll take you to meet the Bergmans in the morning. But I'm delighted to have your company for a light dinner tonight."

Molly giggled. She looked at her big sister. "I like him, Addy."

Rather than take Clifford's hand, Addy took Molly's other hand.

August Olson looked up as Clifford entered Olson's Supply. "Well, well. Clifford, how are you? Are these your new charges from the Orphan Train?"

"Oh, no, no. Their family is the Bergmans on Chambers Island. Probably, this blow kept them home. So, we're all hungry. How about some chicken sandwiches?"

"Coming right up. It's on me, Clifford. I'm assuming you'll need to supervise overnight and deliver them tomorrow. I can help out with dinner. Tell me, young ladies, would you each like to have a piece of candy? I have two jars over there. You can each get one piece from each jar. I'm sorry your family wasn't able to get here. I think you'll like the Bergmans." August waited till the girls walked to the candy jars and discussed which candy they wanted. "Clifford, I talked to the Bergmans when they were here last week. I think they said they were getting one child, and a boy at that."

Clifford shook his head. "They're sisters. Sure hope it works out."

August nodded. "Let me get those sandwiches. I'll get them each a glass of milk. Would you like some coffee? I still have some."

"Thank you."

Molly walked up and leaned against Clifford. "I like you, Mr. Captain."

The girls' eyes grew wide when they saw the sandwiches, piled high with sliced chicken and cheese. August set them on a small table in the corner of the store. Molly squealed when she saw the glasses of milk. "Mister, this is really nice. Thank you."

August smiled and touched his chest. "You just eat up. Maybe we have some cookies in the back for dessert." He winked at the girls and turned to Clifford. "I sure hope the Bergmans appreciate what gifts these children are. I can see big hearts in them." He patted Clifford on his shoulder and went to the back of the store, returning with a cookie for each girl.

The steamer crew had cleaned and prepared the ship for passengers traveling the next day. Even though a new captain would take over, they made accommodations for Clifford and the girls to spend the night. They opened a small cabin for the girls while Clifford bedded down on one of the lounge couches. The blow lessened as the night went on, and by morning the seas calmed.

Clifford rose early, concerned that Addy might just run away if she had the chance. He peeked into their cabin, and the girls remained sound asleep. More than an hour later, they stumbled out of the small cabin rubbing their eyes.

Clifford stood. "Are you hungry? Shall we go back to Olson's Supply and get some breakfast?"

Molly grinned. "You sure take care of us nice. How come?"

Clifford smiled. "That's just what folks do. Kindness is part of life."

Addy raked her hands through her hair. It was shorter than Molly's and a bit darker, but just as unruly. "We ain't seen a whole lot of that. So, we do thank you. Come on, Molly. Let's go."

The girls fetched their small bags, and he folded his blankets, setting them on the pillow provided him. A crewman stood nearby and nodded. "We got it, Captain. Have a good day. Get those little ones to a family."

Addy peered at the young man, then looked at Clifford. "You people up here sure talk nice, too. Do they really mean it?"

"They do, Miss Addy. And I think we can get a pretty good breakfast, but we should get going. Ready?"

"Ready, Mr. Captain." Molly pulled Addy behind her down the plank and hurried toward Olson's.

August grinned as the trio came through the door. Aromas of fresh coffee and baked goods filled the air. "I had a feeling you'd be here before you went to Chambers. I hope you like scrambled eggs and pancakes."

"Pancakes? Really? It's been a mighty long time since I had pancakes." Addy's grin filled her whole face.

The girls licked their sticky fingers covered with syrup and giggled during the whole meal. Clifford got up to get more coffee and stood with August, observing the girls' obvious joy with their breakfast.

August shook his head. "Sure hope this works out with the Bergmans. Like I said last night, those kids are special."

"I hope so, too. It is kind of hard not to fall in love with them in a few minutes. Addy is pretty strong-willed, but that's kept her strong for Molly. They'll do well wherever they are."

Clifford's ferry barge, the *Pearl*, moored close to the steamer. He was glad for once that he had no one seeking passage to Washington Island or any place along the way. He wanted to make sure everything went smoothly at the Bergmans'. The nurses had totally disappeared, so he wasn't quite sure what might happen if the Bergmans didn't want two girls. But surely, that wouldn't happen. Besides, after a few minutes, anyone would take in these girls.

The strong waves from the day before had splashed across Clifford's boat, so he and the girls toweled down the seats and floor before leaving. Then he pulled his boat around to another dock, where he loaded several gallons of gasoline into the tank of his ferry. The trio returned to Olson's Supply once more to pay for the gasoline. Upon reboarding the *Pearl*, Clifford made the girls stand back as he cranked the engine handle that caused ignition. Soon, the pistons drummed their up-and-down motion.

Shortly after the *Pearl* was underway, Addy and Molly stood one on each side of Clifford as he steered. He allowed each girl a turn at the wheel. Molly just held on and grinned. Addy immediately turned the wheel to the right. As often happened with vessels on the water, the turn took place a few seconds after the wheel was turned. Addy kept turning, and then when the boat almost lurched to the right, she turned the wheel back to the left. Clifford placed his hands over hers and explained to her the delay and how to plan for it and not circle the wheel too strongly. Addy turned and looked at Clifford and then set her hands back on the wheel and began steering according to his directions.

"Addy, you're a natural at this. You listened to my instruction and then did it."

"This is fun."

Clifford retook the wheel. "Okay, but now I have to go way north of the island because of a shoal that extends out a long way. Then we'll bring her into the beautiful cove of Chambers Island."

"Can I do it, please?" Addy's big eyes held Clifford's.

"Let me get the boat heading the right way, and then I'll let you bring her around."

"Why do you keep saying 'her'?"

"That's what we call boats and ships—always been that way."

"Okay, let me know when I can bring her around."

Molly leaned against Clifford. "Mr. Captain, do you have any kids?"

"My wife will have our first baby in the fall."

"Oooh, that's nice, Mr. Captain. Just make sure you always keep it. Our mama and papa didn't keep us."

Addy shushed Molly. "Shhh, we don't need to talk about it."

They continued in silence in the calm, blue waters for a few minutes. Clifford pointed out a fishing boat in the distance surrounded by squawking gulls. "As the fishermen clean their fish, the gulls get the leftovers."

"Can I bring her around now?" Addy turned to Clifford.

"You can. Now, go slowly. We don't want to turn sharply and run aground on the shoal we just skirted. That's it. Nice and easy. Okay, straighten out. I know it doesn't seem we've fully turned yet, but, yes, that's it. From here, we go straight in. Do you see that dock up there? That's where we're headed. Almost there. I think I see the Bergmans on the dock. They're probably getting ready to come and get you."

Clifford guided the boat to the dock. Charles Bergman caught the bow line and tied the boat to the dock. Clifford hopped out to secure the stern line.

Charles reached out to shake Clifford's hand. "Did you bring our young charge? Those waters were fairly treacherous yesterday. When we started out, it was relatively calm here in the cove; but as we neared the outer waters, we realized we wouldn't make it safely. Looks like you have a few to deliver. Where do the girls go?"

Clifford held out his hand to assist the girls as they stepped onto the dock. "Charles, I'd like to introduce you to Addy and her sister Molly. They're your new charges."

Charles paused, looked at the girls and then back at Clifford. It seemed a cloud passed over his eyes. "I'm sorry, Clifford. We requested a boy. Well, I guess we mentioned possibly a strong girl. But we want only one. That's all we have room for, and we need someone to help with a lot of tough farm work. Gyda is none too strong, and two children, especially both girls, won't do for us. We'll take the one—the older one—if she's strong."

Addy and Molly backed up and frowned. Addy wrapped her arms protectively around Molly. "Nobody separates us. We're sisters. We're family, and we stay together. Mr. Captain, just take us back. We'll manage."

Clifford placed his hand on Addy's shoulder, and she flinched. "Now, now, just wait." He turned back to Mr. Bergman. "Charles, these girls have traveled a long way. All the other children went to their new homes yesterday. Trust me, you will love these girls, and I'm sure they'll work hard for you. Get Gyda and let her meet them. You'll see. Look, here she comes now."

Gyda walked slowly down the dock to join her husband. Her frailness was evident in her thin body and careful walk. Clifford hadn't seen her for a long time and wondered if she was ill.

"Is our boy here, Charles? Hello, Clifford. Thank you for coming all the way out here."

Charles took her hand. "There's no boy—only two girls, sisters. They refuse to be separated."

Gyda tilted her head. "They can refuse to be separated? That's surprising. But, Charles, we can manage only *one* child. We can't take two."

Clifford stepped closer to the couple. "Gyda, you'll love these girls. They'll help you. Addy is a bit strong-willed, but a fast learner. Molly is a sweetheart. You'll do well with them. They're fairly independent, so you won't have to do everything for them."

Gyda shook her head and started to shake. Charles quickly placed his arm around her. "Don't worry, Gyda; we'll wait for the next one. We can manage. We'll insist on a boy. It'll be okay." He turned back to Clifford. "You'll have to take them back. I'm sorry for the inconvenience, but this just won't work." He stepped away from Clifford's boat and guided his wife back down the dock toward shore, talking softly to her all the way.

Clifford stared after them. How could the Bergmans not even consider taking the girls? Clifford lifted his arm as if he could pull the couple back, then dropped his hand and his head in resignation. What could he do now? What should he do now? The nurses were gone. Who could he even ask? He rubbed his face with both hands, then felt two little people next to him. He looked down at the girls.

"It's okay, Mr. Captain. If they don't want both of us, then we don't want them. Can you take us back to that town we were in? I think I could get a job. We'll be okay."

Clifford dropped down on one knee and took their hands in his. "Addy and Molly, we'll figure this out. But right now, I have to get home. My wife expected me yesterday, although I'm sure she realized the weather kept me away. But rough seas still worry her a bit because her parents died in a shipwreck just south of here."

Molly's eyes grew large. "A shipwreck? Near here? Ohhh."

Addy stared at Clifford. "Her parents died? She was an orphan? Like us? Who took care of her?"

Clifford smiled and stood up. "Well, her aunt and uncle, for a while. But then her uncle broke his leg and lost his job, so they didn't know if they could care for her."

Addy shook her head. "Wow, that's tough. That's what happened to us. Our papa got injured and lost his job, and they couldn't keep us anymore." She leaned in close and whispered. "And Mama was sick.

Papa said she was dying. That's why they sent us away. We don't know if she, well . . . if she . . . you know, if she's still here."

Clifford put his arm around her. "I understand, Addy. My wife was taken in by another family. And you know, that's what will happen with you. We're going to go to my home now, where you can stay a few days. We'll figure out what we need to do and find you a fine family, where you'll be happy."

"Happy? Did he say happy, Addy? Like always having good food and a real bed? That would be really nice." Molly tried to step across to the boat and lost her footing, almost plunging into the water.

Clifford caught her arm. "Whoa, Molly. Let me help you. There you are. Let me give you a hand as well, Addy."

Clifford cranked the engine, warning the girls to never go near the moving pistons. He then untied the bow line. "Addy, can you untie the stern line, so we can move away from the dock?"

Addy moved quickly to the piling near the rear of the boat and removed the line. She looked triumphantly at Clifford. "I did it, Mr. Captain. I think you could hire me."

Clifford laughed. "I think perhaps you could obtain a job as crew one day, young lady. Well, let's get going. It'll take a couple of hours to get to Washington Island."

The calm seas pleased Clifford as he brought the *Pearl* along the Door County coastline. It never got old. He loved being on the water; but coming around the bluff near Gills Rock, knowing home was just a short distance away, was the best part. He knew Lainey would have dinner almost ready, and his mouth started watering.

He'd delivered two families to their Sunset Resort just four days earlier. They'd return to Ephraim with him in the next few days.

Perhaps one of those families would fall in love with Addy and Molly. He began numbering off the families on the island, trying to determine who might take the girls.

His next thought landed on Rose and Niles. They had married a short time after he and Lainey had said their vows. Rose gave birth to a little boy a year later. She continued teaching as her mom watched the little guy. Perhaps they would love the two girls. Clifford also considered Niles' brother, Julius, and his wife, Marla, still the lightkeepers on Pilot Island. They wanted children, but it hadn't worked out just yet. Maybe they would jump at the chance. Pilot Island was so small, Addy might be severely restless. However, Lainey had lived there as a spunky, young girl, and she managed and loved it.

Maybe even August Olson back in Ephraim. He'd talk to him in a few days. As he considered a few other families, Molly pulled on his jacket. "Mr. Captain, I'm hungry."

"Me, too, Miss Molly. We'll be to my home in just a few minutes, and my wife will have lots of food to eat."

"Will she mind if we eat there?" Molly looked up with her big, brown eyes.

Clifford patted her head. "She will be so happy to feed you and your sister."

Molly leaned against him. "I like you, Mr. Captain. Thank you for being so nice."

Clifford chuckled. As they approached the western shore of Washington Island, he gazed at the craggy rock cliff to the north. It reflected white with the sun full on it. He'd heard stories that it was a ridge that somehow crossed the lakes and the land to the Atlantic Ocean and somehow traveled underwater all the way to Ireland. The White

Cliffs of Dover they called them. God's creation baffled him but raised great admiration in his heart. Everything else on the island boasted the lush green of mid-May as the trees were in full, unfurled leaf production.

As Clifford positioned his rig alongside the dock next to the resort, Niles hurried out to grab a line. "Niles, so good to see you."

"We figured the rough seas would detain you. Rose wanted to help Lainey with dinner. Hans is playing with the visiting children." Niles tied off the line and then looked up as another line slapped him in the face.

"Sorry, Mister. I thought you were ready to catch this. I'm learning to be crew. I'm Addy. This is my sister, Molly. Who are you?"

Niles secured the line to another piling, chuckling the whole time. "Well, Miss Addy, I'm Niles, a friend of Clifford's."

"Well, any friend of Mr. Captain is a friend of ours."

Niles raised his eyebrows in Clifford's direction.

Clifford lifted Molly off the boat, while Addy hopped off. He took each girl's hand and walked toward the main building, where the dining room was filled with light and good smells of beef. "Beef stew?" He looked back at Niles.

"It sure is."

"C'mon, Niles. We have a few stories to tell Lainey and Rose."

Addy acted as shy as Molly as they entered the dining room. Several tables covered with red-and-white gingham tablecloths and set with plates and silverware greeted them, while savory smells beckoned from the kitchen. Lainey stood in the kitchen with her back to them but turned around at the sound of the door. Her eyes lit up as she saw Clifford. She rubbed her belly and arched her back just the slightest. Then her eyes fell on the girls.

"Oh my, who are these beautiful young ladies? I hope you'll have dinner with us tonight. Can you stay? I'm Miss Lainey."

Molly pulled her hand out of Clifford's, tore across the room, threw her arms around Lainey's legs, and began to cry. Addy looked up at Clifford. "I think she likes your wife, Mr. Captain."

Lainey dropped down to Molly's eye level. "Can I get you anything . . . " She looked up at Clifford.

"Molly, her name is Molly."

"Well, Molly, can I get—"

"Can you be my mommy? I need a mommy." Molly's sobs filled the room as she buried her face in Lainey's shoulder. Lainey sat on the floor embracing Molly. Her wet eyes probed Clifford's face.

Addy looked from Molly to Clifford. "Mr. Captain, what should we do? Will your wife be mad?"

Clifford smiled. "No, Addy, she'll be fine, but let's help them up. We'll talk over dinner."

The resort guests entered the dining room at that moment, laughing and chatting as they came through the door. They bumped into each other as they took in the scene before them.

Lainey laughed and pried Molly from her strong hug. "Molly, let's eat and find out more about you. Okay?"

Clifford took Molly's hand and dropped down to eye-level, while Addy stood close by. "Molly, it's okay. Let's eat." He let Addy take her sister's hand as he assisted Lainey in rising from the floor.

∽ ∾

Lainey smoothed her apron and turned to the guests. "Looks like we have two more for dinner. Please, take your seats. I will serve as soon as I wash my hands." Lainey hurried to the kitchen and ran her hands in the soapy water she had in the sink, rinsed them, and grabbed a towel to dry. As she turned, Addy stood there.

"Mrs. Captain, that was real nice. My sissy sure likes you. I think I do, too. I helped your husband with his ship. Can I help you serve the dinner? I'm a good worker. Please?"

Lainey took Addy's hands in hers. "I would be delighted to have you help. But let's get your hands washed, too."

Soon, Addy carried the plates out one by one as Lainey dished them up. Rose arrived after tending to their little boy. "So sorry. Hans needed changing. But it looks like you have some help. Who is this young lady?"

Lainey handed Rose two more plates of food. "That's Addy, and her darling sister out there by Clifford is Molly. I actually don't know their story. Clifford will tell us when we join them for dinner."

Lainey, Rose, and Addy made sure each table had rolls, coffee, and water before sitting down.

"Oh dear, we forgot to pray grace over the meal." Lainey looked to Clifford.

He pushed back his chair and stood. "We're a little late in our thanks but just as full of gratefulness. Let's pray. Dear Lord, we thank You for this food and honor You in all our ways. Bless this time, especially our new visitors."

Molly leaned over to Addy. "I think he means us."

A quiet chuckle filled the dining room from all those enjoying the dinner.

Lainey took a few bites, then raised her eyebrows to Clifford.

Addy spoke up. "Mr. Captain, I think Mrs. Captain wants to know why we're here. I can tell her." She turned to look straight at Lainey. "Well, we were on the Orphan Train to Milwaukee."

Lainey pulled her lips between her teeth and tried not to react. The strong memory rose within her. Just ten years previous, she'd overheard Aunt Edith and Uncle Otis in a heated discussion about placing her on the Orphan Train. She straightened her back as Addy continued.

"They were going to split us up there. We pitched a fit. I mean, we're sisters. We lost our mama and papa." Addy paused and put her arm around Molly.

"Well, actually, Mama and Papa gave us up." She swallowed and cleared her throat. "So, anyway, I got Molly on the ship with me, even though I ripped up her tag. It was a wild ride, really rough. Everybody got sick. I kinda liked it, though. Oh, Mr. Captain told us about your parents. That's sad and really tough. We know. So, we got to . . . ah, where was it?"

Clifford smiled. "Ephraim."

Lainey placed her hand over her chin and sent Clifford a sad smile.

"Right, Ephraim. But nobody showed up for us because the people lived out on some island. So, Mr. Captain fed us and let us stay on the ship another night and then took us out there." Addy sighed and took a sip of water. "Well, they didn't want us. They wanted just one boy. It was fine with us. And now, we're here. Mr. Captain said he could find us a family. And we sure have been eating good. Thank you."

Lainey reached over and patted her hand. "Well, we're happy you're here, Miss Addy. You can stay with us until another family is found."

Molly grinned. "I like it here. I like Mr. and Mrs. Captain."

The girls and those present gave the meal their full attention for the next few minutes.

Rose stood and helped Hans down from the table. "Addy and Molly, would you like to play with our little boy? He's three."

The girls looked at Clifford. "Can we?"

"Of course, but don't go near the water. Why don't you just stay inside and play in the other room there?"

The girls climbed down from their chairs, took Hans by the hand, and led him into the adjoining lounge full of overstuffed chairs and couches. Soon, everyone heard giggling and laughing.

Lainey let her eyes go wide. "They're delightful. Did she really help you on the ferry?"

"She did." Clifford set down his coffee. "She is a fast learner and keeps me laughing. Molly is just a sweetie."

Niles and Rose nodded. Niles leaned over and clapped Clifford on the back. "You have room for two more."

Clifford groaned. "I was thinking you and Rose would be perfect."

Rose nodded. "They are quite a pair. I don't know that I'm ready to have four."

Lainey's head jerked up. "You mean three. Wait, do you mean . . . Are you . . . Tell me!"

"Christmas. Just like Tina. Hope this baby is on time, though. Would hate to put her or him in the oven."

The guests at the next table gasped.

Rose laughed. She turned around and explained. "When Lainey's little sister was born early and we were all there in the lighthouse on Rock Island in the middle of a blizzard, she needed to be kept warm.

We used the warming oven on the top of the stove and took turns watching her. Now, she's six."

The guests visibly relaxed and continued visiting with one another as they finished their meal. They stood, thanked Lainey for the dinner, and exited the building.

Lainey hurried around the table to Rose and hugged her. "I'm so excited for you. How wonderful! But wait, what about teaching?"

"Well, I'll take some time off. There is a promising young woman in my school who I think could take my place for a while." She winked. "Then I think perhaps Sunset Resort could be a place my two little ones would thrive a couple days a week while I teach."

"You know I'd love it."

"And my ma will help, too. We went to see her yesterday, and she's so excited. It's funny. I was there when all my siblings were born. I especially remember when David and Catherine were born. My ma was so happy and so in love, just like we were when Hans was born. But for her grandchildren . . . She's so silly. She clapped her hand and hugged me over and over. She even danced around the room."

"I like your little boy, Miss Rose." Rose turned to see Addy holding Hans' hand and standing next to her. "Did you say you're going to have another baby?"

"Why, yes, I did. At Christmas."

"And Mrs. Captain is having one in the fall."

"She is."

Addy stretched to her full height and then gazed around the room before letting her gaze land fully on Rose. "I'm good with little ones. I'd be right honored if you'd let me stay and help you out. I peeked out and saw a bunch of cabins out there. Maybe Molly and I could stay in one and pay for our keep by helping out with these babies. Mr. Captain said I'm a fast learner and a good worker. I'd really like to work on the ships, but I could help out with all the kids if need be. Would you think on it, Miss Rose?" She turned. "You, too, Mrs. Captain?"

Lainey stood. "Miss Addy, we'll think on it. But right now, I could use some help cleaning up this dining room and the kitchen. Would you like to help?"

Addy and Molly cleared the table and returned all the dishes to the kitchen. Rose gathered the leftover food and put it in the cellar ice box. Lainey was finishing up the dishes when Rose joined her in the kitchen.

Lainey extended a tired smile to Rose. "I just sent the girls out to the cabin. Clifford went to get what little belongings they have off the boat. I'll go tuck them in when I'm done here. I'm sure you need to get home soon. It is almost sunset. Maybe we should all watch it together first."

"I hear Hans sounding a little fussy. We should get him home to bed. He sure enjoyed playing with the girls." Rose placed a hand on Lainey's shoulder. Her friend turned to face her. "Lainey, those girls are special. I could be very tempted to take them. But Addy is right. This is an excellent place for them. You would be a perfect mother to them. Whomever you choose to be their next family—and right now, you and Clifford will make that decision—make sure they'll love those girls."

Lainey placed her soapy hand on Rose's. "We will choose well. I don't know if I could take them." She patted her stomach. "This little one will take all my attention, plus tending to the resort—especially when Clifford is gone—and you'll be starting to teach, and then I'll have Hans a couple days, not to mention your next one, on occasion. I think my hands are full. I wonder if Julius and Marla would be the perfect couple. I know they want children so very much. I'm not sure how Addy would do on that tiny island, but it might work out. I don't think it's us, but I will think on it as Addy suggests."

A dish slipped out of Lainey's grasp. "Oh my, I must be tired."

Rose grabbed a broom and swept up the broken pieces. "There. There. All cleaned up. Don't worry. I'll be praying for those girls. God knows where they should be."

Lainey nodded. "You're right, and if He has chosen us, so be it. But we have time to consider, pray, and be sure."

Rose called to Niles and Hans. They said their goodbyes and stepped outdoors. Addy and Molly stood by the front door holding hands. "Oh, girls, I'm glad to get to say goodnight to you. We have to get Hans home to bed. He really enjoyed playing with you. I think Clifford and Lainey want to watch the sunset with you."

Addy tilted her head. "Do what? Isn't this place called Sunset?"

Rose bent over and gave Addy a hug. "They want you to watch the sun go down over the lake. It's usually quite pretty."

"Oh." Addy retook Molly's hand.

As Lainey watched from the dining room, she thought Addy had a frown on her face.

Molly pulled away. "Can I have a hug, too?" She ran into Rose's arms.

Rose hugged Molly, then held her at arm's length. "Don't you worry. You'll have a wonderful family soon."

Addy walked around the resort main building to the waterside. Mr. Captain sat there. Mrs. Captain walked out the door and joined them in the chairs by the water.

Addy put her arm around Molly and squeezed into a chair with her little sister. She heard Mr. and Mrs. Captain converse with the guests of the resort who had joined the group to view the gorgeous sky. Addy had to admit to herself that the purples and oranges on the horizon were probably the most beautiful colors she'd ever seen. But right then, her thoughts screamed louder than the beauty in the sky.

She and Molly had checked out the cabin and thought it was delightful. It had two beds with such pretty quilts. Each had a rosebud pattern on a cream-colored background. Two chairs sat at a little table at the end of one bed. At the end of the other bed sat an overstuffed chair. Another small room held a washstand and a chest to hold clothes. They decided to go back and tell Mrs. Captain how much they liked it.

Approaching the kitchen, she heard Mrs. Captain's voice. The little one would take all her attention. Maybe they could manage on a tiny island, but she didn't think it would be her and Mr. Captain. Addy hoped Molly hadn't heard, but she thought she had. A dish crashed, and she hurried Molly around to the dining room door. She should have known better than to let her hopes get up. This place was perfect, but they probably didn't want them. Just like those people on that other island who wanted a boy.

"Addy, are you okay?" Mr. Captain was watching her face.

"It's a pretty sunset, Mr. Captain, but we're pretty tired. Your food was good, and we like the cabin. Could we go to bed now?"

Mrs. Captain stood. "Can I tuck you in? I could read you a story."

Molly turned hopeful eyes to her big sister, but Addy shook her head. "I'm too sleepy now." She feigned a big yawn and headed toward the cabin. "Good night and thank you."

As the girls rounded the corner and went out of sight. Lainey turned to Clifford. "Did something change there?"

"I think so. Did they say anything? Did they overhear our conversation at dinner?" Clifford placed his arm around his wife. "We'll have a little talk with them in the morning, and then perhaps we should go out to visit Julius and Marla before I take our current guests back to Sturgeon Bay."

Lainey nodded. "Wait." She stepped back and placed her hand over her mouth. "Rose was encouraging me to consider taking them. I went through a whole list of all the reasons why it would be too much for me. They must have overheard." Lainey stretched her neck and scrunched her face. "Those poor girls. They've been through so much. I remember what I went through when I heard my aunt and uncle talking about taking me to the Orphan Train. I was devastated. It was like a cloud descended on me. That's how Addy looked. Should I go talk to them now?"

"Let's have a big breakfast and a talk with them in the morning and then take them right out to meet Julius and Marla."

"Without asking them first about the girls?"

Clifford took her hand and walked toward their room in the main building. "Well, let's just go and let them meet the girls and see what happens."

CHAPTER TWO

THE SUN, FILTERED BY THE many trees, peeked through the window and played on Addy's face. It was later than she'd wanted to get up. She shook Molly. "Let's go. We need to go."

Molly stretched. "I slept really good, Addy. Do you think they'll have breakfast for us?"

"No, Molly. We have to leave. They don't want us."

"But they like us. They said we could stay until they find us a family."

Addy rolled her eyes. "Out on a tiny island? No, we just need to go."

"But where?" Tears streamed down Molly's face.

"It's okay. I can get a job. I can do anything. Don't you worry. I'll take care of you." She gathered her sister into her arms until Molly's sobs subsided. "So, grab your bag, and let's go."

Addy held Molly's hand in hers and stood a moment outside the cabin. "We'll follow the road closest to the water. Maybe we'll find another boat where I could work, or we could get back to that first town we visited. What was its name . . . Ephraim. That's it. Maybe we could go there. So, if we see anyone coming in a wagon, we'll get into the woods, and we can still keep near the water."

Molly pulled away. "I don't want to go in the woods. Papa always talked about bears in the woods."

"Hmmm. But this is an island. I don't think there would be too many bears here. But just in case there are mean dogs, we'll find a good stick, a big stick. We'll be all right, Molly. Let's go."

Molly whimpered but walked with Addy.

As daylight crowned, Addy led Molly into the woods. "They'll probably come look for us, so we should stay in the woods." Addy found a path. It ran about twenty feet from the water and in the direction she thought they needed to travel. "We'll take this; we can go fast."

The sound of gulls cawing filled the air as the sun rose in its journey. The light filtering through the newly unfurled leaves created a fairytale look in the woods. The shadows that remained shivered at their presence, and Molly continually jumped and clung to Addy as they went along. Though a slight breeze whispered through the trees, the stillness of the lake calmed Addy. She held Molly's hand tightly and swallowed the fear that rose within her. She'd conquered a lot so far. She could do it. She could take care of Molly. She had to.

Lost in thought and determination, Addy didn't see a root that rumpled the ground and found herself face down in the dirt. Molly screamed.

"Molly, shush. We don't want them to find us. I'm not hurt. I only tripped. I need to pay more attention where we walk. It's a path, but there sure are a lot of rocks and roots jutting out." Addy stood and brushed her clothes off. Molly had a funny look on her face. "What is it, Molly? You okay?"

Molly giggled. "Addy, you sure look funny. You have dirt all over your face."

Addy grinned. "There, that's the attitude. Let's laugh. Maybe you can help me brush my face off. I'll close my eyes, and you get rid of the dirt." She stood still and let her sister wipe her off. "See what a help you are, Molly? I need you as much as you need me. We'll be okay. Together, we can do just fine."

Addy thought they had traveled a half-hour when she spotted a stick that would serve as a weapon. Addy let go of Molly's hand to retrieve the stick. Molly tripped on a root, falling on her knees. When Addy tried to brush the dirt off, Molly began to cry. "Molly, keep your voice down. They might be looking for us."

Addy examined her sister's bloody knees. "Let's go to the water and wash it off. I can use my other shirt to get it clean. Now, don't cry, Molly."

Addy pulled out her shirt and dipped it in the water. She gently washed Molly's bruised knees, remembering how their mother had washed her knees when she skinned them. Molly grimaced at each touch but slowed her crying to a whimper.

"Look how pretty this little bay is, Molly. The water is so flat. I kinda liked the rough water and big waves, but this is so nice. I wouldn't mind living here, so long as I can find a job. But we better get going. Mr. Captain is sure to be looking for us soon."

"But you said they didn't want us."

"They don't, but he'll feel like he's gotta find us and get us a family. Let's go."

They stood and turned around, and there on the edge of the woods stood a little, old lady in long skirts with a scarf wrapped around her head. Her nose stood out on her face, surrounded by numerous wrinkles. The woman's eyes held kindness, but Molly's cries filled the air. "Is she a witch?"

Addy didn't respond but pulled Molly and tried to escape back the way they'd come.

"Are you girls all right? I heard the little one crying. Can I help you? I just made breakfast. I can share it with you if you're hungry. Are you lost?"

Addy stood straight. "No, we're not lost. Just a morning walk. Thank you, but we must be going."

Molly pulled away from Addy and sniffed. "I hurt my knees. We're running away."

Addy slapped her hand over Molly's mouth. "Kids sure like to make up stories. We're fine."

Molly started crying again. "I'm hungry, Addy. Lady, if you're not a witch, are you sure you have enough food for us?"

"I'm sure. My name is Hilga Figgenschau. I live in this little cabin here all by myself. I'm not a witch—I'm just old—and I can keep your secret. I can give you some food to take with you as well."

Molly giggled. "You have a funny name."

"I know, but when I married my husband years ago, I took his name. He's gone now. Do you think I should go back to the name I had when I was your age?"

Molly smiled and took a step closer. "What was it?"

The woman's eyes lit up. "It was Engebretson."

Addy laughed. "I think I like Figgenschau better."

"Me, too. Can you girls tell me your names?"

"I'm Addy Bickel. This is my sister, Molly." The words were out before Addy considered giving made-up names. She should be more careful.

"Well, I have some ointments that will heal up those knees in no time. My cottage is right here."

The old lady turned and walked down a short, stone path to a tiny, wood cottage. The small window had plants in pots that covered the whole windowsill. Through the open door, Addy could see purple plants hanging upside down in bunches from the ceiling. The fragrance of soup wafted out the door, along with a perfume scent that Addy wasn't familiar with.

Molly stopped when she saw the little home. "It looks like a witch's house. Are you sure you're not a witch?"

Addy again pulled Molly close. "We'll just stay outside. Besides, we can't stay long. They'll be loo—We just need to be on our way soon."

Mrs. Figgenschau disappeared into her home and returned with a bowl of water and a bag of creams and ointments. "I like to sit out here, too, so that's just fine. Let me put some ointment on your knee. May I wash it just a bit more, Molly? Your sister got most of the dirt off, but there's still a little left."

Molly nodded and sat on the bench that stood next to a small table graced with a bowl of wild flowers. She grimaced as the older woman patted and cleaned her scrapes. When she applied the ointment, Molly let out a sigh. "Oh, it doesn't sting anymore. That's a nice cream."

"Thank you. I make a lot of ointments from flowers and plants, and I sell them in town. I know a lot of the families, but I haven't seen you. Are you staying at the Sunset Resort? I know they have a lot of visitors."

Addy blew air out from her cheeks. "Well . . . I mean, well, yes, we stayed there, but we're on our way now. I have to meet a boat and get back to Ephraim. I, er, we have a job there."

Mrs. Figgenschau nodded. "I see. I do believe the man at Sunset Resort takes a boat to Ephraim quite often. Perhaps you could ride with him."

Addy gulped. Molly opened her mouth; but Addy gave her a stern look, and she dropped her head. "Well, he, ah, couldn't take us for a few days, and we need to go right away. Did you say you had breakfast?"

"I do. My ducks have been laying quite a few eggs lately, and I boiled up a few. And I just made bread yesterday. How's that sound?"

Molly squinted. "Ducks? You have ducks? I didn't see any. Do they get mad when you take their eggs?"

"They don't mind. I feed them, so they're happy. I think all the crying made them stay out of sight. But here they come now. Would you like to feed them?"

Molly squealed, and the ducks stopped.

Mrs. Figgenschau stood and walked toward the ducks and tossed some bread to them. They scurried around her and gobbled up the bits of food. When she turned, the ducks waddled behind her right up to the small cottage.

Mrs. Figgenschau handed each girl a handful of bread crumbs. "Now, just toss a few pieces, and you'll be their friends."

Addy did as instructed. "Your ducks are pretty. I didn't realize they had so many colors."

"Ma'am, I'm really hungry. Could I eat some of this bread?"

"Just give it to the ducks. I have more for you. I'll get it now."

Molly sighed deeply after she'd eaten a hard-boiled egg and a chunk of bread slathered in butter. "Everybody has such good food. Can we just stay here, Addy?"

Addy frowned. "Molly. We have to go. Ephraim has good food, too. And there are more roads there. More places to go."

Mrs. Figgenschau laid her hand on Addy's. "In case you decide to run away again?"

Addy pulled her hand away. "Thank you for the food. We have to go. C'mon, Molly." She stood up and grabbed her sister's hand.

The woman remained in her seat. "Addy. Molly. I said I could keep your secret. But can you tell me why you want to leave? From whom are you running?"

A tear slid down Molly's face. "I wanted to stay, but . . . "

"Molly, we're okay. They can't keep us. Thank you, Mrs. Hilga. You've been very nice. We have to go." She grabbed Molly's hand and pulled the girl toward the woods.

Mrs. Hilga stood. "Thank you for telling me. I think you may be wrong. Please let me give you some food for your journey."

Addy hesitated. Molly slipped her hand out of Addy's and ran back to this new friend and wrapped her arms around her skirts. "Yes, thank you for some food." She looked back to Addy. "Right, Addy? We need food."

Addy sighed and walked back to the small house. "I suppose. People here sure like to feed us. That's a good thing in all this mess."

Mrs. Hilga unwrapped Molly and went inside, returning with a small flour sack. "I filled a canning jar with the soup. Be careful; it's hot. I've given you a couple spoons. If you ever come back to visit, you can return them. If not, they're yours to keep. You'll find eggs, cookies, and bread. That should keep you for a while. I also put a little ointment in for your knees, Molly, or any other scrapes you might have. Godspeed."

Addy stuffed the bag in with her few clothes. She nodded to the older lady. "Thank you. Molly, we must go."

The trees blurred as Addy charged into the woods, bag in one hand and Molly's hand in the other. It didn't make sense. She pulled up her fist to rub her eyes and discovered tears. As best she could, she wiped her eyes without letting go of the bag or Molly.

"Addy?" Molly's voice came through a fog. Addy was too busy thinking. She had to find the path, had to go, had to get away from all this niceness. None of it gave them a home, so they had to make their own home, find their own place. She would take care of them. It would be okay. They just needed to find a boat.

"Addy?" Molly wiggled Addy's hand.

"What, Molly?" Addy realized her voice was harsh.

"Are you mad? Why are you hurrying so? The roots and rocks are hard to walk on. I'm kinda scared."

Addy slowed. "I'm sorry, Molly, but we have to hurry. We spent too much time there. We need to find a boat before Mr. Captain finds us."

"But I like Mr. Captain. And his wife. I like Mrs. Hilga, too, even though I thought she was a witch."

"I know, Molly, but we can't work there. It's too much for them, just like for Papa. And Mrs. Hilga doesn't have any room. I'm strong. I can get a job. We just need to get off this island. Don't worry, Sissy."

Addy stopped. Was she going the right direction? The path had disappeared. Her stomach tightened. She took a deep breath. Just stay close to the water. Eventually, she'd find a port, where boats would come and go. She turned a full circle, peering through the woods. There, a glimmer of water through the trees. Not too far away. Good. She needed to keep that on her right. Otherwise, she'd end up right back at Sunset Resort. Working at Sunset Resort and being part of Mr.

and Mrs. Captain's family would have been great. But no, don't think that. She'd had enough of not being wanted. She and Molly would find their own way. Molly stumbled.

"Molly, I'm sorry. I'm going too fast. I'll slow down a bit. We'll find a boat."

"What if it gets dark, Addy?"

"I'm sure we'll find a boat today, but if not, we'll find a place for overnight. There's probably a barn or two we could get in. You'd like that. Maybe cows or sheep."

Molly giggled. "Wouldn't they be surprised if we showed up? Maybe we could feed them some of Mrs. Hilga's bread."

"Yes. Yes. That's what we'll do."

Addy heard the clop-clop of horses. "Shhh, Molly. Let's sit down. We can't let them find us."

Molly's eyes grew big and filled with tears. "But . . . "

Addy put a finger to her mouth. "No, shhh."

She recognized Mr. Captain's voice. "Addy! Molly! Are you there?"

Molly's eyes pleaded with Addy, but Addy shook her head.

As the sound faded in the distance, Addy stood. "Let's go."

Twenty minutes passed with no conversation. The trees grew thicker and the path more difficult to discern. Addy was so preoccupied with climbing over fallen trees and searching the path that she hadn't looked around. Once more, she stopped. "Where did the water go? I don't see the water." She stuffed down the fear that gripped her. Maybe it was hunger, not fear. "Let's have that soup now, Molly. Don't worry. We'll find our way."

"Are we lost?" Molly's chin trembled.

Addy knew tears would soon follow. "No, Molly. Here's a nice log we can sit on." She pulled the jar of soup out of the little bag and felt around inside and located the spoons.

"Those are pretty spoons, Addy. I like them." The silver stems were a bit tarnished but displayed a curvy filigree in the shape of a swan.

Addy smiled as she removed the metal twist cap of the jar. "Mmm. It smells good. Here, you take the first spoonful."

The girls took turns and, with every spoonful, gained courage.

"This is truly the best soup I've ever had." Addy handed the jar back to Molly. "You get the last of it. I bet you could just drink it now."

Molly giggled and tipped the jar up to gulp the remaining soup. "I feel better, Addy."

"Good, time to go now. The sun is pretty high, so it must be getting close to noon. I think we need to go south, and I think south is this way. Papa was going to give me his compass, but he never did. He must've forgot."

Not long after, they came to a clearing. Addy stopped. "There's a house. We don't want to meet anybody now unless there's a boat." Just then, a horn bellowed. The girls jumped. "Molly, I think that's a boat horn. We have to hurry."

They stepped into the clearing and noticed a road in front of the house. Addy chose to take the road. They could return to the woods if they heard a wagon. She saw a port in the distance and a boat at a dock.

"Look, Sissy, a boat. Let's see if we can get a ride." She stopped and turned to face her sister. "I'll do the talking, Molly. No frowning or crying. Okay?"

Molly nodded her head. "Okay."

The sun shone bright overhead. This would work. She would offer to pay for the trip in time or with work on the boat. She was a good worker. Even Mr. Captain said so. She chewed her bottom lip as twinges of guilt swept through her. Mr. Captain had been so nice. But Mrs. Captain couldn't take them. It was okay. She and Molly would manage. She slowed her walk as they approached the boat, hoping to hide her eagerness.

CHAPTER THREE

THE WATER IN THE PORT had a slight chop to it, with a bit of white at the tops of the small waves. The scent of fish and the odor of horse droppings filled the air. Addy decided it must be early afternoon—enough time to get to the mainland and find shelter for the night and a job.

The man on the boat loaded boxes of produce and a few crates full of chickens. He smiled as the girls approached. "Good morning, young ladies. A beautiful day, is it not?"

"Yes, sir." Addy approached and stood as straight as she could. "We would like to go to Ephraim. Do you think you could take us there? I could pay you back once I have job. I'm a good worker, and I can help on your boat if you need it."

"Well, now, that's quite an offer, young lady. I don't go to Ephraim much, but I do visit Newport Town now and then, and that is on the mainland." The man held out his hand. "I'm Rasmus Hanson. Please come aboard. I do have to be on my way. I'm dropping off groceries at Pilot Island and Rock Island, and I could use the help. We can discuss a trip to Newport Town on the way, and I can see how you work. And then we can stop at my home for dinner with my family. My daughter, Catherine, is about your age. Does that sound okay?"

"Thank you, Mr. Rasmus." Addy reached out to take his hand and then pulled back. "Let my sister get on first. I can untie your lines, if that's okay, and jump on."

Molly smiled. "Everyone likes to feed us. That's nice. He looks nice."

Addy nodded. "Go ahead, Sissy."

Molly reached out to take the man's hand, but instead, he picked her up and set her on the boat. "I'm happy to meet you. Your name is Sissy?"

"Well, it's actua—"

"Yes, it's Sissy, and I'm Marie."

Molly's eyes got big, and Addy shook her head. Molly said no more.

"In just a minute, we'll be off. But I need to let the wagon driver know when I'll be back for my next delivery." The man stepped off the boat and approached the wagon as it readied for departure. Addy could not hear their conversation; but the man returned, and the wagon left. She loved the sound of the clop-clop of the horse's hoofs.

"Undo my bow line first, Marie. That's it. Now the stern line. You do have a way with boats. Here, take my hand and hop on." Addy jumped on and looked around. "This is a nice boat, sir."

"Thank you, young lady. I deliver groceries to several places on this island and out to Pilot and Rock Islands, too."

As they exited the port, Mr. Rasmus pointed. "Do you see that little island out there? That's Pilot Island. There's a very important lighthouse there, and a nice young couple are the lighthouse keepers."

"Everyone here is very kind." Addy walked to the bow and let the wind blow in her face. "I love being out on the water. I don't even mind when it's rough. I was the only one who liked it when . . . " Addy let her words trail off. She would not mention how they arrived on Washington Island. She needed to focus on getting off the island.

"I've found most people to be reasonable and kind here, and I've lived here all my life."

Molly moved close and peered up at him. "Do you have any more children?"

"I do. I have four children and one grandchild. Do you have children?"

Molly scrunched up her face. "Uh . . . " Looking up, she saw the grin that spread across the man's face and the shaking of his shoulders. She laughed. "You're funny, too. Do you tease your kids like that?"

Mr. Rasmus chuckled and slapped his knee. "I do, Sissy, all the time. I hope you don't mind."

Addy smiled and took her sister's hand. "I think that means you love your children and that you are very nice to other children, like Mol—er, Sissy and me."

Mr. Hanson patted Addy on the shoulder. "So, what else do you know about boats, Marie?"

"I know how to steer and that the boat turns a little later than the wheel, so you have to make sure you don't crank the wheel too much. And I think, if you can, you should take waves at an angle, so it isn't so bouncy."

"I'm impressed, Marie. You seem very smart."

"And I'm a quick learner. I can listen and follow instructions. Could you use help on your boat?"

Mr. Rasmus tilted his head, then rubbed his neck. "Well, if I did, you'd be a good one. Right now, I'm not sure, but let's see what happens. We'll keep talking about it." He glanced back at Addy. "Is that okay?"

Addy turned away. She placed her arms around Molly. "Sure, Mr. Rasmus."

The young man pulled his wagon to a stop at Sunset Resort. Lainey hurried out. "Arlo, do you have news?"

"Your two girls have just joined Rasmus on his boat. They're seeking passage to the mainland. Rasmus is on his way to Pilot and Rock. Then back to Jackson Harbor. So, it'll be three or four hours till they arrive at Jackson Harbor. He'd like you and Clifford there. I have to pick up a few more supplies back at the Hanson's, so I'll let Hannah know."

Lainey put her face in her hands and took a deep breath. Then she reached up and patted his hand. "Thank you, Arlo. Could you do one more thing? Please look for Clifford and let him know. He's out searching for them. Oh, make that two things. Find Rose and let her know. I'll get dinner for my guests prepared and see if they are willing to serve themselves today. Then we'll get over to the Hansons'." She sighed and brushed a tear from her cheek. "I think it's my fault they fled. I'm so ashamed . . . praying that they'll be all right."

Arlo smiled. "Miss Lainey, they are in good hands with Rasmus. You know that. I think most of the island is keeping an eye out for them; you know how news travels here. Don't you fret, now. You know God will work it out. I'll stop quick at home and send my Sarah over to help you with dinner and serving. Don't want you overworked and over-wrought with that baby coming soon."

Lainey rubbed her protruding stomach and arched her back. "Arlo, you're a godsend. Thank you. Why don't you come and have dinner here today? In fact, come any day. We always have plenty."

"I may just do that. Well, I'll be on my way. I have some deliveries, and I'll send Sarah. I'll let Rose know and see if I can find Clifford. Now, mind you, don't get yourself worked up over this. It'll all work out."

∽ ∽

"Ahoy, the lighthouse. Grocery boat here." Mr. Rasmus' voice rang out as he pulled alongside the small dock at Pilot Island.

Without a word, Addy jumped out and tied the bow line, then scurried to catch the stern line and fastened it expertly to the small piling.

"Marie, you do a great job with the lines."

Addy smiled. "Like I told you, I'm good at this. Even Mr. Cap—er, many have told me that."

Marla hurried out of the lighthouse with two children in tow. She stopped when she saw Addy and Molly. "Why, Rasmus, who are these lovely, young girls?"

Mr. Rasmus stepped off the boat. "I was about to ask who your young charges are. These two young ladies are Marie and Sissy. They're helping me out today."

Molly hid behind Addy. Addy grabbed Molly's hand. "My sister and I are right happy to meet you. This is a really small island." Addy could view the whole perimeter in a single glance around. A few trees provided a bit of shade. Chickens pecked the ground nearby, where two smaller buildings stood. The lighthouse home had a pink tinge to the bricks. "It looks like in a big storm, the waves would swallow this place up."

Marla smiled. "It is a tiny place. These are my cousins, Andrew and Charlotte. They've come to live with us. Would you like them to show you around?" She glanced at Mr. Rasmus. "That is, if you have time. We were also just about to have cookies and milk. I have plenty."

Molly looked up and met Marla's eyes for the first time. "That sounds nice." She turned her face to Mr. Rasmus. "Can we?"

"I think we have a little time."

Charlotte and Andrew clapped their hands. "C'mon with us." The girls followed them as they ran toward the rocky north part of the tiny island.

Marla crossed her arms. "I'm sure there's more to the story." She smiled. "And to ours. My cousin and his wife passed away. Their horse got spooked by a snake, and the wagon tumbled down a hill." She dabbed at a tear. "Both were killed. The townspeople were about to place the children on the Orphan Train in Milwaukee. Thankfully, we heard about it and offered to take them. We'd hoped for children of our own, but it seems God wants to make these two our own." She looked to the sky and sighed. "And we're okay with that."

Rasmus patted her shoulder. "Marla, we don't always see God's great plan for us. You're still young. Children may still come, but what a godsend you are for these children."

"They're still grieving, so life has been a little sad around here while they adjust. I just hope they can handle growing up on this little place."

"Oh, you know there are plenty who will come visit and will invite these kids to their homes. We'll make sure they—and you—are not alone. My Hannah will come help any time, and you know Anna on Rock delights in your company. I have to go there after this. I'll let her know."

The two entered the house attached to the lighthouse. Julius, the lightkeeper, descended the steps from the lantern room. "Rasmus, how good to see you. Did I see four children out there running and laughing and climbing on the rocks?"

"You did." Marla removed cookies from a crock on the counter and set them on a plate on the gingham tablecloth. She opened the ice box and retrieved a pitcher of milk.

Rasmus pulled out a chair and sat. "Well, the two girls are Addy and Molly."

Marla stopped. "I thought you said Marie and Sissy."

Rasmus chuckled. "That's what Addy made up when she asked for a job on my boat. She wants to go to the mainland and get a job. They actually arrived on the Orphan Train—well, the steamer that came from Milwaukee that Clifford captained. The people they were assigned to wanted a boy and wouldn't take them. So, Clifford brought them to Washington. Rose was there and then stopped over last night and told us the story. She thought they wanted to stay with Clifford and Lainey, but Lainey wasn't sure, and then, they ran away this morning. At dinner, she and Clifford and Niles and Rose discussed various possibilities." He raised his eyebrows. "I think they hoped you'd consider taking them."

"Oh, my." Marla poured milk into several glasses and sat down. "We may well have considered it, but . . . well, we just gained two. Julius, we should ask your mom and brothers if they know anyone on the mainland. What about Niles and Rose?"

"She has Hans and just found out she's pregnant."

A pained expression passed across Marla's face, quickly replaced by a smile. "Oh, that's wonderful. Give her our congratulations."

Rasmus patted her hand. "Your time will come. And yes, I'll tell her."

Marla wiped a small tear from her eye. "I'm sorry. It's just . . ." She looked to Julius.

He reached across the table and held her hand. "It's okay, Marla. Everyone understands. We all have our own heartaches. But we are going to love Andrew and Charlotte and trust God. So, Rasmus, what about Lainey and Clifford?"

"From what Rose told us, those two girls fell in love with Clifford; they call him Mr. Captain. I think he fell in love with them, too. But you know, Lainey is due soon and running the resort basically by herself when Clifford is on the water. Perhaps she feels overloaded. I think they would be perfect, but everyone has to make their own decision. Addy is a spunky, capable girl, and Molly is just a sweet thing."

Laughing filled the air outside the entrance, and four children tumbled through the door. They all stopped as they saw the adults. Addy spoke up. "Did you say milk and cookies?"

Marla stood. "I did. Help yourselves. Why don't you take them outside to the little table?"

"Thank you, ma'am. Everyone is so nice here. Sissy, I'll carry your milk. You bring the cookies."

The children retreated. Rasmus pushed back his chair. "I almost forgot I was making deliveries. Julius, can you give me a hand?"

The two men walked to the boat, and before Julius stepped on to retrieve the supplies, Rasmus placed his hand on his arm. "You know, Julius, when Lainey's parents went down in the boat accident, Otis and Edith were overwhelmed with the thought of raising Lainey here on the island. You know Lainey loved it here, and until Otis broke his leg, they were going to keep her. Not sure if you know that they considered the Orphan Train, too, but then Anna and Reinhardt offered to raise her. Despite the heartache, everyone has done well. Give yourselves some time and grace."

Julius nodded. "Thanks, Rasmus; we will."

Soon, Rasmus and the girls were on their way to Rock Island.

"I think I could live on a boat. I love the smells and the wind. The waves are wonderful to look at. May I steer?"

Rasmus stepped back. "You may, Marie."

"Uh, Mr. Rasmus, my middle name is Marie. My first name is Adeline, but everyone calls me Addy. I . . . Well, I was a little nervous when I got on the boat."

"That's just fine, Addy. And Sissy?"

"I call her that a lot, but her name is Molly, short for Amolia."

Addy took the wheel and grinned ear to ear. "I'm really good at this, Mr. Rasmus. I sure hope you can hire me."

"What about the mainland and Ephraim?"

"I guess it doesn't matter. Wherever I can get a job. Everybody we've met sure is nice."

Molly sniffled. "We need a home, Addy. I don't think we can sleep on this boat tonight."

Addy sighed. "Okay, Mr. Rasmus, I guess I should tell you the honest truth." She glanced at Molly, who now leaned against Rasmus. "We're from a long way away; our papa got injured, and then Mama got so sick." Molly buried her face against Rasmus' side. He knelt and embraced her. Addy smiled a thanks to him. "So, we ended up on the Orphan Train, and that brought us here. Well, it brought us to Ephraim; but the people didn't want us, so Mr. Captain brought us here."

"I see." Rasmus directed her to guide the boat around Detroit Island and toward Rock Island. "Now, be careful. There's a huge shoal here that we need to skirt."

Addy grinned. "Mr. Captain showed me how to go around one at Chambers Island. Do all islands have them?"

"Many do. But tell me why you didn't stay at Sunset Resort. Did they ask you to leave?"

Molly sniffled. "No. Addy said she heard Mrs. Captain tell her friend Miss Rose that she couldn't take two kids. She's got a baby in her tummy and too much work at the resort."

"Oh, my. Well, I guess she does have a lot to do. Did she tell you to leave and go find a job?"

Addy looked at Rasmus and rolled her eyes. "Well, no, they wanted us to stay a little while . . . At least, that's what they said to us. But I heard her tell Miss Rose that it wouldn't work, so I knew we had to leave. I know I can get a job and take care of us. I'm good at this boating stuff."

"You are, Addy. You really are. But I think with all the nice folk around, we can help you find a good home where you'll be loved and you don't have to work."

Addy rocked her head side to side. "Well, maybe, but when our papa put us on the Orphan Train, he told me to take care of Molly and work hard. I think he knew Mama was going to d—" She glanced at Molly, who had tears running down her cheeks. "Well, he knew I could take care of us."

"How did your papa get injured?"

"Well, we lived next to a big lake. Lake Huron. They called our town Harrisville. It wasn't too big. Papa worked a bunch of jobs. His favorites were on the water—fishing, building docks, loading ships with lumber. He told me he loved the water. Maybe that's why I love it, too. Said maybe someday, he'd get his own fishing boat, and I could help." Addy swallowed hard. "Then he offered to help rescue a boat that went down north of town. I guess some of the crew fell overboard. It was a gale, but they recovered most everybody. When they returned to the dock, he went to jump out and help secure the lines—Mr. Captain taught me the right words: 'secure the lines' instead of 'tie the ropes.' Anyway, with the wind blowing so, he slipped, and his leg got smashed between the boat and the dock.

"He couldn't walk after that, except a little with crutches. He couldn't get another job, so Mama took in laundry. She did that for a few years. Papa could help her a little, but it was still hard work she said. Then about a year ago, she got real sick and couldn't work either. People helped us some, but we were getting real hungry, and the bank said we'd have to sell or leave the house soon if Papa couldn't pay his note. So, Daddy decided to put us on the Orphan Train, so at least, we could get food. He cried. Mama didn't cry, but I think she was too sick. She had a big fever. Daddy said she didn't know any of us anymore, and she wasn't long for this world. I think that meant he thought she would die. So, that's our story. That's why I have to be strong and take care of Molly."

"I understand." Rasmus let silence carry them for a few minutes. "Addy, do you know when your dad helped rescue the crew from that boat that sunk?"

"I remember because it was the day Molly turned one. We were going to have a birthday party that night. We never had the party. And my birthday wasn't till June 15, but Pa had promised me a horse ride. That never happened either, but Molly's birthday—the day of the accident—was April 20."

Rasmus sucked in his breath. *That was Clifford's boat that went down. That's a fine howdy-do.*

Addy glanced over at Rasmus. "Now, it's your turn. Will you tell us about your family?"

"Yes, I will. And I think it's my turn to take the wheel, too, as we get closer to Rock Island."

Addy stepped back and sat on a small bench with her arm around Molly.

"I've lived on Washington Island all my life. And I actually built this boat with my brother."

"Ohhh. You built it all yourself?" The girls' eyes were big.

"With my brother, yes. I'm married to Hannah and have four kids. My oldest girl is married and doesn't live with us anymore. My son, Sam, is now twenty-three. He built boats in Sturgeon Bay, and recently traveled to Detroit—that's in Michigan, where you came from—and hired on with a company that's developing and building the new motor carriages that are in the news. Catherine is eleven. She'll be so happy to meet both of you. And David is ten."

Addy squeezed Molly's shoulder. "That sounds nice. I'm glad we get to meet them."

Rasmus guided the boat alongside the dock at Rock Island. Addy quickly hopped onto the dock and secured both the bow line and the stern line.

"Thank you, Addy. As I said, you are a natural. Here comes Carter, Miss Lainey's brother, and six-year-old Tina, Miss Lainey's sister."

Addy stopped and turned. "What? These are Mrs. Captain's brother and sister? Wow."

Tina scurried to the boat. "Hi, my name is Tina. Who are you? Did you come to stay a while? Would you like to play? Can you stay?" She turned to her father, who strolled behind her. "Can they stay, Papa? They look like fun."

Reinhardt scratched his beard and chuckled. "Well, young lady, I'm not sure. I think perhaps we should wait to hear from Mr. Hanson."

"Mr. Hanson, can they stay? Why isn't Catherine here?"

Reinhardt took Tina's hand, turning her to face him. He held a finger up to his mouth. "Tina, shh. Let's give Mr. Hanson time to make the introductions."

Rasmus slapped his knee. "Miss Tina, I'll be happy to tell you." He looked up at Reinhardt. "Goodness, I forgot how much Catherine talked at age six."

Reinhardt pulled his lips between his teeth. "Mmm-hmm. It's non-stop."

"Pleeeaaase," begged Tina.

Rasmus laid his hand on Addy's shoulder. "Tina, this is Addy and her sister, Molly. They are visiting us today. I'm sorry; they can't stay. Perhaps they could another time."

Addy's eyes lit up. "Really? This looks like a really nice place. But are there any stores?"

Tina rolled her eyes. "This boat is the store."

Reinhardt stepped onto the boat. "And it's time we unloaded. Are you sure you can't stay a bit? I'm sure Anna would love to see you and meet these young ladies. How did . . . "

Rasmus gave a little shake of his head. "We can't stay today. The day is getting away from me, and I have to get home. The girls will have dinner with us."

Reinhardt nodded. "Well, let's load up the wagon. Thanks for getting it all here."

Tina grabbed the girls' hands. "C'mon. How fast can you run?" The three girls raced along the dock to the grass and started up the hill.

"Not too far, Tina. They can't stay."

With the girls out of earshot, Reinhardt turned toward Rasmus. "Well?"

"It's a long story, but I'll try to tell you as much as I can. We'll need to pray for these girls—and our girls, Lainey and Rose." He related much of the story of Addy and Molly. "Not sure that Rose or Lainey could take them, but we need to find a family for them. Perhaps you and Anna should consider it, too. The girls are delightful, but it's a big responsibility."

"Anna will be sorry she didn't meet them. Do keep us posted. I'm not sure we could do this. Tina would obviously love it, but I can't consider it at this point—at least not until Anna and I talk." He paused as he picked up another box. "What about Marla and Julius? You were just there, right?"

"They have taken in two children. Cousins whose parents died in an accident. They were almost sent to the Orphan Train. Tell Anna. I think Marla needs her encouragement and advice. I'm sure Hannah will want to help out, too. It's all so new for them, plus hearing that Rose is with child almost brought her to tears."

Reinhardt nodded. "Well, we understand loss and new directions. Those kids will bless her. We'll make sure to get together with them. Thanks for letting us know."

Rasmus bent to pick up another box. He shook his head and set the box down. "Keep this under your hat, Reinhardt. When Addy told me how her dad got injured, he'd been out rescuing a ship's crew. She remembered the date as it was Molly's first birthday. I'm pretty sure it was Clifford's ship, the *Horowitz*. That's a kick in the gut. Poor kid."

Reinhardt groaned. "What are the odds and that we'd ever find that out? It does take your breath away. Are you going to tell Clifford?"

"I just don't know. Maybe after a family is found. I'd hate for Clifford and Lainey to take the girls out of guilt. It'll come out soon enough if the girls are taken in by someone in the area."

Reinhardt slapped his friend on the shoulder. "I'll keep you in prayer, Rasmus. He's my son-in-law, but it looks like it's your task to tell him, as you received the first-hand knowledge. That is, if Addy doesn't tell them herself. Anna will pray, too. Like I said, she'll wish she'd come with me." He paused. "You know, we had to make sure we weren't taking Lainey out of guilt, since her parents died saving our son. We were more than grateful, and I think that influenced us; but you know, it came down to being a good fit for everyone involved. And she certainly stole our hearts. I haven't seen much of these girls, but I bet they are a couple of heart-stealers, too."

Rasmus nodded. "They sure are. Thanks, Reinhardt. I appreciate your prayers, and I know Lainey and Clifford probably really need your prayers now."

The men finished loading the wagon, and Rasmus corralled the girls. Tina insisted that they come back and stay a while very soon. Addy and Molly climbed aboard the boat with big grins.

"Hey, where's my first mate?"

Addy looked up. "Your what?"

"My assistant with the lines, so we can travel again."

Addy popped upright. "Oh goodness, Mr. Rasmus, I forgot. We had so much fun just running and running with Tina that I forgot my job. Sorry, sir." Quickly disembarking the boat, she loosened the lines and then hopped back on and sat next to her sister. "I'm a little tired."

"That's what jobs do. But we'll be at my home shortly and have dinner."

Molly smiled. "I'm hungry."

Catherine was waiting as the boat arrived. "Papa, Papa! Mama said you brought company. Oh, look at you. Hi. I'm Catherine. What are your names? Can you stay overnight?"

"Give us a minute, Catherine." Once the lines were tied, he placed his hands on the girls' shoulders. "Catherine, this is Addy and her sister, Molly. Girls, this is my daughter, Catherine."

"Oh, come!" Catherine grabbed both their hands and ran with them to the house.

CHAPTER FOUR

MRS. HANSON TURNED FROM THE stove as Catherine burst through the door. "Mama, Mama, this is Addy, and this is Molly. They're sisters!"

Mrs. Hanson brushed a loose strand of hair back onto her head. "Addy and Molly, I'm delighted to meet you. Dinner will be ready in a few minutes. Did you have a nice boat trip with my husband?"

"Yes, ma'am. I'm hoping maybe he'll give me a job on his boat. I'm real good with the lines and steering, and I'm strong. I listen and follow directions. I could help you, too, if you need it."

"Well, now, I'm glad you're such a good worker. But right now, why don't you let Catherine show you around and just relax. You can help Catherine clean up after supper if you like."

The girls wandered around the property and the house with Catherine chatting the whole time. Mrs. Hanson grinned at Rasmus when he came in the house. "They seem so nice and well-behaved, and Catherine is in heaven."

"Tina was the same way at Rock. And did you know, Marla and Julius at Pilot just took in Marla's cousins, a boy and a little girl? Our population is growing around here." He glanced around to locate the girls. "Did Arlo fill you in?"

"He did. Clifford and Lainey will come as soon as they can. How can we resolve this? They could stay here until we find a family. I talked with Rose. She says Lainey isn't sure she can do it, and Rose has the new baby coming, too. That is amazing about Marla and Julius, and I hope it all works out well for them. They would have been a likely choice." Hannah shook her head. "I'm sure Lainey and Clifford don't know. What about Anna and Reinhardt?"

"I think they'll consider it, but Anna wasn't there to meet them."

The girls ran into the house with David at their heels. "Mama, is dinner ready?"

"Yes, let's sit and pray."

Addy tilted her head. "Pray? Aren't we going to eat?"

Hannah patted her shoulder. "We always pray before we eat and thank God for providing us food."

Addy shrugged her shoulders. "That's nice. I like that. Mrs. Captain did that, too."

Catherine made a face. "Who's Mrs. Captain?"

Molly's little voice piped up. "She's Mr. Captain's wife. I really like her."

Mrs. Hanson set the stewpot on the table. "I think she means Lainey and Clifford."

Hannah took her husband and David's hands and watched as David took Catherine's hand and Catherine took Addy's. Addy looked around and took Molly's hand. Molly didn't hesitate to take Rasmus' hand. Rasmus bowed his head, and one by one, they all bowed their heads.

Rasmus' voice was strong. "Dear Lord, we thank You for providing this food. Most of all, we thank you for bringing Molly and Addy to our home today. We ask You with all our hearts to provide a wonderful, loving home for them. Amen."

Mrs. Hanson spooned stew into the bowls on the table and passed them one by one to each person.

"Oh." Catherine slurped her stew. "It's just the right temperature, Mama."

"Well, then, eat up."

"Sarah, thank you so much helping with dinner. I know the guests appreciate it as well. Is Arlo coming to eat?"

Sarah turned from the pot of soup she was ladling into bowls. "I'm happy to help, and Arlo will be along soon. He'll help with clean-up. Sit down and eat and then go fetch those girls back here. It'll all work out. Don't you worry." She glanced up. "There's Clifford. As soon as he's eaten, you go. Don't worry about us or your guests."

Lainey sat with a sigh. "Thank you again." She took a sip of the soup. "It's delicious, Sarah. You can come help with dinner anytime. And you can come eat absolutely any time you want."

"Well, your bread is divine. I need your recipe." Sarah exited the kitchen carrying bowls of the thick and creamy soup to the guests. She returned after all were served to fetch the large loaves of bread.

Clifford walked through the door a few minutes later, offering Lainey a weary smile. "Well, I have the boat ready to return the guests tomorrow to Ephraim. I can talk to August Olson then to see if he has anyone to take the girls. I talked to a few while I searched this morning. Everyone is sympathetic, but no one is jumping at the opportunity." He sat down and patted Lainey's hand as Sarah set a steaming bowl and fragrant bread in front of him. "I can't believe how much I missed them today. And worried about them."

Lainey hung her head and wiped a tear from her eye. "I feel so awful, so responsible. I'm sure they heard me saying I didn't think I could take them. How could I be so cruel?"

Clifford caught the tear sneaking down her cheek with his thumb. "Lainey, don't blame yourself. You know how easy it is for kids to misinterpret. And we know so little of their background, except they have been hurt. And that Addy is going to take care of Molly." He chuckled. "She is a little firebrand, isn't she?"

Lainey nodded. "Should we, could we . . . ?"

"You know . . . Let's just go get them, talk with them. And then, let them just be here with you tomorrow. I certainly hope they don't want to go with me to Ephraim. And let's find out. Rasmus may have talked to Marla and Julius and your folks, as well." He looked up as Sarah returned to the kitchen. "And there's always Sarah and Arlo."

Sarah put her hands on her hip. "They do sound wonderful. But I have three busy ones returning tomorrow evening after a visit with their grandparents on the other side of the island. However, I know it will work out. I've been praying for those girls ever since I heard their story. There's a place for them. Now, you two need to get going. No, no, I'll get your dishes. You go."

Lainey took her shawl and let Clifford assist her ascent into the wagon. "Not that long ago, I hopped up here so easily. Now it seems almost a chore to climb up."

"Well, it won't be long before I can hold the baby while you hop up there again. Speaking of, your mom is coming to assist with the birth, isn't she?"

Lainey scooted over to sit close to her husband. "She's coming a few days early and bringing Tina. Remember when Tina was born, and somehow, I saw her standing with me when I gave birth?"

"I do. What a day that was. Putting that little baby in the warming oven, the blizzard . . . oh my, the blizzard."

Lainey laid her hand on his arm. "We almost lost you that day."

"Thank God Rasmus and your pa found me. I was starting to get the freezing sickness."

Lainey nudged him. "And then I didn't see you till the Valentine Ball."

Clifford guffawed. "Oh, that is so funny to look back on but so awkward and awful at the time."

"And now look at us—an old married couple."

"I hope we really become an old married couple in about forty years."

Lainey leaned her head on his shoulder and sighed. "Me, too."

After a few minutes, Lainey sat up straight and rubbed her belly. "What are we going to do about Addy and Molly? Are we supposed to take them? I can't believe she overheard me—just like I overheard Aunt Edith and Uncle Otis."

"What does your heart tell you, Lainey?"

"Oh, my heart is ready for them—they're delightful—but is it practical or wise? With you traveling and the baby and the resort?"

"We can afford to hire some more help. The boat has done well and so has the resort. Sarah wants to work, and we have Rose in the summer. And Addy would want to travel with me." Clifford looked over at Lainey and chuckled. "She is such a spunky thing; she could run the boat company or the resort. She is a talented, little businesswoman."

"You saw all that in the short time with her?"

"I did. I'm not sure how I saw it, but it just seemed obvious."

"You've always been a good judge of character. Uncle Otis saw that in you. I wish he were here to add his perspective to ours."

The early evening breeze refreshed the heat of heavy decision-making for Lainey. At moments, she almost couldn't catch a breath. She didn't blame the pregnancy; it was her own foolishness. How could she have said those words and not realized the girls might overhear? She gazed into the fresh leaf growth that made the island so green. Perhaps she could have new growth—not just the baby, but the girls. But could she handle it? She rubbed her belly again.

Clifford gave the horse a little slap with the reins. "Maybe we should discuss this with your aunt and uncle before we make a final decision."

Lainey laid her hand on his arm. "Clifford, yes. Let's do that. Maybe we should talk to Pastor Gunnlerson as well."

"Okay, we're almost to the Hansons'. Let's just love them and bring them home with the promise that a happy home will be theirs whether or not it's us."

Lainey and Clifford quietly opened the door. Addy and Catherine stood at the sink washing dishes and chatting away about their favorite animals. They apparently didn't hear the door.

Then Molly squealed. "Mr. Captain. Mrs. Captain. Ooohh, I missed you." Molly ran and threw her arms around Lainey's skirts. "How did you know we were here?"

Lainey stooped so she could look in Molly's eyes. "We have lots of friends who were looking for you. And now we've found you."

"Did you decide to be my mommy?" Molly's eyes held Lainey's.

Addy scurried over and took Molly's hand. "Pay her no mind, Mrs. Captain. We understand that you have too much to do and that we would probably be a burden. I may be able to help Mr. Rasmus on his boat, and I can take care of Molly." She took a big breath. "So, you don't need to worry about us."

Clifford stepped forward. "Addy, we were worried. We didn't understand why you left this morning."

Addy lifted her head. "Like I said, you have enough to do, and we can take care of ourselves."

Clifford went down on one knee. "Why don't you come back to the resort for a few days, and we can talk about finding the right family while we get to know you better."

Addy turned to Catherine. "We were having a good time."

Catherine's eyes brightened. "Mama, let Addy and Molly stay here. I like playing with them."

Hannah approached Lainey. "Why not let the girls stay here? They can play with Catherine for a couple days until we get it all worked out."

"But we . . . " Lainey's words trailed off, and her eyes pleaded with Hannah.

A tear trickled down Molly's face. "But I've missed Mrs. Captain since forever. I need her."

Lainey drew Molly into her arms. "We missed you, too."

Hannah clapped her hands. "Let's all sit down for some pie, and we'll figure this out."

After cutting the pie and placing the pieces on plates, Hannah shooed the girls outside to eat. The girls scurried through the door chattering all the way. Lainey sat at the table breathing a deep sigh and staring at her piece of pie.

"Lainey, Clifford. Tell us what you're thinking. What do you think is best here?" Hannah set cups of coffee on the table and sat down.

Placing her hand on Lainey's, she smiled. "You don't have to decide this now."

"I don't think I can bear to turn them away. I'm sure they heard me last night when I told Rose I didn't think I could do it. And then when they were gone, I almost couldn't stand it. I've almost fallen in love with them already."

Rasmus nodded. "But think about this, Lainey. Right now, you're deciding based a bit on guilt. You had some similar times as a child and can't bear the thought of the girls not having the right family."

Lainey picked up her fork. "You're right. They need a home, and we could give that; and yet, I'm just not sure I can do it all when Clifford is out on the boat."

Clifford placed his arm around her. "We thought perhaps we should ask Edith and Otis what they think. And Pastor Gunnlerson as well. I can hire more help for Lainey, since our businesses are doing well. But she doesn't need to be overwhelmed by suddenly having three children instead of one."

A tear trickled down Lainey's cheek. "But . . ."

Hannah nodded at her husband. "Then, it's settled. The girls will stay here for two or three days. Catherine will love the company, and we'll plan to get out to Rock and see your folks. Remember, they are a possibility for the girls. Lainey, get some rest and go see your aunt and uncle. You need time to discuss this and not make this decision out of guilt or necessity. Let it be love. It may be that God has another family. Let's all agree and pray that God will show each of us the right family."

Lainey sniffled and stood. Hannah walked over and embraced her. "Lainey, this is emotional. I can see that you are torn. But this stage of pregnancy is often emotional. So, rather than take the girls now and feel obligated, you can take your time to make a decision. They'll be fine here. Don't worry. We'll keep a good eye on them."

Catherine rushed in the door. "Mama, can we go out to see the minks? Addy's never seen one."

Addy followed at Catherine's heels. "I'd really like—Mrs. Captain? Are you okay?" Addy hung her head. "Did we make you cry?" She walked slowly toward Lainey. "It's just, well . . . I didn't think you wanted us . . . I mean . . . we might be too much work for you. I'm really sorry, Mrs. Captain." She burst into tears and threw her arms around Lainey's waist. The two allowed sobs to envelop them. Addy pulled back and looked around. "I'm sorry to cause trouble. My papa said to be strong and not cause trouble, and now that's just what I've done. We can leave again. You've been really nice, but we don't want to be your trouble."

Clifford placed a hand on Addy's shoulder and tipped her chin so she could see his eyes. "Addy, you and Molly are a surprise, but you are no trouble." He tapped her head with one finger. "Well, only when you run away maybe, but it all worked out. You got to meet the Hansons."

"And Marla and Julius on Pilot Island. And I like their kids."

Lainey's head shot up. "Their kids?"

Rasmus nodded. "We haven't had time to tell you. We were surprised. A distant cousin passed, and the family didn't want to put them on the Orph—I mean . . . "

Addy smiled. "It's okay, Mr. Rasmus. I'm glad they didn't have to go on the Orphan Train. I wouldn't wish that on anyone, even though it looks like it might've been okay for us. You wouldn't put us back on it, would you?"

Lainey shook her head. "Not a chance at all. But tell me about these children."

Addy took Lainey's hand and led her outside to a small bench by the water. "Do you love the water, Mrs. Captain? I always liked the water where I grew up, but now, after being out there on the boats, I just can hardly get enough of that. What is that?"

Lainey smiled. "Oh, it's just growing and learning and finding out the loves and the talents God has put in you. And yes, I love being by the water. It always comforts me. Well, except when there's a big storm or a shipwreck. Those things make me afraid, but that's when I pray and trust God."

"There sure is a lot of talking about God here."

"That's because He helps us when times are tough. And we're thankful."

"Mr. Captain sure has helped Molly and me, and we're thankful to him. Do you mean like that?"

"I do. But when people aren't there to help you and you feel all alone, God is always there."

Addy hugged herself. "Hmmm. Molly and I felt pretty lonely on the Orphan Train. Was He with us there?"

"He was, Addy, even though you didn't realize it. I think maybe that's why you ended up here. Whatever family you end up with, we'll make sure that they make you family, not sla—Not just workers."

Addy's head snapped up. "Were you about to say slaves? You know, a lot of kids are slaves and have a rough time."

"I almost ended up on the Orphan Train after my parents died and my uncle broke his leg and couldn't work. I didn't want that to happen, and thank God, the Engelsons took me in."

Addy nodded her head and then looked down.

"You were going to tell me about the new kids on Pilot Island."

Addy chuckled. "That sure is a tiny island. You actually lived there?"

"I did."

"Well, the lighthouse is very cool. And the kids, a boy and a girl, are really nice. I had friends like them before I came here. I think a cousin died, and they were either going on the Orphan Train or coming here. Marla and Julius took them. That's really nice. But I'm kinda glad." Addy rolled her eyes at Lainey. "Otherwise, they might have taken us, and, golly, that island is just too small for me."

Lainey laughed and hugged Addy. "You are funny."

Addy pursed her lips. "Mrs. Captain, I overheard that we're going to stay here with Catherine and then go visit the island where Tina lives, and you're going to talk to your aunt and uncle. I'm sure we could be a lot of work for you, but I hope you know we don't mind helping with the work. We know we wouldn't be slaves. And if you're not our family, I'm pretty sure everybody gets to visit everybody else here, so we'd get to see you. I'd really like to help Mr. Captain on his boat. I helped Mr. Rasmus today on his."

Lainey closed her eyes and fought back the tears. She pulled Addy close. "We'll see, Addy. We'll see."

Lainey took Addy's hand as they returned to the house. Molly sat on Clifford's lap.

Clifford gently lifted Molly to stand next to him as he stood. "We should go. We still have guests, and they need to return to the mainland tomorrow. Rasmus and Hannah, thank you for dessert and watching the girls. We'll be in touch." He took Lainey's hand and turned to go.

Lainey gave a little wave. "Bye, girls. Love you."

Just before the door closed, Lainey heard Addy's voice. "Did she say she loved us? Really?"

Then Molly's sweet giggle reached her ears. "Well, I love her. Don't you, Addy?"

Clifford assisted Lainey onto the wagon and urged the horse to start for home.

Lainey sighed. "I feel wrung out like a dish towel after doing the dishes."

"I know. Me, too. But you need to get some rest. At least, our guests will be gone tomorrow, so you don't have to prepare a lot of food."

"But I have to clean the cottages for the next ones."

"I already asked Sarah to help. She's able to. Maybe you should go with me tomorrow instead. We can swing around to Newport Town to see your aunt and uncle on the way back from Ephraim. I don't pick up the next batch of guests for two days."

Lainey nodded. "I would like to do that. The boat ride will be relaxing. Thank God for Sarah. Clifford?"

He turned. Tears streamed down Lainey's face.

Clifford put his arm around his wife. "I know. I know. We'll figure it out. God will show us."

CHAPTER FIVE

CATHERINE, ADDY, AND MOLLY GIGGLED in the big bed long after Mrs. Hanson tucked them in.

Addy propped up herself on her elbows. "Your mama is nice. I really like helping your pa."

Molly peeked out from under the covers. "This bed is so soft and warm. I like it here."

"Do you want my mama and papa to keep you? That would be really fun."

Addy puffed her cheeks and released the big breath. "It would be okay. I think I'd kind of like to be with Mr. and Mrs. Captain. But they aren't sure. Do you think your ma and pa would want us?"

Catherine fluffed her pillow. "I don't know. I want you, but Lainey and Clifford are like family already. So if you go with them, we'll still get to see you. And we'll be in school together."

"Oh, school. I think I'd rather work." Addy groaned.

Catherine giggled. "You're funny, Addy. School is great. My sister Rose is the teacher, and Lainey is her best friend."

A muffled voice came from under the covers. "I like Miss Rose. And her little boy."

Addy smiled. "Miss Rose is your sister? No wonder your pa knew who we were. Everybody kind of knows everyone else."

Catherine nodded. "Everyone here definitely knows everybody."

Addy pulled the covers up close to her face. "Miss Rose and Niles were there last night, and we played with their little boy."

"I'm his aunt. Isn't he cute?"

"I'm sleepy, Catherine. I think Molly is already asleep. See you in the morning." Addy snuggled down close to Molly.

"Umm, hmmm." Catherine yawned, and soon, all was quiet.

Lainey placed her feet on the floor and shuffled them around until they met her slippers. She stood and grabbed her robe that lay at the foot of the bed. Wrapping the robe around herself, she padded to the kitchen and fired the stove. Soon, the aroma of coffee filled the room. She placed the cinnamon rolls that she'd made two days previous in the oven to warm.

She sighed. "Thank you, Lord. I still have enough for today."

Lainey removed the eggs from the box nestled in the root well, the cold ground water that provided a place to keep foods cool. She chuckled at the awkwardness of bending over due to her growing mid-section.

"Not that long and this bundle will be in my arms."

As she straightened, she felt Clifford's arms slip around her. "Be careful. Don't want you falling in the root well."

"I'm just glad I don't have to go out to the chicken coop like I did on Pilot and Rock and collect eggs from those snappy little hens. Having them delivered is just wonderful."

Clifford laughed. "I already pulled the salt pork out of the pantry. I can start it and stir up the eggs while you get dressed."

Lainey turned and placed a quick kiss on Clifford's lips. "Thank you." She shuffled back to their bedroom and put on her work dress and apron. Her mind wandered back to her time on Pilot Island, when Aunt Edith was overworked and not a happy woman. She had one apron she wore until it was faded and torn before she'd use another one.

Hearing voices in the dining room, she scurried out to greet the guests. "Coffee is ready. I'll bring it out, and breakfast will be ready in a few minutes."

One of the women embraced her. "We've had a wonderful time. We hope to come again. But we must know—did you find the little girls yesterday?"

Lainey ran her hand across her forehead. "Yes, we did." She quickly related the details of the girls' escapades and that they were staying at the Hansons' home. Before they could ask if Lainey and Clifford would take them, she hurried into the kitchen to retrieve the coffee. She placed the pot on one of the tables and returned to cook the eggs. Clifford had the salt pork almost done and had removed the cinnamon rolls from the oven.

Before the eggs were done, Sarah arrived. "Lainey, I'm here for the day, so you can rest. I know yesterday was a tiring one."

Clifford loaded a platter with the bacon. "Actually, I'm going to whisk her away with me on the boat for the day as I return the guests. And then we're going to visit her aunt and uncle. I hope you don't mind getting some of the cleaning down. We have a couple of days before the next group comes, so it doesn't all need to be done today."

"I'll be fine. I think Rose will be stopping by, too. Perhaps together, we can get it all done. You enjoy yourself, Lainey."

Lainey hugged Sarah. "Thank you, my friend."

Clifford held the plate of meat. "I have to get the boat ready and load their luggage now. Sarah, can you take this platter out for them and the rolls?"

As the guests returned to their cottages to ascertain they'd removed all their belongings, Lainey and Sarah cleared the tables and started the dishes.

"Lainey, you need to get all your things. Take a sweater or coat. You know how chilly it can be on the water. And grab a cushion to sit on. Clifford's boat has hard seats."

"Thank you for the reminder. I'll get my things. Sounds like he's cranked it and the pistons are firing. Thank you again."

"I'm happy to help. Arlo might stop over to eat, if that's okay."

"Any time at all."

"And do give your aunt and uncle a hug for me. It's been a while since we last saw them."

Lainey removed her apron and put on a warm sweater. She placed a blanket and a small pillow in a bag and hurried out to the boat. All the passengers were on the boat, and one held out his hand to assist Lainey in boarding.

His wife patted the bench beside her. "We're so glad to have your company for a little while longer."

Before Lainey could respond, she heard a faint voice. "Ahoy the boat. Please wait. Please."

Looking around, she saw Mrs. Figgenschau. "Clifford, look. Wait a minute. Perhaps she needs assistance."

Mrs. Figgenschau shuffled along the dock. "Oh, my dears, I'm so glad I caught you." She placed her hand on her chest and drew some deep breaths. "I don't usually move this fast. Forgive me."

Clifford stepped off the boat. "It's okay. How can we help you? Do you need a ride to the mainland? Are you well?"

"I'm just fine, young man. Just old." She chuckled. "I've been so concerned about the two little girls. Can you tell me how they are? Did you find them?"

Clifford grasped her hand. "They've been found, Mrs. Figgenschau, but how did you know? Did you go into town yesterday?"

She smiled and turned to gaze at Lainey. "Oh, Miss Lainey, how long before the baby comes? Remember, I have herbs that will ease the labor. I'll get them ready and bring them over."

Lainey rubbed her middle. "Thank you, dear, but how did you know about the girls?"

"They came through the woods, running away, as you know. The little one stumbled and cut her knee. They came out to the water right by my cottage." She related the details of the visit, then paused. She gave a toothy grin. "They thought I was a witch." She giggled, and her shoulders shook. "Such sweet things, although the older one is very determined."

Lainey stood at the rail. "Oh, thank you, Mrs. Figgenschau. They got to Rasmus Hanson's boat and spent the day with him. They are staying there a few days, while we consider if we are to adopt them."

A twinkle lit up the old woman's eyes. "Oh, Miss Lainey, that might be a very good idea. Though they tried not to mention you, I could tell they longed for you. When I bring the herbs, I would love to hear how they came to be here, but you need to leave now." She nodded at the guests and patted Clifford's arm. "You're good people, Clifford." She turned and shuffled back down the dock.

Lainey called out. "Mrs. Figgenschau, please go in the resort and have breakfast. Please. Sarah is helping today, and there is plenty of food."

Mrs. Figgenschau stopped, waved to Lainey, and nodded her head before proceeding to the resort door.

Catherine ran into the bedroom. "Wake up, you sleepyheads. We're going out to Rock Island, and Mama wants us to eat breakfast."

Addy's eyes snapped open. "What? Um, where are . . . Oh, I remember where we are. Which island is Rock?"

"It's where Tina lives. And Carter. David's going with us. It's so much fun. If we get there early enough, we can hike around the island. Well, we can just play, too. Anyway, you have to get up." Catherine scurried out of the bedroom. "They're awake now, Ma. I'll help you with breakfast."

Addy shook Molly, who grumbled in her sleep. "Molly, time to get up. We're having a nice breakfast and then going to another island to see Tina and her family."

Molly rolled over. "I like this island. I want to be with Mrs. Captain."

Addy sighed. "I know, but I don't think that will happen. But we'll be okay. Everyone here is nice, and they give us so much food. Let's just get dressed and not worry about things."

Molly whimpered, then sat up. "Okay, Addy. This is a nice bed. I dreamed about Mama and Papa last night. We were playing and happy. Then they stepped back and waved goodbye. Then you woke me up."

"I miss them, too, Molly. Sometimes, I'm just mad at them, but things are just what they are. Can't do too much about it, so we have to be strong. I do wonder if Mama is still alive."

Molly leaned against her sister. "Me, too, Addy. Me, too."

Mrs. Hanson entered the bedroom while wiping her hands on her apron. "Well, sleepyheads. We have breakfast ready and then a big day. Did you sleep well?"

Both girls nodded.

"Well, then, sweethearts, get dressed. We'll wait for you." She turned and walked out.

Molly grinned. "Sweethearts. She called us sweethearts. Mama used to do that."

Addy hugged her sister, and then the girls quickly donned their clothes and joined the family for breakfast.

CHAPTER SIX

RASMUS SLID THE STARBOARD SIDE of the boat alongside the dock of Rock Island. Addy hopped off and held the bow line in her hand and wrapped the piling to prevent movement too far forward. Rasmus nodded at her, and she tied it off. David tossed her the stern line. She wrapped the closest piling and pulled to bring the rear of the boat to touch the dock before tying it off.

David grinned. "You're right, Pa! Addy is really good with boats. I'm okay if you hire her to go with you instead of me. I'd rather hunt and chop wood."

Addy paused and gasped. "Do you really mean that, David?"

Rasmus groaned. "Now, you two, let's just see how things work out. Let's get up to see the Engelsons. Looks like their wagon is almost here."

Catherine squealed. "I see Tina. Hold my hand, Molly. I'll help you off the boat. Then we can run."

The four children ran to meet Tina as she climbed down from the wagon. Reinhardt stepped off the wagon and trotted along the dock, pausing to let the young ones tear by him. Laughing, he shook Rasmus' hand. "Looks like you brought a few more supplies. Let me help you."

Rasmus looked past Reinhardt. "No Carter today. Is all well?"

"Oh, he just had to finish a few chores. We have another small leak in the cistern, so he needed to bring up some extra water."

"I brought the supplies to fix that. We'll work on it while the kids play. Did you and Anna have time to talk about the possibility of keeping Addy and Molly?"

"We just don't know. It's sudden for us to make that decision, although Tina would love it. We did decide rather quickly with Lainey, but there was a strong connection there. Are Lainey and Clifford considering it? They do have their hands full now."

Rasmus placed his hand on Reinhardt's shoulder. "Please, don't feel pressured. I shouldn't have asked you as soon as we arrived. We just want to check with as many as possible. Please just enjoy getting to know the girls. No matter who takes them, I'm sure we'll all see them a lot." He chuckled. "Addy is quite convinced I'm going to hire her. She is quite amazing on a boat. And I may just let her help out."

The men loaded Reinhardt's wagon and watched the children hold a rousing game of tag in the open field beyond the dock. The big, grassy area gently sloped upward to a line of tall trees in every direction. Soon, out of breath, the children flopped on the ground and laughed.

Addy got up and approached the horse, who nickered. Addy giggled. "Does that mean I can pet you?"

Tina followed her. "Missy is very friendly. Rub her head right above her nose. She likes that."

Addy reached up, and before she could touch Missy, the horse leaned forward so her head met Addy's hand. "Ooohh. I like her. I think she likes me."

Rasmus picked up Molly and swung her up to a seat on the wagon. "Yes, she likes you, but now it's time to get to the lighthouse. The men have work, and the children need to play."

Molly smiled. "I like you, Mr. Rasmus. I like to play."

Soon all were loaded on the wagon, and Missy was pulling them up the mile path to the lighthouse. The warm breeze brought scents of the lake and the wildflowers that graced the floor of the woods while the trees towered over them.

Anna stood outside wiping her hands on her apron when the wagon approached the lighthouse. "Addy and Molly, I'm Anna Engelson, Tina and Carter's mom. I've already heard so much about you from Tina, and I'm so happy to meet you."

Molly waited for Rasmus to lower her from the wagon as the other children scrambled down. She looked down, then raised her head. "You look like a nice lady. I'm happy to meet you. Everyone here is so nice to us."

Addy scurried up and took Molly's hand. "I like your island. It seems to be pretty big. It's sure bigger than Pilot Island. I'm kinda glad Marla and Julius have a couple kids and don't need us. I don't think I'd like it there. Do you ever feel that way here? I mean, do you go other places than here? Does a lighthouse take a lot of work? I like working on the boats. Wait. Is this where Mrs. Captain lived? Are you her mom?"

Mrs. Engelson laughed and embraced each girl. "Yes, I like it here. And yes, I'm Lainey's mom, but I'm her adopted mom. Her first mom . . . " She stood and turned to Rasmus. "Does she know?"

Addy straightened. "I know about her parents dying in the shipwreck and that they first saved your little boy . . . I guess he's pretty big now, but he was little then, right? I mean, all that is sad, but it turned out okay 'cause she got you."

Molly leaned against her sister. "I want her for a mama. But, well . . . "

Anna took their hands. "Well, I think there is a wonderful family just waiting for you two. But let's go inside. I have some cookies made.

I think maybe we could each have one and not ruin our lunch. What do you think?"

The other children cheered and ran for the steps leading to the kitchen area of the lighthouse.

Lainey breathed in the slightly fishy fragrance so prevalent on the waters around Door County. "I love the water when it's mostly calm like this. I don't think I could ever move to the city."

One of the guests nodded. "I've loved being here. It's such a breath of fresh air, so relaxing, but I'm actually looking forward to getting back to the city. I like the pace and the many stores and businesses so close. My dress shop has lots of customers there."

Lainey gasped. "How did I miss that you owned a dress shop? Do you have a catalog? I'd love to order from you after the baby, when I get my figure back." She laughed. "How long does that take?"

"It won't take long. But I have a surprise for you. Rose let me look at your dresses to get an idea what you like and what your size will be in a few months. A dress will soon be on its way."

"But . . . how much? I mean, you can't do this for free." She lowered her voice. "You already left a generous tip."

"Rose ordered a dress, and Clifford already paid for yours. Both dresses are at a fifty percent discount. And Rose has the catalog. We didn't want you to see it yet, so you'd be surprised. I just hope you'll show it to others on the Island, and maybe they'll order, too. If there are several orders, I can reduce the cost by twenty percent."

The woman stood and crossed to the bench where Lainey sat. "Tell me, do you think you'll take the girls?"

Lainey sighed. "I just don't know. We're going to visit my aunt and uncle on our return trip. They raised me for a while after my parents died. We value their advice."

She patted Lainey's hand. "It's a big decision. But they are just the cutest things, so smart and sweet. I hope they stay on the island. I will look forward to seeing how they fare." She patted Lainey's hand again. "But now, just breathe in this wonderful air and relax."

Without another word, she returned to her friends and family and began visiting with them. Lainey followed her directions and just absorbed the beauty. The tension in her shoulders flew behind her in the wake of the boat. Her spirit once more soared with the gulls flying overhead. Even the baby within kicked only a few times. The gentle rocking of the boat soothed Lainey and her little one.

An hour and a half later, Clifford brought the boat into the Ephraim dock. After the others had deboarded and loaded their luggage to a waiting carriage, Clifford turned to Lainey. "Let's have lunch at August's place and see if he's interested in the girls. He really liked them."

August's eyes lit up when he saw Lainey. "You look lovely, Miss Lainey. No beauty like that of a woman with child. What can I get you today?"

After ordering sandwiches and finding a seat, August walked to the table. "Clifford, I saw the Bergmans and asked about the girls. He just harrumphed and walked away. What happened?"

Clifford related the events of the past few days, while August alternately chuckled and grimaced. "So, do you have a family in mind?"

Lainey smiled, while Clifford nodded to August. "We thought you might be just the family. Addy would love it here. Not that you need help, but she loves to work, and she especially loves being around the boats."

Lainey chuckled. "She'd probably sneak aboard a boat and become crew if you're not careful."

August's wife, Grace, approached with sandwich plates in each hand. "I heard that. We've raised our children. I sure admire anyone that takes them in, and I understand their plight, but you'll find the right family. August told me how they take to Clifford here. I know you two have a lot going on, but you're young. Do you think perhaps God brought them straight to you?"

Lainey lowered her head and sighed. "I do wonder that, Grace."

August winked at Lainey and then patted Clifford's shoulder. "We will keep you in prayer. But I know that as wonderful or sneaky as those girls are, we are not their family. You'll know. Enjoy your lunch." He paused after taking a few steps away. "Oh, Clifford, we have a shipment of gasoline for the boats at the dock. I would be happy to help you fill up your boat tank. Are you picking up passengers today?"

"No passengers today, just the two of us. I appreciate your offer to assist with the gasoline. We should be back to the boat in half an hour or so."

Carter and David showed Addy and Molly the fifty steps they walked down at least once a day to fetch water for the cistern.

Addy whistled. "That's a long way. Is water heavy? I never thought about it before."

Carter nodded. "Not bad after you get used to it. Want to try it?"

"Sure, let's try it. Are we all going?"

David, Catherine, and Molly all backed away, shaking their heads.

Tina stepped forward. "I can go with you, Addy. I'm used to it. Carter, you can go explore with David. Besides you already did an extra trip today."

Tina and Addy started down the steps each with one bucket. Tina explained the routine. "We actually have shoulder yokes with buckets attached to make it easier most days. We like to do our math facts on the way down and tell stories on the way back up. Lainey did that with Carter even before I was born. So, Carter taught me to do it. That makes the time go faster; plus, it means less time with our studies, though I like school. What about you?"

"I'd rather do things than sit at a desk for learning. I mean, it's okay, but I need to be outside exploring, working, playing . . . anything other than sitting. There are a lot of steps here."

Tina nodded. "Fifty down and fifty back up."

Addy laughed. "Do you like it here on the island?"

"Yes. We explore a lot, and I love the lighthouse. Lainey always helped watching for ships, recording the weather, cleaning the light and the glass; and now, I'm learning to do all that, too. It's fun when we have company or go to Washington Island or the mainland, but I like it here. It's all mine, and I can make up stories about what is happening all the time."

Addy scooped the pail in the water. "Hmmm, it is pretty heavy, but I'm strong. But you do two buckets at a time?"

"Like Carter said, we're used to it."

Addy was silent as she ascended the stairs. Would she like it here? Tina and Carter were nice. Where would she and Molly end up? Mrs. Engelson was very kind.

As they neared the top, Catherine hollered for them to hurry. "David and Carter came back to get us, so we could explore. Pa says we have a couple hours."

Addy stopped. "What should we do with the water?"

"We have to put it in the cistern. I'll show you. They'll wait for us."

CHAPTER SEVEN

ADDY COULDN'T REMEMBER SUCH GREENERY anywhere in her life. The path they walked down was thick with ferns and overhanging with huge, leafy branches. "These trees are so tall. It almost hurts my neck to look up to the top of them."

Carter grinned. "Just wait till we get out to the bluff area. There are rocks that jut out, and we can sit on them and look down at the water."

Tina took Molly's hand. "We don't have to go as fast as everyone else. There are too many rocks and roots to trip on. I'll be seven at Christmas. Addy said you just turned seven a few weeks ago."

Molly squeezed Tina's hand. "I like having someone my age to play with."

Catherine, David, Carter, and Addy jumped over roots and rocks on their way to the rock slab. The twills of birds filled the air as wildflowers poked their heads out of the ground.

"Look at all these flowers. I don't recognize the white ones." Addy stopped to examine the flower in question. "It has three triangles."

"Those are trilliums. Ma said they're special to this area." Catherine bent to run her finger over the petal. "I think that means they don't grow everywhere. They come up every May, no matter what, even if there is still snow on the ground."

"What? You have snow in May?"

Carter turned at the question. "It's happened a few times. I remember it snowing the first week of May once, but sometimes, it's leftover in the deep woods where there isn't much sun, so the snow doesn't melt very quickly."

Addy shook her head. "I sure hope I never see snow in May. But I do like these flowers, the trilliums. Can we pick them?"

David shook his head. "Pa says we're not supposed to 'cause they're special. And Ma says she just loves looking outside and seeing them. She doesn't need a bouquet in the house."

Carter moved ahead. "Let's go, everyone. We're almost there. Be careful. The stones along the path are a little slippery."

Addy's foot slipped on the next stone, and she lurched forward, bumping into David. "Sorry, it is slippery."

David smiled. "It's okay. Just go slower."

Hanging onto tree branches and trunks, the children picked their way down to the rock slab, which jutted straight out from the bluff about four feet. It measured five feet in length so offered plenty of sitting room for all four of them. The surface, mostly smooth, had little dips that held a bit of water from recent rains.

Catherine surveyed the surface. "Looks like we'll get wet clothes if we sit."

Carter rolled his eyes. "Pa always says, 'It's just water.'"

David untied a bag from his waist. "Mrs. Engelson sent some cookies with me."

Addy clapped her hands. "This is the coolest place. I'm going to sit on the far edge." Looking down, she felt a shiver run up her back. "Oohhh, it's a ways down. Do you ever go down there?" She leaned out to better see it all.

Carter grabbed her arm. "Careful, Addy. You could fall. Lainey and I went down once with Pa. But it was when it was dry, and our footing was better."

"But how in the world did you get down there?"

"See that vine there? It's really a root that hangs down. We had to hang on to it, and Pa found the rocks and roots sticking out that we used for footholds. He went first and dug a little dirt out around those spots to make it easier for us. It's real pretty down there closer to the lake, but we don't go very often."

Addy chewed her cookie, alternately gazing out and peeking over the edge. "I'd really like to go down there."

Catherine nodded. "Me, too. We'll come back when it's drier and climb down. Maybe Pa will come with us."

Addy scowled. "Not today?"

Carter shook his head. "Nope. David, do you have more cookies?"

"I do, but we need to make sure we leave enough for Molly and Tina."

Catherine leaned over, along with Carter, to count the cookies.

Addy scooched over to the edge of the rock slab and studied the root vine. Glancing back, she saw the others looking at the cookies. She tentatively reached for the vine. Touching it with one hand, she attempted to get the other hand out and around it while searching for the first foothold. She didn't see it, so she leaned a little further. Just as her eye located it, she found too much of her body was extended out from the rock, and she felt herself sliding. "Ooohhhh, wait. Noooo!" Her hand glanced off the root and slammed against a rock jutting out. Try as she might, she could not grab hold of anything. Rocks and roots smacked her as she tumbled against the bluff, striking her forehead on a protruding rock. Before she could grasp anything, her foot landed on the rock below with a painful twist. Half-screaming and half-moaning, Addy crumpled on the rocky area near the shore at the bottom of the bluff.

Catherine screamed. "Addy, Addy! She fell! Carter, she fell! Addy, are you alive? Can you hear us?"

Carter lay flat on the rock slab and extended his head out over the edge. "I see you, Addy. Are you hurt badly?"

Addy couldn't catch her breath. Every time she tried to respond and call back, the pain stole her voice. She moaned.

"Oh, no. Carter, is she dead? What will we do?"

Carter turned. "Catherine, I see her. I think she's pretty hurt. But stop screaming."

Catherine wrapped her arms around herself. "Okay. Okay. What will we do?"

Carter called out to Addy again. "Addy, can you hear me? How bad are you hurt?"

Addy whimpered. "My ankle really hurts, and my head is bleeding."

Tina and Molly took their time walking the path to the rock slab.

Molly smiled. "Thank you for not going too fast. I tripped when we ran away from Mr. and Mrs. Captain. An old lady helped us. I thought she was a witch at first, but she was just old."

"Really? You ran away from Lainey and Clifford? Did you know she's my sister?"

Molly shook her head no. "But I love her. Addy thought she didn't want us, so we left."

"Well, she is going to have a baby soon. Babies take a lot of work."

Molly squatted down. "Look at all these pretty flowers. They smell sweet."

"I know. Maybe on the way back, we can pick some. Pa taught me which ones we can pick." Tina pulled on Molly's hand. "Look up; there's an eagle flying over. They are so big. He's probably going to catch some fish. Pa says there's a nest not too far from here. Maybe some time, we can go find it."

A scream, followed by yells, emerged from the path up ahead.

Tina grabbed Molly's hand even tighter. "We have to hurry. Try not to slip."

Molly's sobs erupted, and tears coursed down her cheeks. "Is it a monster?"

Tina paused and turned so she could see Molly's face. "No, someone probably slipped and got hurt. Can you stop crying so we can hurry and get there? You can't see if your eyes are blurry. I don't want you to get hurt."

"Okay." Molly sniffled and dragged her sleeve across her eyes.

When Catherine saw them, she began to scream. "Addy fell. Addy fell. She's hurt. David and Carter are trying to get to her. Tina, they want you to go back and get our papas."

"Hold on to Molly and tell me what happened."

"We sat on the rock slab, and Addy wanted to go down. Carter said no, that it was too far down and dangerous. She must've leaned out, and she toppled right off. I think she hurt her ankle. Maybe bad. But David is stuck half-way down, and Carter had to jump the rest of the way. They can't get back up here."

Carter saw Tina. "Tell Pa to bring ropes and bandages. Hurry."

The men finished fixing the leak on the cistern. Reinhardt smiled. "Thanks. We'll need to make a few trips down to the water today before you go, so we can refill the cistern. That is, if you don't mind."

"I don't, but let's sit a bit."

They joined Anna and Hannah in the kitchen. Anna stood. "Come, sit and have some lemonade. We've been talking about these new grandbabies coming. I can't wait to be a grandma. The children are all exploring. Tina sure enjoys Addy and Molly."

Rasmus winked. "Does that mean you'd like to adopt them?"

Anna poured more lemonade. "Oh my, no. But we'd love to have them visit. Wouldn't you want them with you? Catherine and David love them as well. And Addy, I hear, wants to work on your boat."

Hannah shook her head. "I've thought about it and prayed, but I just don't have a peace about it. I sure hope someone nearby takes them because all the children like them. I mean, I love them, but I feel it's a no. Have you prayed about it?"

"We did. Reinhardt met them before I did, and Tina couldn't stop talking about them. But I don't have peace about it, either. And I must say, we probably could handle having them, but I don't think it's us."

Hannah laid her hand on Anna's. "What about Lainey and Clifford? Do you think they can handle having them? Lainey seems anxious about it all—the baby, the resort, Clifford being gone on the boat at times."

Anna rested her elbow on the table and chin in her hands. "I keep thinking that they might be the ones."

Rasmus cleared his throat. "There's a catch, though, that Lainey and Clifford don't even know about. I've shared it with only Reinhardt. When Addy's father was injured, such that he could no longer work, it occurred during the rescue of the crew of a boat that went down. It happened just north of their hometown on Lake Huron—Harrisville, Michigan."

Anna gasped and covered her mouth. "Clifford's ship?"

Rasmus nodded. "I'm pretty sure. She remembers the date because it was Molly's first birthday."

Anna shook her head. "Does Addy know it was his ship?"

"We don't think so, and, of course, neither do Clifford or Lainey."

Reinhardt rubbed his chin. "I didn't tell Anna, as I didn't want it to influence our decision whether to take the girls." He shook his head. "It sure could change things for Lainey and Clifford. They'd adopt out of guilt, or Addy could resent them."

"True. I don't know who should tell them—or if anyone should."

Tina ran through the door. "Ma, Pa! Addy fell from the rock slab, and she's hurt. Carter got down to her, but he had to jump part of the way, and he might be hurt. And David is only part-way down and can't get back up."

All four adults jumped up.

Reinhardt headed through the door. "I'll get the rope. Let's go, Rasmus."

Tina yelled. "Wait, Pa! Carter said to bring bandages."

"I'll get them." Anna rushed to storeroom. "Where are Catherine and Molly?"

"I told Catherine to watch Molly, since I knew the way back better."

Mrs. Hanson grabbed her sweater. "We'll come and get the girls."

Addy wiped her sleeve against her forehead. Blood oozed across her sleeve. "Ouch. I have a big lump on my forehead." She found her breath coming in big gasps. She usually acted tough, but today, the blood made her squeamish. Nausea rose from the pit of her stomach. And everything hurt.

Carter nodded. "We call that a goose egg. Can you move your ankle?"

Addy looked down at her foot. "It's really sore. Did I break it? Why's it so big all of a sudden?"

"It might be a sprain. They can swell up like that real quick. Can you stand on it?"

Addy set her hands on the cool rock surface and got on her knees. "Oooh, I think I scraped my knees, too. I sure messed up."

"You look a mess, too, little sister."

Addy jerked her head up. "Sister. Am I going to be your sister? Do you mean . . . "

"No, no. I mean, I don't know. I don't have any idea. But I call all of Tina's friends that, especially Catherine because our families are so close."

"Oh. Okay. I'll try to stand up."

"Hey, Addy. I didn't mean to upset you with that."

"It's all right. Can you help me?"

Carter got in front of her and grasped her upper arms. "All right, try to go up on your good ankle, then set the other one down. It's awkward, but I'll make sure you don't tip over."

Addy found herself gritting her teeth. She wobbled onto one foot, then put the injured one down. Throbbing pain rose from her ankle to her knee. She closed her eyes and groaned. "That really hurts. I think I need to sit."

Carter helped her return to a seated position. "Let's scooch you over, so your ankle dangles in the cold water. That will help the swelling go down.

Addy looked up. "Thank you, Carter. I never had a big brother, but if I did, I'd hope he'd be like you. Ooohh, that water is cold!" Addy yanked her foot out of water and turned to Carter. "Do I need to do this?"

"Yes, Addy, you do, and you need to keep it there till Pa and Mr. Hanson come to get us out of here."

CHAPTER EIGHT

LAINEY STARED AT THE MESMERIZING blues and greens of the lake and twinkling white spray that arose from the light chop. "Clifford, why am I so confused on this?"

"Sweetheart, it's a lot at once. I think pregnancy makes you more emotional."

Lainey tipped her head and scowled.

Clifford held up a hand. "Now, I didn't mean that quite the way it sounded. I think any woman who's pregnant is just naturally more . . . I mean . . . I mean, I really am not qualified to answer that." He rubbed his mouth with his hand. "You just have a lot going on right now. And pregnancy just puts more stress on everything." He paused and looked at her. "I mean, it's good. It's wonderful. I'm so happy for us and can't wait for this baby. But, well . . . Honey, am I making any sense? I'd like to just sit and hold your hand and tell you everything will be just fine no matter what we decide, but I can't leave the steering."

Lainey laughed. "I do love you, Mr. Captain. Just don't offend the lady with child."

Clifford blew her a kiss.

The two traveled silently for several minutes.

Lainey adjusted her position on the bench. "I think I need to put it in the Lord's hand and trust He'll tell us whether we should be their family or someone else. I think everything has moved so quickly that I haven't taken time to really pray."

"You're right. We're not at Death's Door yet, so we can drift a bit right now. Let's pray."

Clifford surveyed the waters around them. No other vessels were nearby. Sitting next to Lainey, he placed his arm around her and leaned over to kiss her protruding belly. "Be well, little one; go to full term. We can't wait to see you." He kissed Lainey's cheek. "Let's pray, love, but I'm keeping my eyes open."

Lainey nodded and leaned against him. The smell of cotton and fresh air relaxed her. Clifford was her rock in so many ways. "Dear Lord, here we are. You know all the details. You know everything about Addy and Molly, and we know so little, except that You brought them to us and they are wonderful in so many ways. Are we to be their parents? Are we able to be good parents with a new baby, the resort, the ferry business? Help us to hear Your decision."

Clifford squeezed her. "And, Lord, strengthen Lainey. And me. To be good parents to this little one who is here with us right now and to Addy and Molly, if that is Your design. And help us to let go if You have someone else in mind."

"Clifford, that's it."

"What's it?"

"I think I'm so confused because I don't think I can let them go, but I don't think I can handle it all."

"You may have hit the nail on the head." He bowed his head again. "Lord, help us to accept Your plan—whatever is best for the girls."

"Amen. Well, let's see what Uncle Otis and Aunt Edith have to say." Lainey laid her head on his shoulder for a moment longer before releasing him back to the steering.

Death's Door never bothered Clifford. He was seaworthy and respected the currents that roiled in the passage. Currents that, in storms, had brought down several ships. On Pilot Island, Lainey had been tasked with directing the light for one such wreck while her uncle went to rescue the crew. It was after that rescue that Uncle Otis wanted to praise Lainey for a job well done but didn't dry his boots and slipped on the steps. He broke his leg and could no longer be the lighthouse keeper. That was when they had almost sent Lainey to the Orphan Train. Instead, the Engelsons, lighthouse keepers on Rock, took in Lainey. It was a perfect fit. Could Addy and Molly be a perfect fit for Lainey and him? How could he know? What if they took them in, and it didn't work? What if Addy ran away again?

The currents of questions and opposing possibilities roiled within him now, just like the water currents beneath the *Pearl*. What must they be like in the girls' hearts and minds? Where was the calm current, the safe passage for this huge decision? Did storms hide just around the bluff? Should they take this voyage? How could they not? What waters lay ahead for the girls? Were he and Lainey to be their captains? He chuckled silently. Addy and Molly already called them Mr. and Mrs. Captain.

He shook his head. They were almost to Newport Town, where Uncle Otis and Aunt Edith now lived. He'd become the accountant for the lumber company, which thrived at this time. After the Chicago and great Pestigo fires, there'd been such a clamor for lumber, and the great demand for northwoods pine kept the Newport Town port bursting with business. Clifford idled his boat for ten minutes while waiting for an opening to dock. A huge steamer sat low in the water with the steam engine gaining steam enough to route its way to Chicago. Three wagons pulled by huge horses now left the dock, headed back to the woods, perhaps for another load yet today.

Lainey stood by Clifford. "I love those cargo steamers. I always went out onto the gallery at Pilot Lighthouse and waved. They'd honk their horn, and that made my day. Uncle Otis taught me so much about the water, the weather, the ships. It'll be so good to see them."

Clifford docked the boat and jumped out with the stern line and tied the line firmly to the piling. Lainey tossed him the bow line, and as soon as it was secured, he held out his hand to Lainey.

She chuckled. "Once upon a time, I would've just jumped out."

"That's what Addy does. Just like you were a natural in the lighthouse, she is a natural with boats."

Clifford held his wife's hand as they walked toward the home of Lainey's aunt and uncle. Children ran by, laughing and calling out to each other. Wagons went by, some with lumber, some with furniture, others with household supplies. The bustle warmed Lainey's heart. As much as she enjoyed solitude and quiet times near the water, she loved watching the busyness of people living their daily lives.

A voice behind them caught their ears. "Is that my niece? Lainey, is that you? Yes, my Lainey, great with child. Clifford, so good to see you. What brings you here?"

Lainey fell into the arms of her uncle. "I've missed you."

Clifford shook hands. "We have a matter we'd like your advice on—yours and Aunt Edith's."

"Well, this is perfect timing. Now that that last steamer is loaded, I'm done for the day. I think Edith has been doing some flower planting, but I would guess she's done now. Might even have dinner ready. Can you stay?"

"Only an hour or two, and we're still a little full from lunch in Ephraim. I had to return guests today. I'll pick more up day after tomorrow, and there's still work to be done at the resort."

"Well, you know, you'd best not tell Edith you'd rather not eat if she has a meal prepared."

Lainey laughed. "We'll find room. This little one keeps me hungry."

They turned onto the little rock path leading to the house as Aunt Edith came out the door with a lemonade in her hand. When she saw Lainey and Clifford, she almost dropped her lemonade. To grab it with both hands, she let go of the screened door, and it slammed.

Lainey tensed but wouldn't let herself grimace. When she stayed on Pilot Island, the number of bounces the door made when it slammed indicated the level of anger her aunt held. Those days were long past, and in the last few years, Aunt Edith exuded peace and happiness. Still, a bit of the memory and emotion clung to Lainey.

Uncle Otis' voice boomed. "Edith, look who I found."

Aunt Edith hurried down the steps. "Lainey. Clifford. How wonderful to see you! Oh, how I've missed you. Let me look at you. Pregnant women are so beautiful. We're so happy for you. Goodness, listen to me. Come and sit. I'll get more lemonade. Otis, you're home a little early."

"Yes, we got that big load of lumber out today, and the boss sent us all home."

"You know, I put that stew in early today—earlier than usual—and I bet it will be ready if you want to eat."

Otis chuckled. "Lainey says she's always hungry with this little one."

"Wonderful. Then it's settled. Let's just sit for a while first and catch up. I'll get the lemonade."

Soon, they were settled, each with a brimming glass of lemonade.

Edith shared about her quilting group and planting flowers. "You know, I don't have a lot tying me down—well, other than cooking for Otis and any needy families we hear of—so, I'd love to come for a few days when the baby comes if you need assistance. I could help cook or clean for the resort. Is Anna going to come? Have you determined yet?"

Lainey spread her hands out. "Yes, Mama will come early with Tina, but perhaps they can't stay long after with the lighthouse. It would be lovely, Aunt Edith, if you could come as well. Do you mind, Uncle Otis?"

"Not at all, although I may have to come, too. I can't wait to see your baby."

A slight cloud passed over her aunt's eyes, and Lainey saw it. "Aunt Edith?"

She shook her head. "No, no. It's okay. Losing Mandy was the worst thing that ever happened. She was such a dear, little girl. But that will not dampen my joy for this little one. I just hope I can be involved in his or her life."

"Absolutely. We wouldn't have it any other way."

Otis leaned over and patted Lainey's knee. "You two said you had a matter to discuss."

Clifford cleared his throat. "We do. You may know, I sometimes bring the Orphan Train children here on the steamer from Chicago or Milwaukee."

Aunt Edith looked down. "Lainey, I'm still so sorry we considered that."

"No more guilt, Aunt Edith. It all worked out, and you were only trying to see that I was cared for."

Clifford set his lemonade on the small table. "Anyway, there were two girls—sisters—who were . . . well, left over. The people who were supposed to get them wanted a boy, so Addy and Molly ended up going home with me."

Lainey smiled. "They're beautiful girls. Addy is high-spirited, and Molly is so sweet; they just attached themselves to Clifford. They call him Mr. Captain, but they overheard me telling Rose I didn't think I could handle the resort, Clifford gone on the boat, a new baby, and them."

Clifford nodded. "So, they ran away."

Otis coughed. "What? Did you find them?"

"We did. Well, Rasmus did and took them out to Pilot, then to Rock, and back to his house. That's where they are now."

Otis rubbed his hands together and stared off into space. Then he looked Clifford squarely in the eyes. "So, you want to keep them but don't know if you should?" He shifted his gaze to Lainey. "Is this the matter?"

Clifford and Lainey both nodded.

"If it's money you need, we're happy to help."

Lainey shook her head. "No, it's whether we should—whether I can handle it—whether *we* can handle it. I am tired, and I know a baby may tire me more, but . . . well . . . Oh, I just don't know." A tear tracked down Lainey's cheek.

Aunt Edith took her hand. "Lainey, what does your heart tell you? What does the Lord tell you?"

"It's all jumbled up inside me, Aunt Edith."

Uncle Otis stood. "Is the decision yours? I mean, not the Orphan Train people?"

Clifford chuckled, then groaned. "The nurses left. They didn't like the rough seas. So, there is no one that we know of that we can even ask for advice or permission. That leaves me, the ship captain." He gestured to Lainey. "Well, us. We're the deciders."

Uncle Otis chewed his bottom lip for a moment. "Have you considered other families? Rose and Niles? Marla and Julius? The Hansons? Your folks on Rock? Arlo and Sarah?"

Lainey reached to take Clifford's hand. "Yes, Rose is pregnant again and going to continue teaching. Marla and Julius just took in her cousin's children."

"Oh, yes, I did hear that. Jimmy took them out to Pilot. And that's wonderful about Rose. I usually see Niles, but he's been working on the island for a few days. I would think you could still find a family if the girls are as engaging as you say—perhaps a bit too independent . . . They ran away?"

Lainey chuckled. "Yes, and they wandered into Mrs. Figgenschau's cove and thought she was a witch. But she fed them and helped them out, and then they found Rasmus—or he found them, thank the Lord. I was so worried and felt so guilty."

Otis held his chin in his hand. "Okay, let me ask you this." He sat down and leaned forward. "Since the decision as to where they go is yours to make, there's no doubt that you'd choose a good family, right?"

Clifford nodded, and Lainey fidgeted in her seat.

"But giving them to another family makes you uncomfortable, correct?"

"It's just, well, I . . . " Lainey let out a big breath.

Otis smiled. "It's just that they've captured your heart."

Lainey nodded.

Aunt Edith squeezed her hand. "When the Engelsons offered to take you, it was hard to let you go. We loved you, but we knew it was the right fit."

Otis nodded. "At first, I didn't think I could bear to let you go, but we felt the Engelsons were the right ones; and at that point, we didn't know if I'd ever work again and be able to support you."

Lainey breathed in. "So, you think we should let them go to another family that we choose?"

Aunt Edith tilted her head. "Let's say you did that." She paused.

Lainey squirmed in her seat.

Uncle Otis smiled. "That doesn't sit well with you, does it?"

"How do you know that, Uncle?"

"Oh, I know my little girl. I saw that squirm. And I think that you are already so in love with these two girls that no matter how difficult or busy or challenging, you cannot let them go anywhere else. You know, they just might be a big help to you with the baby and the resort."

Lainey worked her ear with her hand and scrunched her face. "I think you might be right. Clifford?"

"You know, when Addy took the wheel on the boat and when Molly ran up to you and asked you to be her mama, I think my heart took hold of them permanently. I tried to be practical, but I may have told the Lord when they ran away that I'd take care of them forever if He'd just get them back to us."

"You didn't tell me that. But when I realized they'd overheard me and that's why they ran away, I think I made the same promise, but I wasn't sure if it was out of guilt or out of love."

Aunt Edith stood. "Oh, Lainey, we knew that guilt when you overheard us talking about the Orphan Train. And now, isn't this strange that the Orphan Train has brought them to you? I rather think you have your answer. You know we'll help in any way we can. But dinner is ready, and you need to get back to your resort before dark."

CHAPTER NINE

REINHARDT KNEW EXACTLY THE SPOT where the accident had occurred. He'd warned Lainey, Carter, and Tina so many times to be careful there. He glanced back toward Rasmus, who marched just a few feet behind him, his face in a determined grimace. "Is young Addy a bit foolhardy?"

"I'd say headstrong and too adventurous. As enjoyable as she is, whoever parents her will have to match that strong will and keep a close eye. She'll go far, but she can certainly go too far. Who knows where she'd be now if she'd happened on someone who'd have taken her to the mainland? I'm so glad we intercepted her."

"I sure hope she's not badly injured." Reinhardt shook his head. "We may have to set up a stretcher of sorts if she can't walk." He slapped his head. "Good grief, I should've brought our stretcher. What was I thinking? Too late now. We're almost there."

As they slowed to pick their way down the stony path to the rock slab, Reinhardt took in the pine smells and caught the fishy smell that wafted from the water. "Almost there. I think I hear crying."

Catherine turned at the sound of men's voices. "Oh, Mr. Engelson, Pa. I think Addy's hurt bad. Carter's with her but can't get back up. David is stuck half-way. Too far to jump down and too far to climb back up. And Molly is scared stiff."

At that, Molly let out a wail.

Catherine held her close. "It'll be okay, Molly. Pa and Mr. Engelson will get them back up."

Reinhardt held on to a tree growing out of the side of the bluff and leaned out. "Carter, what's the situation?"

"Don't think anything is broken, but she twisted her ankle. I've got her soaking it in the cold water, and the swelling has gone down just a bit. A nasty goose egg on her forehead, but like you told me, 'Better the bump extends out rather than dents in.' But not sure how to get back up. Did you bring ropes?"

"I did. Where's David? Oh, I see you. Let's get you back up, and then I'll come down. Rasmus will stay up here, and hopefully, we can get everyone out of harm's way."

A few minutes passed as Rasmus and Reinhardt determined their plan. Then Rasmus called to his son, "Hang in there, David. I've almost got the rope secured in boat half-hitches, just like tying the boat to the pilings. We'll put the noose hook in the other end and lower it."

Reinhardt tossed the finished rope down to David. "Place it over your head and under your arms. We'll pull, and you can almost walk back up."

David did as they instructed. "Okay. I'm ready."

"Good, now lean back a little so your feet and even your hands can work their way up."

David's head emerged over the edge of the bluff, and the men helped him scramble the rest of the way.

Rasmus hugged David. "Son, you all right? Any cuts or bruises?"

David shook his head. "Nah, I'm fine. Just wish I could have gotten down or up without help."

"Nothing to be ashamed of. It wasn't something planned. You tried to help. Good thing Tina knew the way back to get us."

Reinhardt smiled. "She's sure-footed and knows these woods better than any of us."

Anna and Hannah arrived. Molly bolted for Mrs. Hanson and began sobbing again.

"There, there, Molly. I think Addy will be just fine. Don't you worry. Look, Mrs. Engelson brought some cookies."

Molly wiped her eyes with the back of her hand. "Enough for everyone?"

"Yes, enough for everyone. You can have two."

Catherine mouthed a big thank you to her mother and sat down next to Molly.

By now, Reinhardt had lowered himself to the rocky shore, where Addy sat nursing her ankle next to Carter.

Addy winced but stood up with Carter's help. "Mr. Engelson. I'm really sorry to have caused you so much trouble. Will you be sending Molly and me or just me back to the Orphan Train? My pa always said I was a handful. Everyone's been so nice, and now I cause all this trouble."

Reinhardt smiled and placed his hands on her shoulders. "Young lady, accidents happen. No one is sending you back. You may need to learn how to be a little more careful, though. Did my son warn you about not trying to come down here? I've told him that a number of times." He raised his eyes at Carter.

"He did. He told me. But I just . . . Well, I only tried . . . " Addy hung her head. "I'm sorry."

"Okay, enough apologizing. You are forgiven. But now, how injured are you? You are standing. Can you walk on it?"

Carter held out his arm. "Here, lean on me and see."

Addy put her hand on his arm. "Okay." She lifted up the uninjured foot and groaned. She covered her mouth with her free hand and squeezed her eyes shut. "Oh, that hurts, but I can do it if I have to."

"Atta, girl. You have a good and strong attitude. But Carter and I will help you, so you don't have to put much pressure on it. We'll each wrap an arm around you, and you put your arms on us, like we're a crutch. Do you know what a crutch is?"

"I do. My pa used them when he got hurt."

With Carter and his pa's assistance, Addy moved over to where the rope dangled.

"Okay, we need you to lean against this tree. We're going to send Carter up so he can help pull you. Rasmus, I'm going to move the noose more to the middle of the rope, so there's an end that the boys can pull. That will make it more like a pulley and cut the load in half."

"Excellent idea, Reinhardt."

With the help of the rope and Rasmus pulling, Carter scaled the bluff and scrambled over the top. He dropped the noose down but kept hold of the free end of the rope.

"Now, Miss Addy, I'm going to put this over your head and around your waist, just like we did with Carter and David. However, I don't want you to try to use your feet, only your hands. You might get some scrapes, but it can't be helped."

Anna went closer to the edge. "Wait, Reinhardt. I brought a pillow and a bag with a draw string. Slip Addy in there and put the pillow in. That way, she won't scrape her legs, and it will help keep them still." Anna tossed it down.

"What a great idea." Reinhardt lowered the rope over her head and placed it under her arms. "Okay, lift her up just a bit, and I'll get the bag and pillow secured as best we can."

Addy grimaced but said nothing as Mr. Engelson worked. Soon, he had the bag positioned so the drawstring was around her waist and the pillow in the bag in front of her knees and ankles. "Addy, is your ankle okay in the position we have it, or is it more painful?"

She nodded, then shook her head. "It hurts, but no more than it did before. Thank you."

Reinhardt smiled. "All right. Rasmus and boys, pull gently. I'll try to keep her away from the rough spots going up. Addy, use your hands to help."

Addy's eyes blurred, and she tried to wipe them clear with the back of her hand. Soon though, the tears coursed down her cheeks. Was it the pain or the kindness? She truly didn't know. Here, she'd caused so much trouble, and they weren't mad. She was pretty sure that man on Chambers Island who didn't want her wouldn't have been this nice. She hoped the other kids from the Orphan Train had found people like these islanders.

She felt someone's hands under her arms. It was Carter. "Be careful, Addy. Let me pull you over the edge."

When she finally sat back on the rock slab, she took a deep breath. What a relief. But now, how would she get back?

The boys and Mr. Rasmus turned their attention to Mr. Engelson and soon were pulling him up the side of the bluff.

Mrs. Hanson sat next to Addy. "Are you okay, sweetie? You had us so worried. This was quite an ordeal. We brought you cookies."

"Really? I'm so hungry. Thank you." That first bite tasted heavenly. The oatmeal was sweet, and it disappeared too quickly. Mrs. Hanson handed her another one. She took her time to savor the sweetness and the bulk. It made her stop shaking. How long had she been shaking? Why did she feel cold, too? Her ankle didn't throb as much. Maybe she could walk. "I think I can walk." Her eyes pleaded with Mr. Rasmus and Mr. Engelson.

Mr. Engelson shook his head. "I don't think that would be wise."

Mr. Rasmus and Mr. Engelson looked at each other. Mr. Engelson rubbed his chin. "I sure should've thought to bring the stretcher. I don't think using us as crutches will work; she's in quite a bit of pain. I guess we'd better send Carter back for it. He's the fastest."

Just then, Tina called from the top of the stony path. "Pa, I brought the little stretcher, that first one you made you decided was too small. The one you let us play with." Her forehead beaded with sweat as she dragged behind her a canvas material strung between two wooden rods.

"My smart daughter. I forgot all about that one."

The men helped Addy climb onto the stretcher. "Addy, lay down now, and we'll carry you."

"First, I need to wrap that ankle." Mrs. Engelson wound the bandage firmly around the ankle. "I know this might hurt a bit. Putting it in the cold water was a good idea, and we don't want the swelling to increase too much." Addy grimaced as she worked but tried not to react to the pain.

David and Carter grabbed the poles at the front, and their fathers took the back ends of the poles. "All right, one, two, three, lift."

Addy grabbed the sides and hung on for dear life. Momentarily, her ankle lost her attention. "Am I going to fall off? I feel upside down." With the stretcher traveling uphill and her head at the lower end, she felt she would slide right back down the hill. The gait of the men and boys was uneven, so it felt a bit like the boat on rough water.

Molly looked up at Mrs. Engelson. "She looks funny. Can I ride like that sometime?"

Tina laughed. "We used to play with it all the time when friends came. We'll give you a ride sometime."

Molly clapped. "Addy, are you having fun?"

"I . . . I'm not sure. I think walking might be easier on this hill."

Carter wiggled his end of the stretcher, making it feel even more like she rode on the waves out on the lake. "Don't worry, Addy; if you slide off, we'll catch you."

Addy tipped her head up to look at Carter. He winked. Then she laughed. At the top of the hill, the ground became fairly level. It was narrow, and she knew the men were swatting ferns out of the way and several branches. The view upward mesmerized her. The trees canopied over the path and painted a trellis that the blue sky and the sun peeked through. She squinted several times from the occasional glare but refused to blot out the view. A soft breeze wafted through the trail, making the new leaves flutter. The green of the leaves was resplendent. She wanted to sing. Even the slight throb of her ankle couldn't stop the thrill of this ride through the woods.

She heard Catherine whisper, "Did she fall asleep?"

David shook his head. "Her eyes are open. Maybe she hurts too much to say anything."

Addy couldn't respond. She could drift off to sleep, now that she was level, for the most part, and the boys and men had the rhythm down of carrying her. Guilt began to rise again over her foolishness. Would she ever learn to listen? Papa and Mama had to often remind her to pay attention, to listen, to obey. She didn't really ever mean to disobey. It was just that, well, she never was sure, but so many things seemed the obvious thing to do. But then, they cascaded into the wrong thing. She probably shouldn't have run away, and she should have listened to Carter. But she was right to not let Molly be separated from her. And she was right to get on Mr. Hanson's boat. How could she figure out the right thing each time?

She was on the ground. Mr. Rasmus scooped her off the stretcher and carried her into the lighthouse. He passed through the kitchen and dining room to the sitting room, where he placed her on the settee. "Now, let's get a look at this." He unwrapped the bandage that Mrs. Engelson had hastily used to wrap her ankle. "It's pretty red and a bit swollen. Addy, I'm going to move it around a little. Does this hurt?"

Addy grimaced. "Yes. It felt better with the wrap on it."

Every move hurt but not sufficient to make her cry out. Mr. Rasmus stood up. "I don't think anything is broken. It's still a pretty bad sprain, but I think Carter getting it in the cold water helped."

Mrs. Engelson knelt beside Addy. "I'm going to rewrap this now. It might seem tight, but that will help it heal better. Mrs. Hanson is making you some willow bark tea. That will help the swelling to go down. But first, I'm going to rub some herbs and oil on it to assist the healing. Tell me if I'm rubbing too hard and making it hurt."

Addy smiled. "Did you get them from Mrs. Figgenschau?"

Mrs. Engelson looked up. "Why, yes, how did you know? How could you possibly know Mrs. Figgenschau?"

Molly tapped Mrs. Engelson's shoulder. "I cut my knee when we ran away. And she helped me, and she fed us. I thought she was a witch at first, but she was just old."

Mrs. Engelson chuckled. "I can understand why you thought that, but I'm glad you found out she's not. Isn't she nice?"

Molly nodded. "She is."

"Addy, is this hurting at all?"

"It feels good, ma'am. Thank you."

"All right. Now, I'm going to wrap it." When Mrs. Engelson finished, she pushed a pillow under Addy's foot. "Let's keep it elevated for a while. Oh, here's your tea. Just sip it."

Catherine got a pillow to place behind Addy while she sipped her tea. "Well, it's almost a tea party."

"What's a tea party?"

Tina entered the room. "It's for girls. And we all have tea in pretty cups, and we have little pastries with it. Sometimes, we dress up. It's fun."

"I don't think I've ever dressed up. I don't think I ever had a new dress. My mama did a few times. But I'd rather be outside, running and playing and climbing trees."

Carter looked around the corner from the dining room. "And falling off rock slabs."

Addy scrunched her face. "Sorry, Carter. Thanks for helping me."

"You're welcome. I'm going to eat now."

Mrs. Engelson stood. "Well, I was about to make sandwiches when all the commotion began, so I'd better do that now." She turned to Mr. Rasmus. "You probably need to get everyone back to Washington soon."

Rasmus walked out of the room, signaling Anna to follow. He lowered his voice. "She's looking sleepy now. Let her sleep an hour or so. It'll do her good. We can get everyone else fed and then go in a couple hours. We'll be fine."

Hannah set a sandwich in front of Carter. "Don't worry, Anna. I already started making sandwiches. With all that excitement, these young ones will eat you out of house and home."

Anna laughed. "Nonsense. We love to share what we have. I think I'll heat up that soup as well. Everyone needs a little extra to recover from today's escapade."

Tina and Catherine joined the others in the kitchen. "We put a blanket over Addy. She's sound asleep. Molly fell asleep, too. I think she worried herself exhausted."

Hannah smiled. "I'm sure she did. She's had quite a few days. I've no idea how long they were on the Orphan Train before getting on the steamer. Addy said they tried to separate them in Milwaukee, and she put up a fuss and kept Molly with her. Then no one showed up in Ephraim, and the couple out on Chambers refused them. Then they get to Sunset Resort and think perhaps they have a home."

Carter raised his eyebrows. "Aunt Hannah, what happened there? How did they find Uncle Rasmus?"

Hannah lowered her voice. "Carter, she overheard Lainey saying she didn't think she could take them. They have the resort, a baby coming, Clifford often gone on the ferry boat."

Carter sighed. "Oh, that's too bad. I think they'd be perfect."

Hannah patted his shoulder. "That's why they stayed with us. One, to give Clifford and Lainey time to think and pray about it, and two, to see if your folks might be open to it."

Tina grinned. "I wouldn't mind that. Ma?"

Anna put her arm around her daughter's shoulders. "Tina, we prayed. It's not that we're opposed. We just feel the Lord has other plans for them, better plans."

CHAPTER TEN

LAINEY AND CLIFFORD WERE SILENT as they plied their way back through Death's Door to the dock at Sunset Resort.

As they came around to the west side of the island, Clifford glanced over at Lainey. "Calm waters today. I'm always thankful. And it looks like a beautiful sunset."

Lainey stood and walked over to her husband. She leaned against him. "It is gorgeous tonight. This has been such a nice day. It's been too long since we've seen Uncle Otis and Aunt Edith."

"So, what do you think? Do you hear the Lord's voice, His direction?"

"It seems we already promised the Lord. But was it out of guilt or love? I've felt guilty since I realized they overheard us, but I think our first thoughts and commitments were out of love. I think the Lord brought them here. I think they belong to us."

Clifford swooped Lainey into his arms and twirled her around. "I think they do, too. But let's consider this. What if she runs away again? I mean, she has such a strong, independent spirit, she might run off again or just disobey or give us fits. Are we up for that?"

Lainey gazed off into space. "I think that if God has gone to all this effort to make these girls ours, then we are the ones who can handle and shape those young spirits."

Clifford brought the vessel alongside the dock and quieted the engine. He held onto the piling to make sure the boat sat steady. Stepping off, he tied the lines fore and aft, then held out his hand to help Lainey depart. "Let's get some sleep and then go get our girls in the morning."

"Yes, let's do that."

They entered the resort and found it spotless. Everything in the kitchen was scrubbed and put away. A big bouquet of flowers sat on the table. A note sat beside it: "Clifford and Lainey, we hope you had a wonderful day. All the cleaning is done. We think Addy and Molly belong to you, and we hope you think that as well. Love, Arlo and Sarah, Niles and Rose."

A tear tracked down Lainey's cheek, and Clifford caught it with his thumb. "We're a big family now, honey."

Lainey leaned down to inhale the fragrance of the flowers. "We are. Oh, my. Here we go. God has so many adventures for us. Let's pray."

Clifford sat and pulled Lainey onto his lap and wrapped both arms around her. "Lord, we thank you for Addy and Molly. We believe You've brought them to us to be their parents. But they belong to You, Lord, and so right now, we give them back to You as we promise to be good parents. We can't do it without Your help, so we ask for Your great assistance."

"Amen."

"Lainey, your parents will soon know about the girls as Rasmus and Otis are at their store fairly often, and chances are, they may have already heard the story. But we'll need to get to Ellison Bay and let my parents meet their two new grandchildren. And you know, my mother will want to come for the birth."

Lainey sighed. "I'll be well cared for when this little one makes his or her entrance into the world."

Just then a knock sounded at the door. Lainey jumped. "Who in the world could that be at this hour?"

The door cracked open, and a familiar voice called, "Lainey? Clifford? It's the Gunnlersons. Please forgive this late visit. We were returning from an evening at a friend's and felt compelled to stop by."

Clifford swung the door open and shook the pastor's hand. "We are delighted to see you."

Lainey stood. "Come in, come in. Can I fix you a cup of tea?"

"Nothing. Nothing." Mrs. Gunnlerson embraced Lainey.

The four sat down at the table. "I won't take much time, dear ones. We heard the story of the girls who arrived on the Orphan Train, ran away, and then were found by Rasmus. We were even out looking for them when we heard. And we prayed." He paused and looked at Lainey, then Clifford. "We prayed that they'd be found, and we prayed for you. Are you considering keeping them?"

Lainey took a deep sigh and nodded at Clifford.

Clifford steepled his hands and rested his chin on his fingers. "We are, and we think we're supposed to take them. We just decided, but I think we knew. We've prayed, and we went to visit Otis and Edith and talked it through with them. We also craved your perspective, so we're so glad you stopped by.

Pastor Gunnlerson smiled and took his wife's hand in his. "Lainey, Clifford, a verse rose up in me today, and it won't leave. I think it's for you. It's Isaiah 41:10. 'Fear not, for I am with you; be not dismayed, for I am your God. I will strengthen you, I will help you, I will uphold you with My righteous right hand.'"

Lainey found she could no longer see Clifford or the Gunnlersons, for the tears sabotaged her eyes. It seemed they invaded her throat as well. Yet the tension seeped away, and a deep peace beckoned her. She decided to follow that peace. Clifford placed a handkerchief in her hand, and she wiped her eyes and cleared her throat. Upon gazing around, tears dominated every face, but there appeared a shine, almost a light on every face. Could there be an actual light from somewhere above them, or was it within?

Clifford coughed. "Pastor, that was . . . Well, we needed that. I think that sealed our decision." He turned. "Lainey?"

She nodded and reached for Pastor and Mrs. Gunnlerson's hands. "Yes. I was dismayed because I didn't feel strong enough, but I know now where my help is. It is in my God, and I believe He has chosen these girls for us."

The pastor squeezed her hand. "Or perhaps He chose you two for them."

Clifford placed his arm around his wife and drew her close. "Yes, yes, you're right."

"May we pray for you?"

Lainey and Clifford nodded and once more took the Gunnlersons' hands.

The pastor closed his eyes. "Dear Lord, You love children, and You love adoption. You have graced our sweet Lainey and her husband with both. Lainey was adopted, now soon to give birth, and also to adopt. You set the solitary in families, and so we thank You that Addy and Molly will be in this family. Bless them, keep them, help them, and make them all strong in You. Amen."

Lainey and Clifford both added an amen.

"We should go. It will be a dark ride home, but I do have a lantern. It should be fine." Pastor and his wife stood.

Clifford stood as well. "No, it's too dark and not even a moon. You'll stay in one of our cabins. No one is here now, and no one is coming for another day or two."

"But that is more work for you. We know you have to clean and change the bedding. I'm sure we'll be fine."

Lainey tipped her head. "We won't take no for an answer. You will spend the night. You have always been there for us. Now let us be there for you. And don't you dare sneak off before breakfast. Clifford will take care of your horse and I'll show you to your cabin."

Addy stirred as Mr. Rasmus scooped her up. "Well, young lady, how do you feel?"

Addy shook her head. "I think I was sleeping. I forgot all about falling. I'm really sorry. Do you think we'll have to go back to the Orphan Train?"

Mr. Rasmus smiled. "No one is sending you back. Don't you worry about that. We're taking you back to the boat now and back to our house."

Addy nodded. "Okay."

"Are you hungry? We all ate while you slept."

"Oh, well, I am, but that's okay."

Mr. Rasmus carried her outside and set her in the wagon next to Molly. Molly leaned against her. "Mrs. Hanson gave me two sandwiches for you."

Addy gobbled them as they rode along. She gulped as she finished. "I was really hungry." She grinned. "Thank you, Mrs. Hanson."

"You're more than welcome."

Mr. Engelson reined the horse to a stop close to the boat dock.

Addy scooted to the end of the wagon, grimacing as her heel slid across the wood. "Should I walk to the boat? I think I can."

Carter scooted off ahead of her. "Wait, Addy. Mr. Hanson will carry you."

Mr. Rasmus slipped his arms under Addy and lifted her. "You'll be walking on that soon. But we're going to keep you resting for a few days."

Addy waved to the Engelsons as Mr. Rasmus set her on a seat on the boat where she could rest her injured ankle. He turned and lifted Molly onto a seat near her. Catherine and her mother stepped on while David tended the lines.

Addy frowned as they waved back. Would she ever see them again? They helped her so much, but did anyone really want her now? She was trouble. Molly would stay, and they would make her go, even though they said they wouldn't. How could she manage? A tear trickled down her cheek.

"Ma, Addy's crying." Catherine sat next her. "Does it hurt bad?"

"Not that much." She looked down.

Mrs. Hanson smiled and tilted her head. "Don't worry, Addy. Everything will work out."

Confusion filled her mind. How did Mrs. Hanson seem to know and understand her thoughts? So many people in this place overflowed with kindness. And they didn't have to.

The morning sun peeked through the curtains. Molly nudged Addy. "Let's get up. I think I smell breakfast."

Addy sat up and rubbed her eyes. She yawned and, without thinking, swung her legs out of the bed and stood. "Ohhh!" She stumbled and caught herself on a nearby chair. "I forgot about my ankle." She plopped down in the chair and unwound the wrap. She studied her lower leg. "It's still a little swollen and red. I think it was worse yesterday, but it still hurts."

Mrs. Hanson walked in carrying a pan with water. "Oh, Addy, I wanted to get in here before you awoke, but I want you to stay right there in the chair. Catherine will bring your breakfast. This is warm water with Epsom salts in it. It will help bring the swelling down more. The rest of the day you'll keep it elevated. No playing outside today."

Addy groaned. "Thank you, but I don't like this. I wish I hadn't tried to go down to the water."

Mrs. Hanson nodded. "Sometimes, we learn easy. Sometimes, we learn hard."

Addy looked up, examining Mrs. Hanson's expression. She didn't seem angry. Still, Addy was certain nobody would want her now.

Catherine came in carrying two plates with eggs and potatoes. "We get to eat in here. Molly is going to eat with Ma in the kitchen." She set the plate on the little table next to Addy and sat down in the other chair. "This is fun. I know your ankle hurts, but I like having you here. We can read books or play checkers today. I can teach you to embroider, too, if you like. Have you ever done that?"

"My mama said she'd teach me, but then she got sick."

Catherine nodded. "I'd like to teach you."

They heard a wagon arrive outside the window. Catherine pushed the curtain aside. "It's Lainey and Clifford!" She turned and grinned at Addy, then ran out of the bedroom. The door bumped the wall and swung back partway.

Addy sighed. Mr. and Mrs. Captain. Probably here to say they found someone else who would take them, and maybe not, once they heard about her causing more trouble. She touched her forehead. A slight pang of discomfort shot through her head. The goose egg was still there, but not as big.

Molly squealed. She must be hugging them. They might not even want to see her at all. She could hear everyone talking. A silence followed. Addy gulped. *Well, they'll leave now. They won't even say goodbye.*

The door swung open. There stood Mrs. and Mr. Captain. Molly had Mrs. Captain's hand. They were all smiling. Confusion reigned in Addy's head again. So much smiling. Surely, they would soon frown at her.

Mrs. Captain knelt in front of her. "I'm so sorry you're hurt, but as soon as breakfast is over, we're taking you home."

Home? That sounded strange.

Addy studied her face. Was she about to laugh? Was she teasing her?

"Addy, we've come to get our girls. You and Molly are going to live with us. We've decided we love you both. I think we knew it almost as soon as we met you. We can't let you go anywhere else. God brought you to us."

"You heard about my ankle, that I disobeyed Carter and caused so much trouble for everyone? Aren't you mad?"

"Oh, I think you learned a lesson like we all do as we grow. We're not mad. We're just happy to have you be part of our family."

Tears burst from her eyes and poured down her face. Soon, she found herself in Mr. Captain's arms.

He sat on the edge of the bed and held her on his lap. Molly scrambled up next to them. "Mr. Captain, I want to always be with you and Mrs. Captain. Can I call you Ma and Pa?" She raised her eyebrows at Addy. "Is that okay with you, Addy?"

"It's okay, Molly." Addy leaned against Mr. Captain's chest and breathed in his cotton shirt and boat scent. Relief coursed through her. Every muscle relaxed.

Mrs. Captain sat next to Molly and placed her arm around the little girl. "We are now a family of four—well, actually five—and this little one is kicking right now—must be happy about getting two sisters."

Everyone crowded into the bedroom to congratulate the girls. Mrs. Hanson insisted that Addy soak her ankle a few more minutes while finishing her breakfast. Before leaving, Mrs. Hanson dried and rewrapped her ankle and instructed Mr. and Mrs. Captain that she should keep it elevated for a day or two. Mr. Captain carried her out to the wagon when it was time to go.

The ride back to Sunset Resort was quiet. Molly sat on Mrs. Captain's lap, and Addy sat between their new parents with a box to rest her foot on. She alternately leaned on each of them. Deep sighs punctuated the clop-clop of the horses. Addy wanted to laugh and cry at the same time, but she simply breathed deeply. How could she have landed here with Molly and these wonderful people who said they loved her? Her eyes welled. Just four days previous, she and Molly had arrived in Ephraim on the steamer, almost sure they'd be slaves but willing to work hard. And now, here they were, with family and friends and adventures to enjoy. She would still work hard, though. Mrs. Captain deserved that. Addy had caused her a lot of worry, and she would need help. Addy would be her help with all that was within her.

Upon arriving, Addy instructed Molly to grab their little bags and take them to the cottage. She glanced over. "Right, Mrs. Captain? The little cottage we stayed in before?"

Mrs. Captain smiled and shook her head. "No, Addy, we want you close to us. We have a bedroom in the main building for you. You and Molly will be in the same big bed. Is that okay? We can get two smaller beds later if you'd prefer that. The baby's room is right next to us, and the next room is yours. Does that sound good?

Molly looked up at Addy. "I like that, don't you, Addy?"

Addy grinned. "Yes, Molly and Mrs. Captain, that sounds nice. Thank you."

Molly stood and whispered into Addy's ear. "We can call them Ma and Pa, remember?"

"We can; you're right. You can start right now, Molly."

Molly tilted her head. "But what about you?"

Addy hugged her sister. "I will. Soon."

Mr. Captain helped his wife down from the wagon. He then caught Molly under her arms and swung her out and around before setting her down. He laughed, and Molly giggled. Addy scooted herself over to the edge of the wagon seat. Mr. Captain scooped her up and carried her inside with Molly right next to him. Mrs. Captain grabbed their bags. They passed through the dining room into the sitting area, where they'd played with little Hans.

Mrs. Captain pointed to one of the doors. "That's our bedroom there. The baby's room is right next to it. Your room is here." She opened a door to a small room that had a bed big enough for the two of them. A fluffy quilt covered with flower designs and multiple colors was spread across the bed. A chest of drawers stood next to a window that looked out to the woods. An overstuffed chair sat on one wall next to a small table with a wooden chair.

"It's not real big, but we think you'll be cozy. When you have schoolwork, you can work here or out in the sitting room. I think we may need a bigger chest of drawers sometime, but . . . oooh!" Mrs. Captain reached down as Molly threw her arms around her and sobbed. "Oh, Molly, it's all right. We're so glad you're here."

Addy then buried her face in Mr. Captain's shoulder and began to cry in great gasps.

Mr. Captain sat down on the settee in the sitting room, and Mrs. Captain sat next to them, while Molly climbed up beside her. Mrs. Captain took Addy's hands in hers. "Addy, Addy, we love you. I'm hoping these are happy tears. Does your ankle hurt?" She looked up to her husband. "Let's get her set up out here with her foot elevated. Are you all right?"

"It's too nice. I mean, thank you. I don't know . . . I mean, I don't know what I should do. I've been so awful, and yet you want us."

"Oh, Addy, we do want you and Molly. You don't have to do anything." Lainey winked. "Except sit with your foot up. I think that might be the hardest thing we'll ask of you. But soon, that ankle will be back to normal." She tapped Addy's nose. "No need to cry. We are now family. This is your home, and once that ankle is good, you'll be able to explore and play all day long."

Addy sniffed. "I promise to help you and not cause trouble."

Mr. Captain chuckled. "Don't you worry about that."

The next two days, the girls settled in. Addy longed to explore, while Molly was content to stay close to Mrs. Captain. Mrs. Captain provided books for Addy to read the first afternoon. Addy pushed the books away at first, but when Mrs. Captain took a nap and Molly fell asleep as well, Addy picked up *The Adventures of Huckleberry Finn.* Before she knew it, she was well into it, recognizing that she was of a similar spirit as Huck. *At least, I haven't gotten in as much trouble as he did.*

Mr. Rasmus brought Catherine over the next day to sit with Addy and teach her to embroider. Molly asked to learn as well. Soon, Addy found that this agreed with her. She determined to make something for the baby. Whispering, she asked Catherine what she might do.

Catherine rubbed the side of her face. "Well, you could make a pillow. One side would be what you embroider, and the other would just be plain fabric. My mama could help with the sewing part. Do you know how to sew?"

"I watched my mama sew some but never did learn. But if I can embroider, I could probably sew, too, don't you think?"

"Yes, but what would you embroider? We don't know the name or whether it's a boy or girl."

"Hmmm, that's true. Maybe just a picture of Mrs. Captain holding a baby or saying, 'God bless this baby.' They like Bible verses. Do you know a Bible verse I could embroider?"

Catherine grinned. "That's a great idea. Let me ask Ma and Pa. I know an angel came to Mary in the Bible to tell her about having Jesus as a baby. Maybe there's a verse there you could use."

Molly's eyes grew big. "An angel. Oooh. Didn't Mama have a picture of one? Could you make an embroidery drawing of that, Addy?"

"Well, maybe. Angels have wings, don't they? I think I saw another picture of angels in Mama's Bible. Mama told us stories from the Bible, but I remember only a few of them."

"Addy, do you think you'll call Miss Lainey *Ma?*"

Molly grinned. "I call her Ma. You said it was okay, right, Addy?"

Addy smiled. "Yes, Molly, it's okay." She looked at Catherine and shrugged her shoulders. "I'm sure I will soon."

Mrs. Captain walked into the sitting room. "Oh, look at you girls. Do you like to embroider?"

Addy held up her cloth. "I do like it. It's not as hard as I thought."

Molly ran over to hug her new mother. "I like it, too, Ma."

"Are you ready for cookies and milk?"

A chorus of yes rang out just as a knock came on the door. There stood Mrs. Figgenschau.

Mrs. Captain went quickly to greet her. "Come in. Come in. I was just about to get the girls some cookies and milk. Would you please join us?"

"Oh, none for me, but I would love to sit with you for a few minutes. The walk here seems just a bit longer each time. That must be what getting older does to one's ability to get around. But no more about me. Has a home been determined for these young ladies?"

"Yes, yes, it has. And this is now their home. They are now our daughters."

Mrs. Figgenschau lowered herself in a nearby chair. "I'm delighted to hear it. I knew this was to be your home from the time I met you two."

Molly stood and walked over to her. "How did you know that?"

Mrs. Figgenschau patted her shoulder. "Oh, sometimes we just know things as we get older. I talk a lot to the Lord, and I get a sense about things. But I heard about the young lady's fall and brought some herbs and salve for your ankle. Looks like you got a bruise on your forehead, too."

"I did. I had a duck egg . . . Wait, what do you call it, a goose egg?"

Catherine laughed. "Addy, you're so funny. But the goose egg is almost gone, even though it's still a little black and blue."

Mrs. Figgenschau stood. "I have salve for that as well. May I?" She looked first to Mrs. Captain and then to Addy.

"Please do. And thank you. I'll get the cookies and milk now. Molly, would you like to help me?"

Catherine moved off the footstool next to Addy, and Mrs. Figgenschau sat down. "Let's unwrap that ankle and see how it looks." She carefully untied the wrap and took it off. It still looked red to Addy but not nearly as swollen.

Mrs. Figgenschau had Addy turn so her ankle lay across her lap. "I'm going to rub it a bit to just get the blood flowing again through there."

Addy gulped. "You're going to make it bleed?"

"Oh, no, no. When you sit a long time, the blood doesn't flow as well on the inside to the area of injury. So, rubbing it helps get things back to normal. That is, if it doesn't hurt too much when I rub."

Addy shook her head. "That doesn't hurt. It feels good. It hurt so much before. Does that mean it's healed?"

"Well, it's in the recovery process. Now, I'm going to rub my salve on it. It's made of oils and herbs that can help with healing."

"Mrs. Engelson on Rock Island, where I fell, used some of your salve on it the first day."

"Oh, I'm so glad to hear that. I do recall she has purchased some of my salves."

Mrs. Captain arrived with a tray heaping with cookies while Molly carried a small pitcher of milk. "Oh, do let me pay you for your salve. Then I can apply it as often as you suggest."

"Cookies and milk and your fine company are payment enough. I will leave this here. I would suggest a morning and evening application, but I don't think she needs the wrap anymore."

Addy clapped. "Does that mean I can walk on it now?"

Mrs. Captain set the tray down and extended her hand to Addy. "Let's see."

Addy placed both feet on the floor and let Catherine take her other hand. Putting her weight on her feet to stand felt strange. She'd been carried or sitting for almost three days. She felt a little wobbly, but stood. "It feels a little strange, but it doesn't hurt."

Mrs. Captain put her hand under her arm. "Okay, let's take a small step. Maybe a shuffle step. See if it's strong enough."

Addy shuffled across to the table, never fully lifting her foot. "It tingles a bit, almost itches, but it doesn't hurt."

Mrs. Figgenschau smiled. "The itchy feeling is just the healing and getting back to normal. I'll leave an extra salve to help with that. It may take a few days for the itchiness to leave. Try holding on to the back of that chair and place your full weight on the injured ankle. That way, you won't fall if it isn't strong enough yet."

Addy followed instructions and winced as she stood on her injured side. Her eyes grew big. "It doesn't hurt."

Molly scrunched her face. "But you just winced."

"I expected it to hurt, but it didn't."

Mrs. Captain came to stand beside her. "Well, let's try walking then."

The tingling continued, as did the itchiness. Addy took three steps, stopped, and bent down to rub her ankle. She then walked the rest of the way to the settee. "It still feels a little weird, but it doesn't hurt."

Mrs. Figgenschau smiled. "Well, I think you'll be just fine. I wouldn't advise running for a couple days. Use the salve for a few days. I think you'll be good as new before you know it. Now, I think I'd like some cookies and milk before I go home."

Addy spent the rest of the day alternating walking and sitting, determined to follow instructions and not make her ankle worse. More than anything, she wanted to please Mr. and Mrs. Captain and not disappoint them.

She begged Mr. Captain to let her go with him the next day on the boat. At first, he said no, then relented but made her promise not to jump out of the boat to tie the lines. She promised. "I'll still be out on the water, and I'll learn more of what needs to be done as a first mate."

"And you'll sit a lot of the time. And you'll bring the salve." Mr. Captain's voice was a bit stern, and his eyes held hers.

"Okay, Mr. Captain . . . Pa."

His face softened, and a tear filled his eye. He scooped her up in his arms and twirled her around. "Did you say *Pa?*"

Addy nodded and buried her face in his shoulder. She was home.

CHAPTER ELEVEN

THE NEXT MORNING ARRIVED COOL and dry. Mrs. Captain insisted she wear a sweater. As she went out the door, she paused and turned. "Bye, Ma."

Ma got the sweetest expression on her face and blew her a kiss.

Addy kept her promise not to jump out and tie the lines, though she dearly wanted to. Instead, she moved to the stern quickly to toss the lines to Pa. *Pa.* That felt really good to say. It brought a tinge of sadness as she wondered where her first papa might be. If Mama had died. If Papa was okay. But this was her life now, and Mr. Captain was her pa. It was good. Maybe someday she'd find out her parents' fate, but she would have a good life here.

To Addy's surprise, after the guests boarded the boat and found their seats, Pa brought the boat around to another dock, where a wide plank was placed from the dock to the boat. A man drove a horse and a small wagon onto the boat. Addy watched with wide eyes. No one else seemed surprised.

Pa grinned and patted Addy's shoulder. "We sometimes transport horses and wagons. We're going to unhook the horse now and place the wagon between him and the water. We'll put blinders on him, so he doesn't see the water. That can make him nervous. The wagon driver will sit on his seat and talk to the horse along the way."

Addy waited until they were underway, then went to the front of the wagon and caught the eye of the driver. He smiled and nodded. Addy shuffled up to the front of the horse and whispered a hello. The horse nickered. She took a step forward and placed her hand on his forehead as Tina had instructed her with Missy. "Good boy. You're a good boy." The horse pressed against her hand, so she rubbed his face up and down.

The wagon driver smiled. "So, you know horses. I can see he likes you already."

Addy squinted. "Well, this is only the second time I've petted a horse. My friend told me how."

"Well, looks like you were born for it. Here, give him a carrot, but be careful he doesn't bite you. His name is Midnight."

"Here, Midnight. I like your name." Addy held the carrot and giggled as the horse scarfed it down. She pulled her hand back just in time so as to not be part of the snack. The horse nickered again and nudged her hand. She patted his forehead again.

The wind picked up and caused some rocking of the barge. The wagon driver laid his hand on the horse's neck. "He's pretty good on the boat, but when it's rough, he can get a little spooked. That's why we have the blinders on him, so he doesn't see the waves, but he can feel them. Young lady, you should take your seat."

Addy grinned. "I like it when it's rough. It doesn't scare me or make me seasick. And if Midnight might get spooked, then I'll just stay here." She laid both hands on Midnight's face, one on each side. "Don't you worry, Midnight. We'll be fine. Just a little rocking." Midnight nickered and closed his eyes, breathing deep.

The driver shook his head. "Girl, you sure have a gift. I've never seen anyone, not even me, calm a horse like that. If you ever need a job, you might want to check out a horse stable. Tell them Jack Figgenschau recommended you."

Addy's head jerked up. "Figgenschau? Are you Mrs. Figgenschau's son?"

"The one on Washington Island? Hilga? She's my aunt. She's a little strange to some. You know her?"

"Yes, she helped my ankle with her salve." Addy chuckled. "We thought she was a witch at first."

"Oh no. Does she know that?"

Addy laughed. "My sister told her—asked her if she was a witch. She said she was just old."

"Well, it's good to hear she has her sense of humor intact. Do you live on Washington Island?"

"I do now. We just came . . . on the Orphan Train."

Pa called out over his shoulder. "Jack, Miss Addy is now my daughter."

"Oh my, so good to hear that." Jack smiled down at Addy. "We have two boys who came to us on the Orphan Train—Forrest and Roy. They're a little older, came to us two years ago. They're with my wife and helping out on our farm right now. That is, when they're not pulling antics in Ephraim." He chuckled and shook his head. "They manage to sneak on the big steamers that come in, and then they go to the top deck and jump in the water. Ship management folks are pretty upset about it, but they never catch them. A good portion of Ephraim people think it's hilarious. I'm hoping they'll end their shenanigans soon. So, if you meet them, don't try to join them in their trouble-making."

Addy's eyes grew big. "They actually do that?"

The man winked at Addy. "They do. Maybe next time I come, I'll bring them along. They've gotten to know a few of the others who came on the 'O Train,' as they call it. We thought it would be good to have all the children get to know each other a bit. It gives them a bit of support and friendship and allows us to make sure they're treated right and not . . . well . . . "

Addy raised her eyebrows. "Not made slaves?"

Jack hung his head. "Well, yes, we've heard stories and even intervened once with one family. But for the most part, the children are well cared for. Sometimes overworked. But I was not aware that Clifford and Lainey were looking for help."

Pa turned. "Addy, the wind has settled a bit. Can you take the wheel for a minute?"

Addy grinned. "I think Pa wants to tell you that my sister and I are surprises. They weren't looking for help, but they decided they wanted us. Another family didn't want us. It worked out pretty good."

"Addy." Clifford's voice held a sternness.

"Yes, Pa. It's okay; I told him already how we got here. But I can take the wheel." She walked with a slight limp to her new pa.

"Your ankle still hurt?"

"No, just not quite as strong as the other yet. And walking on the boat is a little uneven. Everyone said it'll be strong again soon."

Pa smiled. "It will. Just hold the boat straight on this path. You up for it."

"I love it. Mr. Jack said I was a natural with horses, too."

Pa kissed her head. "You are a very talented young woman. I'll be right back."

Addy strained to hear their conversation. She caught snippets of the Bergman's refusal, but soon realized he was discussing the idea of all the children getting together with their new families, a picnic sometime. Pa soon returned and took the wheel.

CHAPTER TWELVE

JUNE PASSED QUICKLY. EVERY WEEK, at least once and perhaps twice, Mr. Rasmus or Pa would collect Addy, Molly, Catherine, and David from Washington; Andrew and Charlotte from Pilot Island; and Tina and Carter from Rock Island. Arlo and Sarah's children—Hattie, Harry, and Helen—joined them as well. Each time, they would spend the day at the home of one of the families. Addy found herself developing strong friendships with each of the children.

Andrew was twelve and disclosed some of his anger and hurt at losing his parents. Addy marveled that she and Andrew had so much in common besides the loss of their parents. They loved to explore and longed to live on the sea. Andrew didn't mind the smallness of Pilot Island but delighted to hike the perimeter of Rock Island when they spent the day there. That day, Carter shared the history, while Catherine and the younger girls picked flowers and lagged behind.

As they sat on the small beach on the eastern side of Rock, Carter told the younger ones scary stories at the small cemetery just a short distance away. Addy and Andrew sat in the sand letting the small granules run through their fingers. A few fishing boats could be seen in the distance.

"Would you want to be a fisherman out on one of those boats?"

Andrew shook his head. "Not really. I want to travel on the steamers that go through the passage. I mean, some go to Milwaukee and Chicago. Some go over to Lake Huron and down to Detroit. I'd even like to travel on the Atlantic Ocean."

Addy nodded. "I think I'd like that, too. I think the ocean sounds scary, but if I learned well on the Lakes, I might want to go there."

"Do you think they'd let girls go?"

Addy punched his arm. "Why not? I'm better than some men, well, boys. Mr. Rasmus and Pa say I'm a natural, but I still have a lot to learn. Pa learned on his uncle's fishing boat."

"I haven't been on too many boats. I want to be. Right now, I really enjoy learning all about them from Uncle Julius. I haven't called him Pa yet. I mean, he's really a cousin. Actually, Marla is my cousin. I think they didn't want to put any pressure on us, so they suggested we call them Aunt and Uncle. I think Charlotte wants to call them Ma and Pa. I'm just not sure yet."

"Yeah, Molly called Mr. and Mrs. Captain Ma and Pa right away. It took a few days for me, but they were fine with that. But did you know Ma, Mrs. Captain, lost her parents in a shipwreck? In fact, before they drowned, they saved Carter from drowning. He was real little then. And Ma lived on Pilot with her aunt and uncle before Carter's parents adopted her."

"Wow. I didn't know all that. I think Aunt Marla mentioned something along that line, but I didn't quite get the whole story. Do you think the next time we come to Sunset Resort, she'd let me talk to her about it?"

"I think she would, and guess what? She's written stories or articles about it. I guess she studied writing in college, and some of her stories have been published in magazines. She just showed them to me the other day. I haven't read them yet, but I plan to."

Carter and the girls joined them. "C'mon. Let's get down to the south end. There are dunes and caves, and we can swim there, too, if we want."

Andrew, David, and Catherine wanted to play in the water, but Addy followed Carter to the cave area with the rest of the girls and ran her hands over the smooth roughness of the rock walls. The etchings in the stone by the early Indian residents amazed her. Carter made sure everyone was careful with the rocks and water. He said that waves often plummeted this shore of Rock Island. "Thankfully, it's fairly calm today, so it's safe."

Addy noticed that as much as she had in common with Andrew—loss of parents and longing for sea life—it was Carter who made her feel secure. He was kind and funny. His warnings, rescue, and protectiveness when she fell had imprinted her heart somehow. She never wanted to disappoint him again and listened to his every word. She loved when he would tease her. She didn't quite understand it, but this summer was outstanding.

Lainey welcomed the children with cookies and milk, promising lunch about 1:00 p.m. Two weeks had passed since Rasmus had taken them to Rock Island. Clifford was taking guests back to Ephraim, and Addy had stayed home to be with her friends. Lainey had only a few guests and needed to do some cleaning, so she left the kids to their snack and went out to one of the cottages.

Andrew followed her. "Miss Lainey, Addy told me a bit about your parents." He shifted his feet. "You know, my parents died, too. Do you think it's okay for me to call my cousins Uncle and Aunt rather than Ma and Pa? I know Addy and Molly call you Ma and Pa now."

Lainey sat her basket of cleaning supplies on the ground next to the cottage. She placed her hand on Andrew's shoulder. "Oh, Andrew, it's okay. You and Charlotte, as well as Addy and Molly, have been through so much." She straightened up and stretched her back. "And it was an awful shock to lose my parents. I lived, at that time, on Pilot Island." She tapped his nose. "Right where you live now. I grieved greatly. Uncle Otis was my rock, as well as Rose—she's Catherine's sister and married to Julius' brother. It's good to talk about it. Don't worry about not calling them Ma and Pa. If that comes, that's wonderful. It took me over a year to do that with Carter's parents, who took me in after my uncle broke his leg and had to leave the lighthouse."

Andrew took a deep breath. "Addy said you wrote stories about it. Would you . . . I mean . . . Well, do you mind if I read them? I do like to read."

Lainey turned and steered him back to the main building. "I would be delighted. I have more than one copy of each of those, so let me get them. You can take them back with you."

Andrew looked up and grinned at her. "I'll be sure to return them after I read them."

"Thank you, Andrew." She walked into her bedroom and came out with three magazines. "Andrew, here they are. I'll place them on the table here, and let's make sure you don't forget them when it's time to return home."

Addy stood in the doorway. "Ma, I'm going to take them for a walk to Mrs. Figgenschau's little house. We won't stay long."

"Oh, let me get some money. Get some of her salve that she gave us for your ankle. I'd like to have some on hand in case any guests or any of you hurt yourselves."

Addy and Molly had returned to Mrs. Figgenschau's home twice since coming to live on Washington Island. They'd discovered a well-worn path they hadn't noticed when running away. This day, they sang and skipped along the path with all the children in tow. Addy loved that she and Molly had grown adept at traveling the wooded and rocky paths of the island and that they rarely tripped anymore.

When they arrived at Figgenschau Cove, Mrs. Figgenschau stood grinning with her hands on her hips. "I heard you coming twenty minutes ago. I like your singing. A little birdie told me earlier you were coming, and I have cookies and bread and soup enough for all of you."

Charlotte stopped. "A birdie told you? Really?"

Mrs. Figgenschau laughed. "It's only an expression, sweet one. But I'm sure glad I felt like baking this morning."

Carter held up a hand. "Mrs. Figgenschau, are you sure you want to feed all of us? I mean, there are eleven of us. Ma would say we'd eat you out of house and home."

Mrs. Figgenschau placed her arms around Molly and Addy. "I'm delighted to share all I have with each of you. I don't think my little house will hold all of you, though, so we'll eat outside."

The children ate and played on the water's edge. David removed his shoes and ventured out in the water. "Hey, everyone. It's really sandy on the bottom. Come on out."

Each one shucked off their shoes and waded out to their knees, the girls pulling up their skirts and the boys their knickers. David had already waded deeper and was wet almost to his waist.

Catherine shook her head. "David, don't get too wet. Ma might not like that."

"Don't worry, Sis; I'll dry." Just then, his foot struck a rock, and he tumbled into the water, head first. He came up, blubbering and laughing. "Well, there's one rock here, but the water's great."

Laughing, each one ran deeper in the water and dove in. A splashing game soon followed. Addy waded out of the water, her hair dripping water over her face and her clothes adding weight. "Oh, that was fun, but these clothes are heavy when they're wet."

Mrs. Figgenschau set cookies on a small table. "You are having so much fun. It warms my heart to watch you play in the water. Be sure to sit a while before you head home, though, so you can dry. There's little sun in the woods but plenty here to dry you off."

The rest of the kids tumbled out of the water, laughing and dripping. Most sprawled on the grassy area near the water. The sun warmed them, and their clothes began to dry as they continued to consume cookies.

Tina groaned. "I think I ate too many cookies. My tummy is rumbling."

Catherine grinned. "But they were so good. Thank you, Mrs. Figgenschau."

"You are so welcome, Catherine. Tina, I have some herbal tea to help settle your stomach. I make it whenever I make cookies because . . . " She winked. "Sometimes, I eat too many cookies, too."

Everyone had a cup of Mrs. Figgenschau's tea. After an hour, they trekked back to Sunset Resort. Before leaving, each child wrapped their arms around the older woman and thanked her for a grand time.

Charlotte paused after hugging. "Mrs. Figgenschau, you are like a grandma to me. May I call you Grandma?"

A tear leaked out of Mrs. Figgenschau's eye. "Oh, Charlotte, I would be honored to have you call me Grandma. Thank you."

Addy stopped and turned. "Oh, I almost forgot. Ma wants some of those herbs that you put on my ankle. She sent some money with me." Her face went white. "Oh no, what if I lost the money in the water." She ran her hands into her pockets, then breathed a sigh of relief. "Here it is. It's all wet."

Mrs. Figgenschau laughed. "That's just fine. I made some of the salve earlier this week. And even if you had lost the money, I wouldn't have minded. Your mama is a wonderful woman, and anything I have is hers, money or not." She went inside and came out with two small jars for Addy to take home.

Addy turned again before leaving. "Mrs. Figgenschau. I met your nephew. He brought his wagon and horse over on Pa's barge boat. He let me talk with his horse. He said I was gifted with horses."

The elderly woman placed her hand on Addy's shoulder. "He came by to visit and told me all about it. You're a talented young lady."

Addy didn't even feel the heaviness of the damp clothes as the children trudged along the trail back to Sunset Resort. She was as tired and full as the rest of them; but Mrs. Figgenschau's praise penetrated deep in her soul, and a joy lightened her heart.

Ma hung clothes on the line as the children returned. Pa's boat idled at the dock, ready to return everyone home. Ma placed her hands on the sides of her back and stretched. She turned upon hearing the chatter. She burst out laughing. "You are a bedraggled-looking bunch, but I see smiles. Well, tired smiles. Did you all go swimming?"

Addy squinted her eyes and raised her shoulders. "We did. It was so much fun, Ma. David started it."

"But I'm almost dry. Glad I don't have to wear skirts."

"Well, sit in the sun for a few minutes. It's always a little chillier on the water. Wouldn't want you to go home with a cold."

Tina grinned. "It's okay; the wind will help dry us. Thank you for letting us go to Mrs. Figgenschau's house. She is so nice, even though . . . "

A chorus finished her sentence. "She looks like a witch." Everyone laughed, while Ma shook her head.

Charlotte walked up to Ma. "I asked if I could call her Grandma. She said yes. Could I call you Aunt Lainey, not just Miss Lainey? Please."

Ma drew her into her arms. "Of course, I'm delighted to have you do that. And lunch is ready if you have room left. Sandwiches are on the table. I think you've had enough cookies for one day."

CHAPTER THIRTEEN

THE NEXT MORNING, PA LEFT early with the remainder of the guests. The girls rose late, tuckered out from all the fun with their friends the day before. Addy stumbled out of the bedroom rubbing her eyes. Ma was in the kitchen.

"There you are, sleepyheads. I think I burned the bacon waiting for you to arise."

"It's okay. I like crisp bacon. I think the smoke woke me up."

Molly trailed behind. "I smell smoke, and why does the sky look red?"

Addy stretched and yawned. "The sunrise is red sometimes, right, Ma?"

Ma chuckled. "The sun rose more than an hour ago. You're sleepyheads today."

Molly shook her head. "But look." She pointed out the dining room windows to the south.

Ma's face turned white. "Oh no, that looks like a fire. I didn't notice the smoke because of the bacon burning. Oh my, the smoke is stronger now."

Bells rang in the distance. Ma wiped her hands on her apron. "The church bells ring when there's an emergency, and everyone else with a bell rings theirs, too, alerting all the island. We need to go. That fire may be coming our way. Get dressed as fast as you can. We'll need to get the horse and wagon ready as soon as I slow the fire in the stove."

Addy fought to remain calm. Her stomach seemed to be in her throat. She didn't want Molly to be scared but hurried her to get dressed. "Molly, everything will be all right, but we have to leave right now."

They dressed and scurried out to help Ma with the horse and wagon. Addy had spent more time with Nellie since she had talked with Mrs. Figgenschau's nephew. Addy ran to the barn and patted Nellie on her forehead. *Don't let the horse feel my worry. I wish Pa was here.* She led the horse to the wagon, and Ma hooked her up.

Addy helped her mama climb to the wagon seat. Molly scrambled up after her.

"Addy, you're so good with the horse. I love how you keep her calm."

"I know. Me, too. Ever since I met Mrs. Figgenschau's nephew on Pa's boat." Addy's face drained of color. "Wait, Mrs. Figgenschau won't hear the bells. She might not know. The fire is south. She is south. I have to go help her."

Ma's eyes grew large. "Addy, no. She may have already left. She's wise. She may have already left."

Addy stood still, her hand on the side of the wagon. "No, I have to go." She walked to the horse. "Nellie, get Ma and Molly to a safe place. Stay calm, even if smoke gets strong. Okay?" The horse nickered. Addy looked at her new mother. "I have to, Ma. I'll be careful. Molly, be strong for Ma, okay?"

Molly nodded. "But . . . "

"Don't cry, Molly. Help Ma."

"Come up on the wagon, Addy." Ma's voice was stern. "We'll send someone to help Mrs. Figgenschau."

Addy began to run toward the woods. She called over her shoulder. "I'm the someone, Ma."

The smoke was stronger than she thought it would be. It disoriented her vision and clouded her mind. "I know the way. I have to go. She needs me." Coughing, she paused to rip a part of her skirt and wrap it around her mouth and nose. For a moment, uncertainty filled her mind. She slapped the side of her head. "You know the way, girl. You know the way. Focus. Move your feet." Uncertainty began to tug at her heart and scream in her mind. *Turn around. You can't do this.* She fell to her knees. Breathing was easier. She remembered her first papa telling her that smoke rises and that if ever their home caught fire and filled with smoke, she should crawl, as the air lower to the floor would be easier to breathe.

"Thank you." She wasn't quite sure who she was thanking. Maybe God, maybe her papa, who let her go. It didn't matter. Crawling wouldn't work, but she could run hunched over. That she did. Her shoulders ached, but determination pulled her forward. Would Mrs. Figgenschau be okay? *Let her be okay, God. She was nice to me. So nice. And don't let Ma worry too much.*

The end of the woods came upon Addy suddenly. She sprawled on the sandy beach. Part of her wanted to just sleep. The soft sand cradled her and brought relief to her hard run. Running with her back hunched prevented her from fully seeing where she was going, but she focused on the path she knew. Hard work. She needed a break. Just a few moments. A movement caught her eye. Addy jerked her head up. She'd arrived at Mrs. Figgenschau's home. She glanced past the cottage and saw flames tickling the sky. The smoke had lessened but still made her cough.

Wait. I saw movement. Wake up, Addy. She forced her eyes to shift back to the beach, and there lay Mrs. Figgenschau in a heap. Addy stood and almost passed out. Too much smoke. She squatted back down and crawled to the older woman.

"Mrs. Figgenschau. Wake up. I'm here to help you. We have to leave. Can you walk? Can you crawl?" Nothing. Addy shook her. "Please, Mrs. Figgenschau, wake up. I'll help you." Her tears mixed with the smoke, and when she wiped her eyes to see better, her fingers came back muddy.

Mrs. Figgenschau groaned. Her eyes fluttered. Addy got down inches from her face and yelled. "We have to go. I'll help you."

The older woman's hand touched Addy's arm. "Oh, dear one. Save yourself. Do leave me here. It's all right. I'm half-dead already. I can hardly breathe. You go." She coughed and closed her eyes and went limp.

"No!" The scream emanated from the depths of Addy's soul. She pulled herself up on her knees, placed her hands under Mrs. Figgenschau's arms, and backed up toward the water, dragging Mrs. Figgenschau inch by inch. Coughing overtook her. She paused and looked up. "I must. I must save her. God, help me." The orange flames were all but licking Mrs. Figgenschau's cottage. Tears made it hard to see. Addy kept backing up. Upon reaching the water, she gave a final heave and stumbled into the chilled and welcoming water. She splashed water on Mrs. Figgenschau's face and her own. The woman's eyes opened.

"Yes, Addy, the water." Her voice was weak. "Thank you. I tried to get here, but the smoke."

"It's okay, Mrs. Figgenschau. You don't need to talk. I'm going to take us deeper."

Mrs. Figgenschau nodded but then began to cry. "Oh, Addy, look at my cottage."

Addy looked. The flames now consumed the little, beautiful home of her dear friend. "I'm so sorry. So sorry."

Mrs. Figgenschau smiled and coughed. "Thank you." Her raspy voice barely reached Addy's ears. Addy bent close to hear her. "You saved me." Sobs and gasps convulsed the older woman. Then a few more words. "Can replace cottage." Another smile crossed her face, accompanied with coughs. "Guess I can't be replaced."

Addy laughed and then cried. "No one can take your place. I had to come. Ma is so worried."

Mrs. Figgenschau looked around. "Wind going south." She coughed and placed her gnarled hand on Addy's arm. "The little island." She turned to face Addy. "I'm cold. Dry there."

Addy shivered. "I'm a little cold, too. Do we have to swim? Can you swim?"

Mrs. Figgenschau struggled to stand, leaning hard on Addy. She coughed again. "We walk. Sand bar, then shallow."

Fortunately, very few stones marred the walk to the tiny island. Addy's foot connected with one rather large stone, and she tumbled headfirst into the little bay. The water moved with a slight chop, and Addy quickly surfaced and shook her head to send the water out of her face and hair. Mrs. Figgenschau took her arm and smiled. "Better you than me."

The water reached Addy's chest in depth before the floor of the bay slanted upward. The two, arm-in-arm, waded to the tiny island. A small bench awaited them, and they slumped onto it.

Mrs. Figgenschau sighed deeply. "So glad my husband built this bench." She put her hand to her chest and took several long breaths. "Look, smoke is almost gone." Mrs. Figgenschau patted Addy's knee.

"It sure smells bad, though." Addy hung her head. "I'm so sorry about your cottage. It's still burning. I wish I could put out that fire."

The older woman nodded and took Addy's hand. "Will burn and smolder for days." She swiped the tears running down her face, then smiled. "And smell even worse. Fires are like that. At least I can breathe better." The two sat hand in hand a few minutes. "If we had help, we could throw sand on it to slow the burning."

Addy looked up. "Not water? Sand?"

"Sand would help smother the fire." She shook her head. "Too bad I didn't realize it was coming. I might've thrown water on the roof and walls to slow the destruction." She patted Addy's knee again. "But I'm alive, thanks to you. The smoke would've killed me. And now, I've rested a bit. The warmth we still feel from the fire and the sun should dry us fairly well. Are you chilled, Addy?"

"I'm starting to warm up now. My throat still hurts a little. I think it was the smoke."

"I sure hope there aren't too many homes in the path of that fire. May God bring rain to put it out. You mentioned your ma. What about your pa?"

"He went to Ephraim to drop off guests. Maybe he's back and helping fight the fire now."

A yell rose up from the north.

Addy and Mrs. Figgenschau looked at each other. Addy tilted her head. "What . . . "

"I heard it, too. Can you yell back?"

Addy stood and turned full circle. There was the *Pearl* and Pa standing in the bow waving to her.

Addy jumped up and down and grabbed Mrs. Figgenschau's hand. "We're saved. It's my pa." Addy grew quiet.

Mrs. Figgenschau stood up. "Addy, what's wrong."

A smile spread across Addy's face. "Look, Mrs. Figgenschau. You can see Sunset Resort from out here. Home is right up there." She turned to the older woman. "Did you know that you could see it from here?"

"Probably, but I haven't been out here for many years. I have watched your pa and his boat out on the water from my cottage many times."

Pa hollered. "Mrs. Figgenschau, is it mostly sand coming up there?"

Mrs. Figgenschau nodded. "Tell your pa that it is. My voice is too weak for him to hear."

"She says it is, Pa. There are a couple rocks, so be careful."

"Are you able to walk out to meet me, so I don't take the chance to run aground?"

Addy and Mrs. Figgenschau held hands and waded into the water once more. Their skirts already heavy with dampness made their movement slow.

"Here's a ladder, Mrs. Figgenschau. Can you get up it?"

Addy grinned. "I'll help her, Pa."

With some effort, they pushed and pulled and got her into the boat. Addy scrambled up behind her and fell into Pa's arms. "How did you know? Is Ma back?"

"She went over to Sarah and Arlo's just before Arlo went to fight the fire. He was working on the water's edge at the harbor entrance between Washington and Detroit Islands. I had no guests, so I headed there to help fight. He told me what you had done." He paused and placed his hands on each of Addy's shoulders. "Young lady, what you did was rather foolish. You could have been killed."

Addy hung her head. "I know, Pa; it was scary. The smoke made it hard to breathe. But, Pa, I couldn't let . . . "

Pa embraced her. "I know, Addy. What you did was also very brave, and now, seeing her cottage burned, I'm sure you may have saved her life."

"She did, dear Clifford. I succumbed to the smoke trying to get to the water. It came up so fast. I was barely breathing when this young girl arrived. Not only did she shake me awake, but she also dragged me to the water. I'm not a big person, but I was a dead weight."

"Well, we are so glad you're alive. You will stay at Sunset until we can rebuild your place." He turned to Addy. "But now, we're getting you home. Your ma is beside herself, and we don't need that baby coming early. It's too early right now."

Addy's eyes grew big. "Oh, Pa, is she okay?"

"Both she and Molly are worried about you. Here we are, and there they are."

Ma stood on the dock, arms wrapped around herself, and Molly leaning against her. When they caught sight of Addy waving to them, Ma went limp and almost fell.

"Ma, Ma, it's okay. I'm okay. Are you all right?" Addy jumped from the boat to the dock and ran to her new mother. "I'm sorry, Ma, but I had to go. And look, Mrs. Figgenschau is alive. She almost died, Ma. I had to go." Tears burst out of Addy's eyes, and she buried her face in her mama's chest.

Ma hugged her and breathed in deep gasps. "Oh, Addy. I don't know what I would have done if anything happened to you." She looked up at her husband, still on the boat.

Pa shook his head then nodded. "She saved Mrs. Figgenschau's life. Addy, can you help me with the lines?"

Ma pulled away from Addy's embrace and gave her a big smile. "I think you forgot your job as first mate. Better grab those lines, young lady."

Addy sighed and looked up. "Yes, ma'am. I'll return to my duties." Chuckling, she turned and tied off the stern and bow lines. By then, Pa had descended from the boat and held out his hand to Mrs. Figgenschau.

"I must look a sight. Do forgive me. But your new daughter is a true heroine. She has a wonderful heart to think of me and then to run through the smoke and find me."

Ma rubbed her belly. "You must be exhausted. I have dry clothes you can get into, and we'll have lunch." She took Mrs. Figgenschau's arm and walked with her toward the resort.

"Wait a moment." Pa hurried to his wife and gave her a kiss. "The fire has definitely turned south, and I think it's dying down, but there's still a great deal of work to make sure all fronts are covered and contained. I'll be gone a while. Keep an eye on the wind direction. If it shifts again, head back to Sarah and Arlo's. I'll be back as soon as I can."

Ma nodded. "God keep you and everyone in that area safe."

"Pa, I could go with you and help."

Pa tapped her nose. "You will stay here, do you understand? You've saved a life, and we're proud of you; but now, go get dry, eat, and take care of your ma, sister, and Mrs. Figgenschau."

"Yes, Pa." Addy threw her arms around him and sobbed.

Pa went down on one knee. "Addy, we love you, but you've been through a lot today. You need to just rest and be here with Ma."

"Okay. Love you, Pa." She stood a moment, then turned and joined the others waiting for her at the end of the dock.

Addy and Mrs. Figgenschau changed into dry clothes while Molly helped Ma put lunch on the table. The four sat down to eat chicken sandwiches and soup. Everyone seemed too tired to talk.

Ma took Mrs. Figgenschau into one of their guest rooms and insisted she lay down for a while. Mrs. Figgenschau fell asleep almost instantly. Ma sat down on one of the over-stuffed chairs. Addy moved a foot stool in front of her so she could rest her feet. Ma was asleep in minutes.

Molly put her hands on her hip. "Are you going to sleep, too, Addy?"

"No, I'm going to go out to see Nellie."

"Pa said to stay here. You can't take the horse and go try to fight the fire."

"Oh, I know. I won't. I promise. I just like to talk to the horse."

"Okay. I'm going to practice my reading and writing."

Addy stepped outside and turned full-circle. Though the sun was overhead in a relatively blue sky, the haze from the smoke made the sky blurry. Gazing to the south, she could no longer see licks of fire. She shivered, remembering how close those flames were when she dragged Mrs. Figgenschau into the water. They were orange monsters threatening to eat her while they consumed the wonderful, little cottage. How sad Mrs. Figgenschau must be now. Addy hoped no one else lost their home, but surely, other homes were in the path. *Please keep Pa and all the others safe.* She thought for a moment the smoke had returned but then realized that tears filled her eyes, not smoke.

"How are you, Nellie?" Addy patted the horse's forehead across the stall door. Nellie nickered and pushed her head against Addy's hand. "I'll keep rubbing your head as long as you want. Were you scared, too? We were all pretty frightened of that fire. Thank you for getting Ma and Molly to Sarah's house safely." The horse backed up and stamped the ground with one of her front hooves and shook her head. "I know, Nellie. I made everyone worry about me, but I had to go."

The horse nuzzled Addy's hand again. Addy opened the gate and joined Nellie in the stall. "Would you like a rub down? I bet Ma didn't have time." Addy picked up the brush and began stroking the horse. Nellie turned her head and rested her muzzle on Addy's shoulder. Addy took a deep sigh and just stood there leaning against the horse for a few minutes.

"You know, Nellie, I didn't realize how wonderful horses were until I met Missy and Midnight. And, all the while, you were right here. I love being with you. I promise to always help take care of you."

Nellie nickered and laid herself down in the straw. Addy sat next to her. Soon, with her head on the horse's shoulder, Addy was sound asleep.

CHAPTER FOURTEEN

CLIFFORD SIGHED. HE WAS DEAD tired, but the fire only smoldered now. A few men were rotating times of observance to make sure there were no new flare-ups. Many dug trenches for hours along the spreading front edge of the burn and threw the dug-up dirt on the approaching flames. Others brought buckets and set up a line to pass them full of water to be dumped in the trenches. Exhaustion, dirt, and heat covered all the workers, but the fire had waned. Good news. He would return on the wagon in the morning to do another shift and walk the perimeter to make sure there were no stray fires springing up. Every farmer brought his bell and spaced them along the roadways to make sure everyone would hear if there was another alarm.

He stood on his dock after tying the *Pearl*. Sunset occurred as he left the fire, but the hazy afterglow continued with deep purples and oranges. It soothed his tired muscles somehow. Maybe his heart as well. When he'd learned that Addy had run to help Mrs. Figgenschau, his heart had risen to his throat. He almost couldn't breathe. That girl. Would she always be so headstrong? Or was it heart-strong? It wasn't so much that she acted so impulsively, but that she was in his heart as if he'd been her pa forever. How was that possible? And now, he'd thought he'd lost her twice. When she hollered from the little island, relief and anger rose up together. It didn't make sense. But then, he'd not been a pa before. What would this new baby be like—a boy or a girl, thoughtful or passionate about life, kind, silly, all of it? He stirred from his thoughts. Where was everyone? Was Lainey okay after all the excitement? The girls? Mrs. Figgenschau?

He entered the dining room in the semi darkness. No candles or lanterns burning. No noise. Had they gone somewhere? "Lainey?"

He heard a shuffle from the sitting room. Lainey emerged rubbing her eyes and smoothing her hair. "Oh my, Clifford. There you are. Is the fire out? We were all exhausted and fell asleep. I'll get some food. I may have left the soup simmering. Goodness, I must look a sight."

Clifford crossed the room and wrapped his arms around her. "A sight for sore eyes. How are you? The girls? Mrs. Figgenschau?"

A soft voice came from one of the bedrooms. "I'm all right. Did I sleep all day? Forgive me. I don't usually do that."

Lainey smiled. "We all slept. Except for Clifford. I think the soup may still be warm. Are you hungry?"

"Soup sounds delightful. How are the girls?"

"Molly's right there on that chair." Lainey chuckled. "Look how she's curled up. She must have started reading and fell asleep. And Addy, well . . . maybe in her room."

"I'll check. You get the soup." Clifford entered the room the girls shared. The beds were unmade. Usually, the girls were good about making them, but he knew they'd left in a hurry upon discovering the danger of the fire. A tickle of fear rose once more in Clifford. He mumbled to himself, "Must be around somewhere. Probably fell asleep in one of the other rooms just like Molly." He made himself take deep breaths as he checked all the rooms. He looked out all the windows to see if she was on the swing or the hammock. Nothing. He went into the kitchen. She would most likely be in there with Lainey.

"Addy in here?"

Lainey jerked her head around. "No. She's not in her bed? Maybe outside on the swing or chairs?"

"The chairs outside. I didn't check there." Clifford forced himself to walk, not run, to the chairs around the campfire area. In the dim light and exhaustion of the day, he must have missed her curled up in those big chairs. "Addy, are you there, girl?" She wasn't. He turned around. Lainey was right behind him.

"Where could she be, Clifford? She wouldn't have gone back to the fire, would she?"

"I can't imagine that she would." Clifford ran his hands through his hair. "Let's wake up Molly. Maybe she knows. Otherwise, we'll have to go looking, and it'll be too dark soon."

Lainey placed both hands on her belly. "Ooh. This little one is concerned, too. He or she is kicking." Lainey paused and arched her back. "Maybe he or she just needs a little room." She smiled in the dimming light at Clifford. "It's getting a little crowded in there, I think."

"Do you think there are two? Are you going to have twins?" Molly stood in the doorway, hair and clothes rumpled. "I just woke up. Did we sleep all day? I don't think I've ever done that. Where's Addy?"

Lainey's shoulders slumped. "We hoped you'd be able to tell us. We can't find her."

Molly slapped her hands to her cheeks. "Oh, no. She wouldn't have gone back to . . . Wait, Mrs. Figgenschau is here. Why would she go back there? Do you think she thought she could help Pa?" Molly looked up at the darkening sky. "Oh, wait, she said she was going to see Nellie. She really likes horses now."

"The barn!" Clifford ran toward the building and swung open the door. "Addy, you in here?" He stopped. Nellie was not standing in her stall. He swung around as Lainey and Molly came through the door.

"What is it, Clifford?"

"Look. Nellie's not there. She must've taken her." He got down on one knee. "Molly, did she say she wanted to come help me or go check on someone?"

Molly shook her head.

Clifford stood. "We can't even take the wagon because the horse is gone."

A groggy voice came from the horse's stall. "Where do you need to go? Nellie's right here."

Clifford and Lainey whirled around. Clifford ran to the stall and looked in. His shoulders slumped, and he breathed in deep gasps. Then he laughed, a big, hearty laugh. "Girl, you just keep giving us scares. Somehow, we need to limit this to once a week, not twice in a day."

By then, Lainey was standing and peering into the stall. She pulled the stable gate open. "Oh, Addy, come here."

Once Addy pushed herself up into a standing position, the horse brought herself up as well. Nellie nudged Addy over to Lainey and then nickered.

Lainey patted the horse's forehead. "You were keeping an eye on her, weren't you? I don't think you usually spend the day sleeping."

Nellie placed her chin on Addy's shoulder.

Addy grinned. "I came out and rubbed her down. I thought maybe with all the worry about me and the fire that you didn't have time to do it. And then, she just laid down, and I did, too. Is it nighttime?"

"Yes, it is. I got back from the fire a few minutes ago. Everyone was just waking up, and we couldn't find you." Clifford patted Nellie and then guided Addy out of the stall. "Thank you, Nellie, for keeping an eye on her." He winked at Addy. "I think there's some soup waiting for all of us, and I'm famished."

"Wait." Molly held up a bucket filled with grasses, some hay, and a few cut-up carrots. "Nellie needs some food, too. I think she already has water."

"Okay, Molly, but come right back to the house." Clifford took Addy's hand, wrapped his other arm around Lainey's shoulders, and walked to the kitchen.

Mrs. Figgenschau stood stirring the pot of soup. "There you are. I found some biscuits and heated them. I'll have this in bowls in a minute."

Soon, all sat at the table munching biscuits and sipping the soup.

Addy sighed. "This is so good. So, Pa, is the fire all done?"

"They're keeping an eye on it along its border to make sure it doesn't flare again. They've dug trenches, run as much water in as they could, and thrown dirt on the edges of the fire."

Addy lifted her head. "Do they know what started it? Did anybody get hurt or lose their house? Did anybody . . . Did anyone . . . "

Clifford reached across the table and patted her hand. "Two more homes were lost. The community will work together to rebuild them." He looked over at Mrs. Figgenschau. "Yours, too. We'll build you a new one, and until then, you'll stay here."

Mrs. Figgenschau nodded and wiped a tear from her eye. "Thank you. I'm glad I'm alive. So, no one was hurt?"

"Unfortunately, a few firefighters got burns; one passed out from the smoke, but he recovered." He turned to Lainey. "But you remember old Mr. Jorgenson? His house burned, and, well, he didn't make it."

Lainey placed her hand over her mouth. "Oh, I'm so sorry."

Mrs. Figgenschau hung her head. "Oh, Bernie. He was a good man. His wife and I were close. After she passed, he would still come visit every once in a while, and we'd chat about our early days. We'd have a cup of tea and a scone; then he would walk back to his house."

"Do you know what started it?" Addy reached for another biscuit.

"A pine snake." Clifford shook his head.

Lainey squinted her eyes. "How in the world?"

"It was at the other house that burned. Otto Weiss. He escaped and told us what happened. He was about to go pick up supplies and was looking for something in the corner of his barn. He lit a lantern so he could see better, as it was still fairly dark. He set the lantern down and put the items in the wagon, then went back to get his horse. Just as he was walking by the lantern and reminding himself to put the lantern out before he left, a pine snake slithered right in front of him.

"Horses get skittish around pine snakes. You usually know when they're around because the horses smell them and snort. But this one seemed to come from nowhere, and the horse actually reared up, snorted, backed up, and then took off. In the process, the horse kicked over the lantern. Otto was so concerned about catching his horse that he didn't even realize the fire had started. Once he grabbed the horse and turned, half his barn was in flames. All he could do was ring his alarm bell and then climb on the horse and get away and alert everyone he could. He's lost everything except the horse and feels very responsible."

"That's so sad. I hope everyone assured him that they don't blame him. Accidents happen. What an unfortunate situation. I really hate pine snakes." Lainey stood. "I think I might have some pie. I'll be right back."

"What about Otto's family?" Mrs. Figgenschau dabbed her eyes again.

"They had all gone to the mainland to visit his wife's sister, so thankfully, they missed it. But they might not even know yet. He's staying with another family tonight. I offered to take him to Ellison Bay day after tomorrow, so he could let them know, and he can stay there until we can rebuild his place."

Addy's eyes got big. "Ellison Bay. Isn't that where your parents live? In a store?"

"Above a store. A store that they own. And yes, it's in Ellison Bay, and it's time you met them. We'll go to Newport Town first to see Aunt Edith and Uncle Otis. We have a standing offer to take his wagon over to Ellison Bay for the day. Arlo and Rasmus are going over early for supplies, so I asked them to let Otis know we're coming, and he may pass the word on to my folks. Also, Uncle Otis knows Otto well and may know of job openings in Newport Town if Otto decides to stay there. I thought we'd all go. You, too, Mrs. Figgenschau."

"Oh, please. I've had enough excitement for a while. Is it all right if I just stay here?"

Lainey set a pie on the table. "It's just fine. Please make yourself at home and eat whatever is here. I bet Nellie would love you to rub her forehead a couple of times."

Mrs. Figgenschau grinned. "No pine snakes here?"

Lainey rubbed her arms. "Oh, I hope the fire burned them all up. But truly, I haven't seen any here at all."

Addy tapped Molly's arm. "Come with me. We forgot something."

Molly followed her into the kitchen, and they returned with their hands behind their backs. Addy grinned. "Mrs. Figgenschau, you didn't lose everything from your house."

Together, the girls revealed what was in their hands—Mrs. Figgenschau's spoons.

"Oh, girls, this warms my heart. These spoons are now so very special to me. They helped you on your way the day you ran away, and now they will help me on my way as I wait to have my little cottage rebuilt. Thank you so much." She held out her arms and hugged them both.

CHAPTER FIFTEEN

PA DOCKED THE *PEARL* ALONG the pier in Newport Town. As always, Addy hopped out of the boat and expertly tied the lines to the pilings. Otto Weiss stepped off and shook hands with Uncle Otis. Addy held out a hand for Molly. Pa stepped onto the dock and held out his arms to assist his wife. Before Ma was fully off the boat, she was in Uncle Otis' arms.

Ma laughed. "Oh, you surprised me, being here to meet us. I'm so glad to see you, Uncle."

Aunt Edith grasped her hand. "You've brought your girls." She turned to Addy and Molly. "I'm so glad you are with Lainey and Clifford. I'm so happy you're here for visit. I made you cinnamon rolls."

A slow smile spread across Addy's face. "I think I'll like it at your house. Did you really live on that tiny, little island? And did you really think about putting Ma on the Orphan Train? Did you know what it's like for some kids?"

Aunt Edith took a deep breath and stooped so she was eye level with Addy. "I did think about it, but I had no idea what it might have been like for her. I'm so sorry that I thought that." She straightened and looked over to Ma. "But I'm glad God had other plans for her."

Addy nodded. "Me, too. Or else, who knows what would've happened to us? But you said it was God's plan? Her parents dying?"

Ma laid a hand on Addy's shoulder. "Addy."

Aunt Edith shook her head. "You have big questions, don't you? I don't think God wanted her parents to die. I don't believe that at all. Life in this world has a lot of obstacles and problems, but God always has a plan to help us out of our deepest troubles. He provided for Lainey, and He provided for us; and I'm quite sure He provided for you."

Addy grinned. "Did you say cinnamon rolls?"

Uncle Otis doubled over in laughter. "Oh my, what spirited girls you have." He slapped Pa on the back and then took Addy's hand. "Yes, let's go get some. I wasn't allowed to have any until you arrived. Otto, please join us."

Otto smiled. "I think I will. Thank you."

Aunt Edith put her arm around Ma. "Looks like you have your work cut out for you. She is something."

Molly took Aunt Edith's hand. "I like you. Can I call you Aunt Edith?"

"Yes, you can, because that's who I am." She winked. "When Lainey was younger, she called me Auntie Edith. So, if you prefer that, it's just fine, too."

"Auntie Edith. I like that."

A short time later, Addy paused between bites and laughter. "I love cinnamon rolls. Thank you. And you have a happy house here." Aunt Edith beamed.

Molly nodded. "I like how Uncle Otis teases us." Uncle Otis stood. "Molly and Addy, let's go meet Fresnel, my horse. Otto, please join us."

Addy pushed her chair back. "Oh yes, I'm good with horses." She and Molly followed Uncle Otis out the door. Otto snagged another cinnamon roll and joined the threesome.

Aunt Edith refilled her coffee cup. "You know I'll be there for you and the baby. What would help you the most? I know your mother and Clifford's mother will be there, too. I'll do whatever you need."

"I've been thinking more about this, and what would really help me is if you came early and helped with all the household chores and any organization that needs to be done for guests or scheduling. I'm trying to make sure we have no guests for the week before and after, but if this little one comes early or late, those plans may go awry. You would be the best person I know who could handle it." Lainey bit her lip. "Would you consider it?"

"I would absolutely love to do that. And I'd be delighted to cook for all those who will be there. Two grandmas, one father, two sisters, one aunt—Tina's coming, right?—and me, the great-aunt. And then all those who want to visit the baby and you."

Clifford took another sip of coffee. "And Mrs. Figgenschau. Don't forget Mrs. Figgenschau."

Aunt Edith tilted her head. "Hilga?"

Clifford grimaced. "You heard about the fire?"

"Oh yes, I can't believe I haven't asked you. We were so excited to see the girls, and then Addy's questions took over the conversation. Was the fire close to you? It was all over before we heard about it."

Clifford nodded. "It came toward us, and then the wind changed. Lost three homes and Bernie Jorgenson. One of the homes was Otto's. He's going with us to Ellison Bay, where his family is staying. Thank God, they missed the fire. I think he wants to check with Otis about jobs in the area."

"I'm so sorry. No wonder Otto was so quiet today." She turned to Lainey. "Were you scared?"

"Yes, but mainly because Addy ran to help Mrs. Figgenschau. She's such a sweet, older woman, and rather eccentric."

"I do remember her. She makes and sells herbs and teas. Not too far from your resort. But wait. Addy ran to help her? From the fire?"

Lainey stared at the ceiling for a moment. "Yes. She saw the flames and realized Mrs. Figgenschau lived that way. She ran. There was no stopping her. And I couldn't chase her. I had Molly, and the smoke had already reached us."

"Well, Addy's here and looks well. Was Hilga okay?"

Clifford shook his head and closed his eyes. "Addy saved her life. She had almost succumbed to the smoke and lay on the beach trying to get to the water when Addy got there." He glanced at Lainey. "Addy told me she fell once because the smoke made it hard to breathe."

Clifford took a deep breath. "She dragged Mrs. Figgenschau into the water and over to a little island. Then they watched the flames burn her cottage. When I returned from Ephraim, Arlo informed me that Addy went there, and I took the boat over and retrieved them. Mrs. Figgenschau is staying at the resort until we build her a new cottage."

Aunt Edith rested her chin in her hand. "Oh my. She is one strong, little girl. And you have your hands full."

Lainey chewed her bottom lip and looked skyward. "Addy is so strong-willed. Impetuous."

Clifford grinned. "But she and Molly are ours now, so we know God will give us the wisdom we need."

"So, you'll have a full house when that baby arrives, even without resort guests. I look forward to helping out."

"I'm sure Mrs. Hanson and Rose and Sarah will all be bringing food, so you won't have to cook everything."

Clifford stood. "We should go, so we can see my parents at the store. Thanks so much for letting us use the horse and wagon. I sure hope you have no need of it while we're gone."

Aunt Edith laughed. "I'm not sure you knew. We now have another horse, and as you did know, we have the surrey if we need anything." She paused and looked at Lainey. "You can probably guess what Otis named the new horse—Pilot."

"Oh, Aunt Edith. So perfect. Fresnel and Pilot, so his lighthouse days are still with him."

"Yes, and he still takes care of them as he did before." Aunt Edith smiled.

"Does he miss it still, Aunt Edith? Does his leg hurt at all? I see him walking with the cane and sometimes not."

Aunt Edith patted her hand. "He has no regrets and no pain—just a little gimpy some days. But he delights in his remembrances and his time on Pilot Island. You know, I do as well. It took me longer, but we are in such a good place in every way—except we miss you. But he just enjoys his horses named Pilot and Fresnel. I think he chuckles every time he says their names."

Lainey felt her uncle's hands on her shoulder. "Edith is right. We miss you. We're so happy here, and I think I picked the perfect names for the horses. But you should get going before Addy runs off with Fresnel. She told me she's a natural with horses, and she's right. She'll probably want to handle the reins." He laughed. "Clifford, you'll need to hold the reins on that girl. She is something."

Clifford nodded. "Yes, Aunt Edith will have to tell you the latest escapade."

"Oh, between Otto and Addy, I heard all about it. Sure hope things work out for Otto and Hilga. I'm not much help in physically helping rebuild those homes, but I can contribute financially. And I want to. Let me know what is needed."

"You're the best, Uncle Otis. Thanks for the wagon. We'll be back early enough, so we can take the boat back to Sunset before dark."

Addy sat perched on the wagon in the driver's seat. "Pa, can I drive the wagon? I'm good with horses."

"Let's wait until our return trip."

The girls moved to the back seat. After Clifford assisted Lainey so she could sit next to him, Otto climbed up next to Lainey. "Otis is truly a kind man. He gave me money to help cover the cost of staying wherever we can until we get a new house."

Clifford nodded. "He said he would contribute to the rebuilding, too. He's a generous one."

The leaves waved gently as they journeyed the well-traveled dirt roads to Ellison Bay. Cherry trees boasted their maturing, small fruit—some still orange and others already bright red, promising an abundance of red cherries in the near future. The air was fresh and delivered a peaceful breeze as a few clouds passed overhead.

They stopped just outside of Ellison Bay to drop off Otto. His family ran to embrace him with tears. They all stood by the water for a few minutes, listening to the quiet whoosh of the waves meeting the rocky shoreline before retreating. Otto shook Clifford's hand. "Thank you again for your kindness."

"Otto, we're just so glad we didn't lose you. Your house will be rebuilt, and life will be full again."

Mrs. Weiss hugged Lainey. "Thank you for bringing Otto here. We were so scared."

"You know, we're available if you need anything; and Uncle Otis is just in Newport Town, and Clifford's parents are right here at the store. Don't hesitate to ask."

A woman ran out the front door of Ruckert's Supply Store, wiping her hands on her apron. "It is so wonderful to see all of you. It has been too long." She stopped and let her gaze fall on each one in the wagon. "Lainey, look at you. Full with child. I'll be a grandma. Wait! I am a grandma. This must be Addy and Molly. I am so happy to meet you girls."

Pa climbed from the wagon and embraced his mother. "Ma, so good to see you as well. I do apologize that it took so long to come for a visit." He bent down and kissed his mother on her cheek. "Yes, this is Addy and Molly, our new daughters." He turned and moved close to his mother's ear. "We are so in love with these girls. You'll soon be in love, too."

Addy smiled. She heard the whisper. She stood and climbed down from the wagon. She started to come around to greet Pa's mother but then turned and offered to help her own mother. "Ma, take my hand."

Ma grinned. "You are such a help, Addy. Thank you. Molly, are you okay?"

"Yes, Ma. I can climb down. I can't wait to hug Pa's mama."

Grandma Ruckert stooped down and caught Molly in her arms. "You know, my arms have been telling me that they need to hug you and your sister."

Molly widened her eyes. "Really? Your arms? They told you?" She turned to Ma and splayed her hands. "Her arms wanted me, just like mine wanted you. Did you hear that?"

Lainey chewed her bottom lip as a tear tracked down her cheek. "Yes, Molly, just like that." She hugged her mother-in-law. "Oh, Ma, so very good to see you."

Addy hovered behind her mama. When Ma stepped aside, Addy walked up to Grandma Ruckert. "Did you say you're my grandma now? I don't think I ever had a grandma." She stopped and looked at Ma. "Mrs. Figgenschau is like a grandma, right? I mean, that's what they're supposed to be like. Always helping and don't mind you being around. Right?"

Grandma Ruckert tilted her head and then took Addy's hand. "That's exactly right. And I promise to always help you and Molly, and I will never mind having you around. In fact, I hope you're around often." She nodded at her son. "I see what you mean. They are wonderful."

Molly skipped up the stairs to the porch that fronted the store, then turned. "Did he say we were wonderful?" She grinned. "That's nice. He's the best, nicest man we know. And now, he's our pa."

Grandma Ruckert moved up the stairs and grasped Molly's hand in her other hand. "Now, grandchildren, let's introduce you to the store."

Addy gazed at the windows lined with lamps and books. When Pa went ahead and opened the door, Addy sighed. "What do I smell? Cinnamon? Chocolate? Stew? I've never smelled so many things at once."

Grandma Ruckert laughed. "We sell many things and have a bakery. We also have lunch ready upstairs, where we live."

Molly squealed. "Look! Dolls. Candy. Toys. This is all yours, ah, Mrs.—I mean, Grandma?"

The woman tapped her nose. "Yes, it is, but it's for other people to buy."

Pa looked around. "Where's Pa?"

"Oh, he had to get some supplies from the basement. Here he comes now."

The tall, lean man came through a door in the back carrying several boxes. He peeked around his load. "Are these my granddaughters? I have been waiting to meet you. Let me set these boxes down."

Pa hurried to assist his father. "I'll go get the rest. Piled at the bottom of the stairs as usual?"

"Thank you, Son. You know exactly."

Molly drew back against Ma and looked down. Addy walked forward. "I like your store, sir— I mean, Grandpa. Grandpa. That has a nice sound. I never had a grandpa before. Thank you."

Grandpa Ruckert sighed. "Addy and Molly, welcome to our family, to our store, and to our home. Tell you what. If your folks don't mind, you can each pick a couple pieces of candy to eat after lunch. Now, mind you, *after* lunch."

Molly clapped her hands and turned to her parents. "Can we? Please?"

Ma laughed. "Of course. Just wait till after lunch to eat them."

By the end of lunch, Molly sat on Grandpa's lap, while Addy kept everyone laughing and groaning with the stories of her many escapades in recent weeks.

Grandma Ruckert went to get the cherry crisp. Grandpa looked from Addy to her parents. "I don't think life will ever be dull again with these two. But I think they'll be great help when the baby arrives. How are you feeling, Lainey?"

"I'm pretty good. Lots of back—well, not pain, but discomfort. I'm hungry all the time." She hung her head and chuckled.

"You know, I'll be there right away when the baby comes." Grandma set plates on the table and returned to bring the dessert. She dished a healthy portion on each plate. "I cannot wait to see this child. You're carrying high, which sometimes means a girl, but you still have some time." She sat down. "Now, Lainey, I know your ma and Tina will be coming from Rock Island. And your Aunt Edith. I'm assuming Anna and Tina will come early, but if for any reason they can't make it early, I am more than willing to be there whenever you want me."

"Thank you. Ma and Tina are planning to come at least a week before the day we think this little one will arrive; but this is your grandbaby, too, so you feel free to come as early as you want. Even if just for the company. We've not scheduled guests for that time, but truly, if the baby comes early, we could still have guests. Aunt Edith has offered to come early and manage the business of the resort and help with cooking and cleaning, whether we have guests or not."

Grandma took a bite of dessert and nodded. "I can help with the cooking as well. I know you have a wonderful kitchen at the resort. Maybe we can put up some food for the winter while we're there. The apples will probably be ready. I'll bring some recipes and jars for canning. And I'll talk with Edith, too."

"That would be truly wonderful." Lainey rubbed her belly with one hand while using the other to enjoy the cherry crisp. "Ahh, the baby is kicking."

Addy stood. "Ma, I saw your belly move. Is that the baby?"

"It is, Addy. It is. Come feel it."

"Me, too." Molly jumped from Grandpa's lap and placed her hand on the protruding stomach of her mother. She jumped and laughed. "The baby kicked me. Quick, Addy, put your hand here."

Addy complied. She shook her head. "That's amazing. There's a real baby in there. A real, little person. How does that happen?"

The adults grinned but said nothing. Then Grandma laid her hand on her daughter-in-law's belly. "Isn't it wonderful how God knits a baby together in a womb?"

Molly tilted her head. "Knit? Womb?"

"The womb is the place inside a mama's body that holds the baby. By *knit*, we mean there's growth, and nourishment, and protection there. It's so wonderful."

"My first mama knit a sweater once. It protected me from cold, but it didn't grow." Molly stared off in space.

Ma put her arms around Molly. "It's what we call an expression or a way of describing something. We don't see the baby grow, except to see my belly get bigger and bigger and see the baby kicking. We know that God designed His creation to grow this way, and we think it's marvelous."

Molly nodded. "Yes, marvelous." She raised her eyes at Grandma Ruckert. "Can we have more cherry crisp, please?"

"You can, if your mama and papa are okay with it." She looked to her daughter-in-law, who nodded.

Molly clapped her hands. "It's so good. Thank you."

CHAPTER SIXTEEN

LATE JULY BROUGHT LONG, HOT days. Ma sat more and stretched a lot. Addy did all she could to help keep the guests happy and the dishes done. Sarah and Rose assisted with much of the cleaning and cooking. As Mrs. Figgenschau waited for her new home, she helped with the cooking.

One day, as Addy watched Pa bring in the boat and ran to tie the lines, he grinned. "We have a surprise we need to discuss."

Addy stopped. "A good surprise?"

He tapped her on the nose. "Of course, a good one. How's your ma? Is she feeling good? You know, I miss you on the boat, but I so appreciate how much help you give her."

"Thanks, Pa. I love the *Pearl*, but Ma needs me now." She smiled at Pa. This was home. She belonged here. She still wondered about her father back in Michigan. Although she'd decided her mother had died, she sometimes imagined she and Molly were back there and her folks were healthy and happy. Still, this life on Washington Island was good.

"Addy, you still in there? Are you daydreaming?"

"Oh, sorry, Pa. What's the surprise?"

"Here comes part of it."

Addy turned as a wagon arrived at the resort. "Oh, it's Mr. Figgenschau. Did he come to see his aunt? Is he going to help build her cottage?"

Clifford laughed. "Hold on, Addy. We'll discuss it over cookies. Are there any cookies?"

Addy grinned. "Mrs. Figgenschau taught me how to make them. They're really good."

"Excellent. Let's go greet Jack and have cookies." Pa took her hand, and they walked to the wagon.

"Well, Addy. It's so good to see you. I think Midnight remembers you. How about you give him this carrot and tie him up?"

The horse nudged Addy and nickered. She wrapped her arms around the horse's neck and breathed in his scent. "I love horses." Mr. Figgenschau climbed from the wagon and handed her the carrot, which she offered to the horse. "Ooh. His tongue feels so funny, but he doesn't try to bite me."

Clifford shook his head. "That's good. Tie him up. We have a surprise to discuss."

Addy hurried into the house after lingering a bit as she tied Midnight to the rail. Jack Figgenschau hugged his aunt and doffed his hat to Ma. Molly sat next to Ma and looked down.

Mrs. Figgenschau took Molly's hand. "Molly, this is my nephew, Jack."

Molly extended her hand to him. He brought it to his lips. "You are a lovely, young lady, Miss Molly. So pleased to meet you."

Molly giggled and scurried back to her seat and buried her face in Ma's shoulder.

"Let's all get to the table. We have a surprise to discuss." Pa reached out a hand to help Ma get up, and Mr. Figgenschau held out a chair for his aunt. "Oh, wait. Addy, get the cookies, would you? Jack, coffee?"

"Point me in the direction, Clifford. I'll get it." He returned with cups and coffee and poured some for each adult. "First, Aunt Hilga,

I stopped by your place on the way, and the progress on your new cottage is going well."

"Is that the surprise? Is Mrs. Figgenschau's house ready?" Addy reached for a cookie.

"No, the surprise is we're going to have a big picnic for all the Orphan Train children."

Addy puckered her lips. "I don't know if I like being called that. I mean, I know we are . . . But it just makes us sound like we're not really wanted."

Pa patted her hand. "We understand that, Addy; and some of the children who came that day with you and some who came before that and since then, well, they still aren't well cared for."

"You mean, they're just workers, right?"

Mr. Figgenschau nodded. "Yes, and some are mistreated. That's why we're doing this. It's to let the kids know—and their new parents—that they are worth having some fun. We want to give them a chance to get to know other kids, and, well . . . "

"To check up on them." Pa drummed his fingers on the table. "We want to make sure that they are being provided for and not treated only as workers."

Addy looked Pa straight in the eye. "But you know, some are. We heard stories. And I think that man on that other island that was supposed to take us . . . I bet we would've just been workers. I mean, some of the kids on the steamer said they expected to have to sleep in barns." She hung her head.

Pa nodded. "That's why this event is so important. That couple now has a boy, and we're making a special attempt to get them to the picnic. August Olson, who owns the store in Ephraim, is planning it.

He has some property just east of town, and that's where the picnic will be. He let Mr. Bergman know when he came in for supplies and is pretty sure they're going to come."

Mr. Figgenschau looked at Addy. "Your pa tells me you are very perceptive. I see it with the horses, but we have a feeling that you may have it with the kids as well. We're hoping that you'll be able to get to know a few and find out if everyone is okay and provided for."

Addy frowned. "Okay, but what if they're not?"

Clifford placed his hand on hers. "That's where the adults will step in. We are planning an organization that keeps an eye on these kids. Maybe greet them when they arrive, visit the families every once in a while, plan these gatherings maybe once a month."

Ma set her coffee cup down. "Clifford, Jack, that's a wonderful idea. As we know, these children arriving are wonderful and also hurting, grieving the loss of family and friends. They can't just be workers to pay for their food and shelter. You know I'll be a part." She laughed and patted her belly. "That is, after this little one arrives."

"I'll donate cookies and my creams. Those children, if they are working farms and lands, probably have many bruises and sores."

"Thank you, Aunt Hilga. We hope that any bruises are from minor mishaps while working, not at the hand of a cruel caretaker."

Ma stood. "So, when is this event? It's time for me to start dinner."

Everyone stood. Mr. Figgenschau picked up his hat. "In two weeks. May I ask when your baby is scheduled to arrive?"

Ma smiled. "A little over a month. I probably won't attend this picnic, but I think it'll be wonderful for our girls. Clifford, could you let Julius and Marla know on Pilot? Charlotte and Andrew should be there."

"Yes, I'm planning to spread the word, and then Rasmus and I will transport as many as can make it."

The day arrived with steamy heat. Wispy clouds flew overhead, and the gulls cawed a greeting as the *Pearl* was readied for departure.

"Those gulls hope you're a fishing boat, Pa. Don't they know by now?"

Pa laughed. "They always hope."

Excitement bubbled inside Addy. She would meet up with some of the kids who were on the steamer with her. A few had been on the train from Michigan, too. Would she recognize them? It had been only a few months, but it seemed a lifetime. She hugged herself. Could she be a help if some of these kids were in hurtful situations? Pa and Ma had warned her to keep her mouth in line. If she saw a kid with bruises or that sadness that she knew too well, the hurt that dwelled deep and surfaced only now and again, well, she'd be tempted to give the parents a tongue-lashing. Pa let her know that wouldn't help anyone and might make it worse. She'd actually prayed and asked God to help her with that. Did the people on that island, Chambers, who didn't want her care about the boy they now had? Did they love him? She blew out a big breath. Why was she nervous about this?

"Pa?"

"Yes, Addy?" He steered the boat into the chop. A slight northwest wind would keep the waters a bit stirred but shouldn't keep anyone from attending the picnic. "I can let you steer when we get out a little further."

"Thanks, but I have a question."

He turned from the steering wheel and tilted his head. "Sure, what is it?"

"Well, I'm worried that not all of the kids have it as good as we do. I mean, you and Ma take really good care of me. I still miss my first mama and papa. But what about some of the kids who aren't doing so well? I mean, will they be jealous?"

"You know, young lady, some might be. But this is why we're having the picnic. We want every single one of these kids to have a happy life, a good life. We realize some may be working really hard for their new parents, but that's another reason for our gathering—so they can have some fun."

Addy nodded and stared at the water. All the kids so far that she met were nice and fun. But she knew if she'd ended up with that family on Chambers, she might've turned mean. Trying to protect her little sister and finding ways to be happy could've made her mad about lots of things. Losing parents, stuck with mean people, working harder than most adults—that can really give someone a bad attitude.

"Addy?"

"Yes, Pa?"

"You okay?"

"Just hoping that all the kids aren't becoming mean because they get stuck in a bad family."

"Come here, Addy." Pa had her take the wheel but stood close behind her. "Addy, you're a smart girl. You sense things about others. You let me know today what you sense. As we've told you, we don't want you to try to fix it. Let the adults handle it, okay?"

"Okay, Pa. It's just . . . It makes me feel bad if life is rotten for them. I mean, it's been really good for us, even when I've gotten in trouble and even when I get mad that my first papa got hurt and my first mama probably died. But you and Ma have really helped me. So, I want to play and have fun today, but I'm nervous about finding some who have it rough."

Pa gripped her shoulders tighter. "You have a good heart. Listen to it. But don't . . . "

Addy grinned and leaned her head back to look up at him. "I know. I know."

As Pa pulled the boat along the dock and Addy jumped out to tie the lines, Molly gripped the boat rail. "Do you think Ma will have the baby while we're gone?"

Addy's head jerked. "Oh, I sure hope not. This is way early, isn't it?"

"But why didn't she come?" Molly straightened her skirts.

Pa stepped off the boat and lifted Molly to the dock. "Don't you worry. She still has time before the baby comes. But she's tired, and Mrs. Figgenschau is with her. We'll be back before dark." He stepped back on the boat. "Better not forget the food she made for us." He returned to the dock and chucked Molly on the chin and laughed. "We'd be in big trouble, then."

The threesome made their way the short distance to the main roadway, a widened dirt path that ran through the town.

Addy pointed down the road. "I don't think we've been here since we arrived. There's Mr. Olson's store. That sure was good food."

Pa patted Addy on the head. "What a day or two that was."

Addy turned around and nodded at Pa. "It sure was." Then her face fell, and goosebumps traveled down her spine. "Pa, look. It's the Bergmans."

Pa turned. Charles and Gyda walked a short distance back. A young man with a sullen face trailed behind. Pa extended his hand. "So good to see you. Are you here for the picnic?"

Mr. Bergman shook Pa's hand. "We are. Seemed like a nice gesture on the part of August and Jack. It's a good day for a little diversion."

Addy stepped toward Mr. Bergman. "Are you working hard these days?"

Pa cast a stern look in her direction. "Mr. and Mrs. Bergman, you may remember our girls, Addy and Molly. Yes, they are now our family, our daughters. And is this your son?"

Mr. Bergman coughed, and Mrs. Bergman touched her husband's arm. "Yes, this is Frederick. We call him Freddy. And, uh, yes, he's our responsibility now."

Addy flinched. "Respon—"

Pa reached his hand to Freddy. "Great to meet you, young man. We're hoping all the families have a wonderful time today. We'll see you up in Mr. Olson's field." He turned and grabbed Addy's hand and quickened his pace up the hill. When a bit further from the Bergmans, Pa spoke while looking straight ahead. "Addy, be careful with your attitude."

Molly skipped along. "I think this is fun."

As they crested the hill, dozens of people milled around. The boys called to one another to start a baseball game, and a few of the men placed bases and offered to umpire the game.

August Olson's twin nieces ran up, their dark red hair bounding off their shoulders. "We're Irene and Doreen. We thought we'd have races. Do you want to run?" Molly and Addy hurried off with the twins to gather other girls as they arrived and set up races.

August shook Clifford's hand. "Glad you're here. I see the Bergmans approaching. There are only three or four families we're concerned about, and that's one of them. Charles comes into the store and lets him buy a few things, but the boy is not a happy one. Saw a bruise on his forearm the other day, and when he saw me noticing, he quickly rolled down his sleeve. If it was a bruise from working hard—the plow slipped and hit his arm—I don't think he'd try to cover it up."

"I met him on our way from the docks, and you're right—he's not happy. Charles and Gyda were quite pleased about the picnic, but when I introduced the girls as our daughters, Gyda said Freddy, the boy, was their responsibility. Not son, not new to the family, not good worker—just a responsibility. Any idea how we can do this and help some of these situations change?"

"Well, today, we'll observe and get to know people. It'd be good to talk more the next time you come to Ephraim. I know Jack has some ideas, too."

CHAPTER SEVENTEEN

THE GIRLS SET UP TWO boards to mark the start and finish of the race. Irene whispered to Addy as Doreen had Molly help her decide where the end of the race should be. "Uncle August told us about checking to see if any of the kids are treated badly. And he said you'd be helping. Said you were very perspective, or precepting, or prespective—you could figure that kind of thing out."

Doreen returned holding Molly's hand. "You mean *perceptive.*" She rolled her eyes at her sister.

Irene shook her head. "She knew what I meant." She turned to Addy. "Didn't you?"

"Yeah. The one I'm most worried about right now is Freddy over there. I hope he has fun with the boys. He doesn't look happy."

Irene raised her eyebrows. "Well, anyone stuck with the Bergmans wouldn't be happy."

Doreen jabbed her sister.

"Oh, wait, sorry. You almost ended up there, didn't you? Our uncle told us. Well, I bet you're glad you got the Ruckerts instead. Do you like it on the island?"

"I do. I didn't think I'd like it, and Ma—my new ma—lived a while on Pilot Island. Now, that's small. I don't think I'd do well there. But, yeah, we like our family here."

"Oh, look." Doreen grabbed Addy's hand. "Here comes Flossy. She's the most fun of all the girls."

Flossy's pigtails bounced as she skipped over to the girls. Her calico dress had a petticoat, and her boots and leggings were shiny black. "This is so exciting. I love picnics. And I had to walk only a short distance."

Irene pointed. "See that fence over there, Addy? Flossy's farm is right on the other side of it. We are really looking forward to being in school every day together in a few weeks. When does your school start?"

Addy shrugged her shoulders. "It's in a few weeks. But Ma is going to have a baby soon, so I'm not sure if Molly and I'll get there right at the start. But the teacher is a good friend of Ma, so I think it'll be okay."

Flossy clapped her hands. "Oh, a baby. I wish I could come and visit. Did you say your name is Addy?"

"Yes, and this is my sister, Molly."

Flossy stood on her tiptoes and then rocked back on her heels. "Addy, are you and Molly Otters? Are they, Irene?" She looked from face to face.

Addy squinted. "Otters? Why would you say that? Is that what you call people on the islands?"

Flossy doubled over in laughter. "No, no. That's what we call the Orphan Train kids. We didn't really like being called Orphan Train kids, so we took the *O* and the *T*, and then we just thought of Otter. We like it."

Addy laughed. "I like it. But you said 'we.' Are you an Orph—I mean, are you an Otter?"

Flossy grinned. "I am. The Logerquists got me, and I help with the little ones and some of the cooking, but they told me I'm family and gave me their last name."

"I haven't quite gotten used to having a different last name, but I think I'll be Addy Ruckert when school starts. I mean, I'm really happy here, but I do miss my first papa and mama a lot."

Flossy took Addy's hand and walked a short distance away. "My ma and pa died in Indiana. I had two older brothers, and we were all put on the Orphan Train. Lots of people wanted farm workers, so my brothers ended up getting chosen—two different families. I worry about them. I hope someday I can find them. My new ma and pa said they'd help. I've been here two years. How about you?"

"Just since May."

"Your little sister is really cute. What's her name again?"

"Molly. They wanted to separate us, but I wouldn't let them."

"Oh, I wish I could have my brothers here, but Mr. Figgenschau's boys, Forrest and Roy, are like brothers. And they're so much fun." Flossy giggled. "They are kind of troublemakers, though. They're always pulling pranks."

Addy smiled. "Their pa told me how they jump off the steamers."

"That's right. They're fun. I really hope my brothers are more than okay, that they're having fun. But hey, let's get in the races. Looks like Molly and the younger girls have found dolls to play with. My ma makes dolls and gives them away, so she'll probably bring one home."

Addy pointed. "Look, there are my friends from the islands. Mr. Rasmus brought them all. Charlotte and Andrew are on Pilot Island. They were almost Otters. Then David and Catherine are Mr. Rasmus' kids, and Tina and Carter are from Rock Island. They are my new ma's brother and sister. Ma was almost an Otter."

Flossy waved, and the girls joined her and Addy. Irene and Doreen called to them to join the races. The boys headed straight for the makeshift ballfield and chose up sides. Soon, the cheering and laughing from the races and ball game filled the air.

Clifford ate the last few bites of his second piece of cherry pie. He smiled at the abundant food provided. No one seemed to go hungry, and he noticed many of the women trading recipes. He probably should get some for Lainey and the resort. The sun still shone brightly—what a gift, along with the light breeze that refreshed the sweaty faces and arms. Several of the kids plopped on the ground catching their breath after the games and food. Soon, the wagons and boats would be carrying these happy participants home.

August Olson joined Clifford. "This is a great success. I like that it's not just the Orphan Train kids— I've been informed they call themselves Otters." He chuckled. "But so many from the communities around have joined in. I think we need to make this a monthly event, don't you?"

Clifford nodded as he swallowed the last of the pie. "It would be nice if we could do this in several places to make sure we include everyone."

Pastor Iverson walked up. Tall and thin, he always had a welcoming smile. "Clifford, that's a good idea. I think in the winter, we could meet at Clayton Hall in Ellison Bay. I saw William the other day, and he offered it for any of these events. I think it's so important to make sure these kids are made a part of the community, accepted as family members."

"Tell me, Pastor, are you noticing any kids who aren't being accepted?"

"I do see a few. A couple families didn't come today, and those are two of the ones I'm concerned about. August sees them at the store, and I go out to visit. They were invited. Hopefully, we can persuade them to come next time. And with school starting soon, we can put a little pressure to make sure the kids are allowed to attend. That will help with the assimilation."

August tipped his head. "I'm glad and a bit surprised to see the Bergmans here. Their boy seemed to get along well with the others and has a strong swing; I think he hit a homer."

"That'll make him want to come again, and the others will want him on their team. Oh, oh." August nudged Clifford's arm. "Addy is talking to Bergman's boy."

Clifford groaned. "We warned her. She can be so impetuous sometimes."

Addy held a cookie in each hand. "Hi, you're with the Bergmans on Chambers, right?"

The young man looked down his nose. "Yeah, what of it?"

"Oh, nothing. Just thought you might like a cookie. I saw you hit that homer." Addy extended the cookie. He seemed a few years older than Addy. Maybe Carter's age. His hair fell in unruly strands around his face. Perhaps he was sweaty from the ballgame. Maybe he needed a haircut.

He grinned. "Thanks. The food here is really great. It's been a long time since I played ball. That was fun."

"I'm Addy. I live on Washington Island. What's your name?"

"Freddy."

"So, Freddy, I'm an Otter. Are you?"

Freddy's head jerked up. "What are you talking about?"

Addy grinned. "Well, I learned today that we Orphan Train kids are called Otters. I kinda like it."

Freddy shook his head. "I don't know. I guess that's okay. Yeah, I came on the Train, then the steamer . . . you did, too? You like your family?"

Addy grabbed his arm to make him sit on the grass, then turned to face him. "I have a great family. I'm lucky, and my sister Molly is with me. Do you have any brothers or sisters?"

Freddy plucked some grass and tore off little pieces. "Had a sister, Frieda. They sent her somewhere else. And now I'm with . . . well . . . I'm glad you got to keep your sister and get a nice family. Not everyone does."

"I know, Freddy. And I have to apologize."

Freddy looked askance at her. "For what?"

"I was supposed to go to the Bergmans, but they refused us because of my sister. They almost took me; but there was no way I would go without my sister, so they said they'd wait for a boy 'cause that's what they really wanted. But, Freddy, they didn't look none too nice."

"They aren't. But I'm glad they didn't take you. It would've been hard."

"I'm tough, but Molly is just a little girl who needs attention."

"Yeah, Frieda is like that, but she's your age. Don't know if I'll ever see her again."

Addy lowered her head and whispered, "Well, just so you know, the adults are doing these picnics so they can help make sure all the Otters are well cared for. Not sure just what they'll do if kids are being treated bad . . . Maybe talk to the parents. But at least try to make sure you get to the picnics, and school, and even church."

Freddy shook his head and smiled. "Otters—that's kinda funny."

Carter plopped down next to them. "Hi, I'm Carter and a friend of Addy. I saw your homer. You're Freddy?"

Freddy smiled. "Yeah, I'm with the Bergmans out on Chambers Island. I guess I'm an Otter. You?"

"No, but my sister almost was. Lainey, Addy's new ma. Her parents saved me from drowning, and then, sadly, they drowned in a shipwreck."

"That's tough. My parents died in a fire. Pa got my sister and me out of the house and went back in to help Ma but didn't make it." He looked down. "I still have nightmares. Sometimes, I yell out in the dreams, and . . . well . . . the Bergmans get really mad when I do that and make me sleep outside."

Addy made fists. "Well, that's wrong. I'd like to tell them . . . "

Carter put his hand on Addy's arm. "Addy, you can't. Tell your pa. Let the adults take care of it."

Freddy let out a deep sigh. "I don't think anything will change them. Hopefully, I won't have any more nightmares when winter comes."

Carter shook his head. "Right, way too cold to sleep outside. You like Chambers?"

"Yeah, it's a pretty neat island. It has a lake, and the lake has a little island. The Bergmans did give me a day off, and I went swimming and met Jake and Matilda Dennett. Their dad bought a bunch of land there and is going to build a resort right on the lake. They had a canoe and let me go with them out to the island. It was so much fun. They were there only a short time. I think they're from Chicago and went back already."

Carter looked from Addy to Freddy. "Maybe we could come out sometime. That would be so neat. I heard they also do a lot of lumbering on Chambers."

Freddy nodded. "Yes, I'm hoping that once we get the Bergmans' farm cleared and producing that maybe I could work with the lumbering, be a lumberjack."

"I think I'd like that as well." Carter looked at Addy. "I think Daniel Claflin, Julius and Niles' brother, is a lumberjack on Chambers. Hey, who's that man over there talking to your pa, Addy?"

"Hmm, don't know."

Freddy grinned. "I know. That's Mr. Dennett, the man who's going to build the resort."

Addy hopped up. "Let's go meet him. C'mon."

The threesome approached the men.

"Hey, Pa, this is Freddy. He's an Otter, too."

Mr. Dennett raised his eyebrows, and Clifford responded, "Orphan Train kids. They call themselves Otters. Freddy, Carter, Addy, this is Mr. Dennett."

"Nice to meet you." Carter extended his hand. Freddy and Addy did the same.

Mr. Dennett's gaze lingered on Freddy. "I do believe I've seen you before."

"Yes, sir. I played with Jake and Matilda one day. I'm with the Bergmans."

Addy noticed the shadow that passed over Mr. Dennett's face.

"Ah, yes, the Bergmans." He stretched his neck. "You know, I've plans to build a resort on Chambers Island. Maybe I could steal you away a couple days a week to do some work for me. I'd pay you, of course."

Freddy's eyes grew big. "That would be amazing if they let me."

"I think I could make it well worth their time. I might even have a job for Mr. Bergman. Don't say anything. Let me talk to them. I bet there are more cookies over there."

The kids ran over to the food table. Addy slapped Freddy on the back. "I would be so happy for you if you . . . " She lowered her voice. "If you could get away from them."

"I sure would like to work for him."

Carter handed him a cookie. "I hope it happens, too. Will they bring you in for school or church? I know it's hard for us on Rock Island to get in for everything."

"Yeah, not sure about school. Maybe church once in a while, especially if there are picnics afterward."

Carter finished a cookie. "Sometimes, my sister and I come to Washington Island and stay with the Hansons for a week so we can go to school and church. My ma also teaches us. Then from Christmas to April, we close our lighthouse, and the whole family stays with the Hansons. Then we can do church and school. My parents help them with building boats and cooking for their café while there."

"I've never been in a lighthouse. I've seen the one on Chambers but haven't visited. Maybe someday, I could . . . Well, I don't know if they'd let me."

Carter glanced back at the men. "Well, they're talking. I know they want to help the Otters. Maybe things will work out. Give it some time. I think I overheard the adults planning to have a picnic every month. We should be at all of them."

"Yes, we'll be at the next one." Addy bit her lip. "Wait. If the baby comes right around then, we might not be able to come. But lots of others will be here." Addy pointed at Charlotte, Andrew, Tina, David, and Catherine. "I think they'll all be here. And do you already know Flossy or the twins, Irene and Doreen?"

Freddy laughed. "Everybody knows the triplets."

Addy scrunched her face and spread her hands. "The triplets?"

"Flossy is always with the twins, and they are everywhere you go in Ephraim. So, I've heard people call them the triplets."

"Freddy!"

All the kids turned. Mr. Bergman stood with arms folded. "It's time to go, Freddy. Say goodbye, and let's return to the boat."

Freddy hung his head. "I have to go. Thanks for talking to me. Hope I see you next time." He turned and walked with slumped shoulders over to Mr. Bergman.

Addy gritted her teeth. "That could've been me. And Molly."

Carter patted her shoulder. "I'm so glad you're not there. But I hope . . . Wait, look. Mr. Dennett is talking to Mr. Bergman."

Addy wanted to run over and listen, but she stood still. Mr. Dennett talked to Freddy. She turned to Carter. "Maybe he's offering that job. I hope so."

CHAPTER EIGHTEEN

THE COLORS ON THE TREES released tips of red as school announced its regathering. Addy shook her head. School did not hold any allure for her. Molly delighted in the thought and loved that Miss Rose would be her teacher. Molly often found a few minutes to sit on Rose's lap when she came to assist with cooking and cleaning. Her belly now revealed the growth of another baby, but there was still room for Molly. Ma's belly left no room for Molly or Hans to sit. Addy offered numerous times to stay home and help instead of going to school, but Ma and Pa insisted she go. Sarah would be helping, and soon, grandmas and aunts would arrive. Mrs. Figgenschau's home was almost rebuilt, but she determined to stay till after the baby came in order to be of any assistance possible.

On the first day of school, Miss Rose introduced Miss Genevieve Seiler, who would take over for her once her baby arrived. The children greeted Miss Genevieve cordially but gathered around Miss Rose to rejoice in her news of a baby on the way.

Addy already knew, so she hung back as the other students hugged Miss Rose or asked about Hans and when this baby would arrive and if she wanted a boy or girl. Gazing out the window, she didn't notice Miss Genevieve arrive behind her.

"Addy, is it?"

Addy jumped. Her grin was sheepish as she turned to face the new teacher. "Yes, Addy. Molly is my sister."

"You don't seem too interested in the new baby or, perhaps, even school."

Addy dropped her head and then looked up. "I know Miss Rose. She's Ma's best friend, so I know all about the baby. And, well, I'd rather be outside, feeding the animals, helping Pa on his ferry boat, or helping Ma at the resort. Her baby is coming soon, and I'd like to just be there."

Miss Genevieve sat down at the nearest desk. "I'm somewhat the same way. There's so much to be learned outdoors. Miss Rose is having me take a day or two each week, and I'm planning to do a lot of outdoor lessons. About trees and leaves, and the lakes, and animals. I'll need someone to assist me with some of those."

Addy's eyes brightened. "I like to help. Maybe I could be your assistor."

Miss Genevieve smiled. "Assistant. I think you could be a big help to me. Shall I plan on it? Can I depend on you?"

Addy nodded. "You can. Well, except when the baby comes. I might miss a few days."

"That will be fine. I'll tell you what. As I plan my lessons, I'll talk with you after school the day before, and we'll see what you can help with. Okay?"

"I'd like that, Miss Genevieve."

All the students returned to their seats, and Addy sat next to Molly. She sighed and whispered to Molly, "I think this will be okay."

Molly giggled. "I love it already."

Addy awoke to moaning. Her mind grappling to understand, she peered through the semi-darkness to Molly who breathed easily in her sleep.

"The baby!" Addy tried not to yell. She piled out of bed, fighting with sheets that had somehow wrapped themselves around her legs. Almost falling, she stood and straightened her nightgown and tiptoed into Ma's room. It was already full of people.

Mrs. Figgenschau shuffled in behind Addy. She patted Addy's shoulder. "Don't be alarmed, child. I'm going to rub some creams on your mama's body to ease the birthing process. I might have you help me fetch and mix a few more things as the day goes by."

Addy's eyes grew big, and she found her voice shaky. "Okay. How long does it take?"

"Well, that we never truly know. We pray not too long and not too painful."

"It hurts?"

Mrs. Figgenschau stopped. "Weren't you there when Molly was born?"

"They sent me next door. I was four, so I don't remember too much."

Tina grabbed Addy's hand. "This is so exciting. Lainey was there when I was born, and she had a vision, or a dream, or something that I would be beside her when she gave birth. Isn't that cool?"

Addy gulped. "It is. Do you know what we should do?"

Tina giggled. "I asked that. And she just said to hold her hand and pray or run errands when they need towels or water or anything."

"Okay."

Tina frowned. "Addy, you look a little whiter than usual. And your forehead looks like it has tears. Are you all right?"

Grandma Engelson turned. "Addy, sit down. Tina, get a cool cloth for her forehead."

Ma grimaced as a contraction tightened around her. Then she reached a hand to Addy. "Come sit by me, Addy. Of course, you can leave anytime and come back. I want Tina on one side and you on the other."

Aunt Edith pulled a chair over for Addy to sit in. "This is exciting, isn't it? You're going to have a little brother or sister."

Addy nodded but found it hard to breathe. She looked at Grandma Engelson, who smiled. "Addy, you'll be all right. Just breathe."

Tina returned and handed Addy a cool cloth to lay on her forehead. Then she sat on the other side of the bed and stroked her sister's face and forehead with another cool cloth.

Pa stood beaming but wringing his hands near the foot of the bed. His mother patted him on the shoulder. "All will be well. It's the natural flow of things. And soon, you'll be holding this little one in your arms."

Ma groaned again as another contraction embraced her whole body. Pa clenched his fists and moved next to Addy and knelt down. "What can I do? I don't like seeing you in pain."

Ma smiled and patted his hand. "It hurts, but it's for a good purpose. You can pray it goes quickly."

But it didn't. Around 8:00 a.m., after several hours of sporadic contractions several minutes apart, Addy and Molly were shooed out to go get dressed and have some breakfast. Tina joined them. Aunt Edith and Mrs. Figgenschau made sure that food was plentiful.

The baby had decided to come two weeks late, so guests had arrived. Clifford had prayed fervently the baby would not arrive on the day he had to pick them up. He allowed the girls to stay home from school that day, just in case, but when he returned around noon and there still seemed to be no indication that the baby would make an appearance, he gathered Addy, Molly, and Tina and dropped them off at school.

Tina and her mother had arrived a week earlier. Grandma Engelson sat and visited with Ma and made sure she didn't do anything strenuous or go anywhere alone. The girls played together, went to school together, and came home each day hoping the baby would soon make an appearance. Aunt Edith and Grandma Ruckert arrived together shortly after the Engelsons and took over the running of the resort. Mrs. Figgenschau remained ever ready with a kind word and assistance wherever needed. With the abundance of apples on the island in the fall, the women made enough applesauce to last the winter. Preserving it in canning jars kept everyone busy when they weren't preparing food for the family and guests or tending to Ma. Addy decided there was nothing on earth that tasted better than the warm applesauce that was made at Sunset Resort.

After breakfast, the girls returned to their seats by Ma. Pa never left the room. Grandma Ruckert brought soup, sandwiches, and applesauce as often as anyone expressed that perhaps they were hungry. Ma had no appetite, but her mother insisted she take sips of water as the day wore on. Pa would eat a couple bites or take a few sips of soup and then set it aside.

About 3:00 p.m., the girls visited the horse.

Addy petted her forehead. "You know, Nellie, we're waiting for a baby. It's taking so long."

Nellie nickered and laid her nose on Addy's shoulder. Addy sighed, and the immense tension seeped out of her body like rain running off the roof.

Molly opened the stall door, pulled the girls in, and shut the door. She and Tina each took a side and rubbed the horse with the brushes hanging on the wall. Addy wrapped her arms around Nellie's neck.

"Nellie really loves you, Addy." Tina brushed Nellie's flank with long deliberate strokes.

"I know, and I love her."

Tina nodded. "She knows that."

Mrs. Figgenschau appeared at the door. "I think it's time, girls. The baby is coming."

The girls dropped their brushes and then hurriedly retrieved them and hung them on the wall. Mrs. Figgenschau waited for them to exit the stall and made sure the gate was closed properly. "Girls, wash your hands before you go in."

Addy ran through the kitchen door and immersed her hands in the sudsy water left from washing dishes. Tina and Molly joined her. They looked at each other with big eyes and then, hand-in-hand, entered the bedroom. Ma had her eyes closed, but Addy could see tears on her face. Ma hollered, and Tina and Addy jumped. Then they took their seats and grasped her hands. Addy grimaced at how hard her ma squeezed. She opened her eyes and smiled and then groaned again. She tried to sit up, but Mrs. Figgenschau gently restrained her.

"You know it's close when you decide to get up and leave." Mrs. Figgenschau held a cool compress on Ma's forehead.

Ma looked up at Mrs. Figgenschau. Her voice was barely a whisper. "Thank you."

Grandma Engelson had her hand on Ma's belly. She pressed lightly. "Okay, sweetheart, this is the painful part, but it's time to push."

Aunt Edith stood next to Pa at the foot of the bed and prayed. "Lord, bring this child into the world with ease. Help our Lainey . . . please."

Addy looked at Aunt Edith and Grandma Ruckert. Their eyes were full of tears. Alarm rose up in her, and she locked eyes with Aunt Edith.

Aunt Edith's expression softened. "No need to worry, Addy. All is well. These are tears of joy at the new life about to arrive, and little bit of concern over your ma's pain."

Grandma Ruckert stretched her neck. "Yes, this is how birth is. There is agony—the pain—and there is uncontainable joy at the child about to be born."

"Push!" Grandma Engelson's voice silenced them all.

Pa positioned his hands; and moments later, a wrinkled, red, beautiful baby girl emerged into his hands.

The women quickly cut the cord and wiped the baby off. Just then, she let out a wail.

Addy couldn't figure out why she couldn't see and then realized she was blubbering. Pa brought the baby over and laid her on Ma's chest. The baby's mouth was already working.

Grandma Engelson helped Ma direct the baby to her breast. "She's late, and she's worked up a big appetite."

Addy stood and stared with mouth agape. She had no words. How could this be? Just moments before, this complete, little person dwelt inside Ma's belly; and now, here she was suckling and crying. Just then, the baby pulled away, and her eyes met Addy's. Addy's whole body tingled, and she knew that this child was and always would be her sister, just like Molly. And a fierceness of determination to look out for that sister enveloped her.

When the baby started to suckle again, Ma looked at Addy. "I know what you feel, Addy. I felt the same way when Tina was born. Even though you and I are both adopted, there is a connection that's greater than the bloodline. I think it's God's blessing." The baby stopped nursing. Ma then looked at Aunt Edith. "This child is truly your bloodline, Aunt Edith. I want you to hold her." Pa lifted the child and handed her to their aunt, whose face was awash with tears.

"Thank you. She's beautiful. I'm so happy to be here. She even looks like . . . like . . . " Aunt Edith's voice cracked. "Like Mandy."

Addy had heard the story that Aunt Edith and Uncle Otis' only child had somehow gotten outdoors and then fallen into the rocks and water on the north end of Pilot Island. By the time they found her, she was gone.

Ma nodded and sniffed. "Clifford, tell her."

Aunt Edith looked up. "Tell me what?"

Pa placed his arm around her shoulder and touched the baby's nose. "If it's all right with you, her name is Emma Mandy. We'll call her Emmy. But we wanted Lainey's first mother—your sister Emma—and little Mandy's name to be hers."

A slow smile spread across Aunt Edith's face, while tears flowed down her cheeks. "That is wonderful, just, so kind. Thank you. Well, little Emma Mandy, we are going to have some special times together."

Grandma Engelson spoke up. "And now, we are going to shoo all of you out of the room to finish cleaning Lainey and making sure the afterbirth is out of her."

Addy squinted. "The what?"

Grandma Ruckert took her hand. "Enough questions. Just part of the birthing process. Let's go take turns holding Emmy."

Addy, Tina, and Molly all sat on the settee next to each other and gently passed the baby one to the other.

"I like her little nose." Molly touched it and grinned. "Pa always touches my nose like that."

Tina grinned. "I'm glad she came late. I was born early, and it was winter, and they had to put me in the warming oven to keep me warm."

Addy giggled. "That would be so strange. I can't imagine doing that with Emmy." She took Emmy in her arms. "You are our sister, little one, and I promise we will always take care of you and protect you."

"That's beautiful, Addy. The grandmas need to hold her now, and there are cookies in the kitchen." Grandma Ruckert picked up Emmy from Addy, and the girls ran to the kitchen.

Addy grabbed a cookie and then stood in the doorway watching the adults. Grandma Ruckert sat on the settee and unwrapped Emmy. The other women gathered around and oohed and aahed over her little body and counted her toes and fingers. Grandma Ruckert wrapped her again and offered her to Aunt Edith.

"Oh, let Hilga hold her first. I know the girls think of you as a grandma." Aunt Edith stood back as Mrs. Figgenschau took the baby.

"Thank you so much for letting me be here." Mrs. Figgenschau held the baby for a few moments, then handed her to Aunt Edith. "She's probably getting hungry again. Look at that face."

As Aunt Edith took the little one in her arms, Emmy let out a wail, and her face turned red. Aunt Edith grinned. "Well, she's not shy. We all know what she wants. I'll take her back to Lainey."

Fifteen minutes later, Grandma Engelson and Pa emerged from the room. Pa barely looked where he walked, his eyes on his baby girl.

Aunt Edith stood. "How's Lainey?"

"She's exhausted. She just nursed Emmy and is falling asleep. We'll let her rest till the baby needs to feed again."

Pa sat down, and the girls gathered around him.

"She's so cute, Pa. She has blue eyes and blonde hair like Ma and you." Molly climbed up on the arm of the overstuffed chair.

He reached over and tapped her nose. "Yes, she does, just like you. And, Addy, she looks deep in my eyes just like you. I think she'll fit right in with you two."

Aunt Edith put her hand over her mouth and then wiped a tear drifting down her cheek. "Yes, you are sisters."

Tina grinned. "And like Aunt Edith, I'm Emmy's aunt."

Aunt Edith clapped her hands. "Yes, we have two aunts here."

Addy tightened her mouth and squinted. "Okay, wait now. We have two sisters, two aunts, and three grandmas. Mrs. Figgenschau, we think of you as a grandma."

Tina shifted her position on the chair arm. "Well, I've started calling her Grandma Hilga. That's easier than Mrs. Figgenschau."

Everyone laughed. Then they heard a knock on the door.

Aunt Edith threw up her hands. "Oh my, we have guests to feed." She, Grandma Ruckert, and Grandma Hilga hurried to the kitchen.

Addy got up. "I'll help with the guests, too." She bent over and kissed Emmy's forehead. "I won't be long, little sis."

Grandma Engelson greeted the guests. "Come in. As you know, we've been waiting for a baby. She has arrived and is in the sitting room with her father and the girls. We'll have dinner ready for you in a few moments. Do forgive us for being a little late."

One of the women spoke up. "Oh, we're more eager to see the baby than we are to eat." She looked at her friends. "Although, we are ready to eat. Shall we stay in the dining area?"

Addy waved from the sitting room doorway. "Right this way. Follow me to see the baby, and then you can sit at the table there by the window. It's a little early for sunset, but you may stay right there if you prefer to watch it from inside. The evening air has a bit of a chill now."

"Why, you are such a good hostess, young lady. What is your name?"

"I'm Addy. My baby sister is right in here. Her name is Emmy."

Later in the evening, Ma came out to the sitting room with Emmy. They all gathered around to ooh and aah once more. Addy slipped out of the room and came back with a small package in her hands. "Ma, I made something for you and the baby. It's the only thing I've ever made, and I couldn't get all the words on, but Catherine and Mrs. Hanson helped me and . . . Well, here it is. I just wrapped it in a towel, so I'll take that off. Pa made a little frame for it. I hope you like it."

Lainey held it up for everyone to see. It was an embroidered plaque with most of the words from Luke 2:52. "This child will grow in wisdom and favor with God and man. Luke 2:52."

"Oh, Addy, I love it, and we'll all cherish it. I'll put it over the baby's crib."

Ma allowed the girls to remain home from school the day after the birth. Addy reveled in the warmth of love that seemed to emanate from everyone and was surprised at how exhausted she felt from all the excitement. She could already see that babies required a lot of attention, but the happiness that oozed around the resort filled her. She, Molly, and Tina could not get enough of holding Emmy. She loved counting her fingers and touching her soft face. And the baby's smiles sent tingles all through her. She wanted to do anything and everything she could to help take care of Ma and this baby. It confounded her but gave her so much joy.

Molly skipped around the house, and no matter who had the baby, she would run up and kiss her. Addy laughed that Tina and the adults were the same way. Even the guests tiptoed into the main dining room between meals asking to see the baby. Aunt Edith would beam and go retrieve Emmy and bring her out to see them. Aunt Edith kept the dining room and kitchen clean, while the other women did most of the cooking.

Pa sat with Ma and held Emmy as much as he could. When she nursed, Pa shut the door. Addy could hear them whispering to each other when she went by the door. She marveled at his care for his wife. Her first papa was good to Mama, but she never noticed a connection like she saw here. Maybe it was because she was older now. She wondered if Molly was aware of this great love between their new parents. Almost every time Pa held the baby, he sang songs to her. Molly, Tina, and Addy would run and sit at his feet, loving the songs.

Addy dragged her feet the next day as they prepared to go to school, but she surprised herself noticing that she actually looked forward to school. Tina and Molly, though disappointed to not be with Emmy, gushed with excitement about the return to school.

Book-learning had never appealed to Addy, but Miss Genevieve made it more practical and used the outdoors to teach. Addy could handle that. And Pa had told her that even though she was a natural and quick learner when it came to boats and horses, she needed to learn more about those things, and books would help. Because he complimented her when she followed his instruction, she decided that she would give school her best try. Somehow, watching someone do something, showing her how it worked, helped her get it and retain it. Sometimes, the words in the book went in her head and got lost. But she would try. And she wouldn't complain.

CHAPTER NINETEEN

THE NEXT OTTER PICNIC WAS scheduled for Washington Island. Pa had contacted people as he traveled back and forth ferrying people and some supplies. He checked in with August Olson every trip. He delivered messages between Rev. Gunnlerson and Rev. Iverson as they each focused on means to possibly counsel Otter families. Mr. Olson and Rev. Iverson informed everyone they knew when the event would take place. And of course, Irene, Doreen, and Flossy talked with as many kids as they could.

Pa laughed as he shared details of these communications with his family. "Those girls, the triplets, will make sure everyone and anyone knows. They can be pretty persuasive."

Molly ducked her head. "I like those girls; they're pretty and flouncy."

Addy squinted. "Flouncy?"

Ma laughed. "I would say a bit prissy, aware of how cute they are, and ready to make sure everyone does their bidding. Not necessarily mean, but a little bossy." She looked at Pa and winked.

Pa tipped his head. "What?"

"Your cousin, Miss Pritchard, my teacher—whom I love dearly now, but . . ."

Pa slapped his knee. "Oh, yes, I guess she could well have been considered flouncy."

Molly and Addy looked from face to face. "What?"

"Oh, when your pa and I were starting to fall in love, I got a beautiful new dress for the Valentine's dance. But when your pa arrived, he was on the arm of my teacher, whom I would have considered flouncy that night." Ma shifted her seat and moved Emmy to the other arm. "I, of course, assumed he was her beau."

Pa held up his hand. "Now, I tried several times to say Miss Juliet Pritchard was my cousin, but your ma here would not give me the time of day."

Addy clapped her hands. "So, what happened?"

Ma grinned. "Well, I was heartbroken until a few weeks later when I learned that they were cousins. And then I let him dance with me."

"And I was confused." Pa laid his hand against his forehead, feigning helplessness. "But we soon got it figured out."

Addy's eyes brightened. "Ma, have you written about it?"

"I have, but my piece still needs some work. And I want Juliet, his cousin, to look it over with me. I hope we see her soon. She went downstate to teach and married a couple years ago."

Pa picked up the baby and bounced her a little on his knees. "Now, back to the Otter picnic. I've even talked to Mr. Dennett. He will help transport families."

"What about Freddy? Is he okay?"

Pa smiled. "He was able to hire Freddy two days a week to help clear land and learn a little about building. He also hired Charles Bergman, two different days a week, to do some of the same and learn a little about bookkeeping. Charles seems very good with numbers. Mr. Dennett's given the Bergmans some farm equipment that makes their clearing and plowing easier and faster. I think Dennett got new items and just gave the others to Charles, saying he'd otherwise get rid of the older pieces. They've seen a softening in Charles already, and even his wife, Gyda, seems a little stronger and happier. I think the life they chose there was simply harder than they expected, and now, life is better."

Addy wrapped her arms around herself. "That's good. I'm glad to hear that."

"So, Mr. Dennett and I will transport from Ephraim. I'll also pick up some in Ellison Bay. My folks are letting people know when they come to their store. Mr. Hogenson, who owns a hotel in Ephraim, is bringing people from Fish Creek on his schooner, the *Ebenezer*. Rasmus will bring Rock and Pilot and any from Newport Town. Pastor Gunnlerson has several women from church lined up to bring food and serve it. Jack Figgenschau and Arlo will transport everyone from the boat docks to the church."

"Pa, I could take people in our wagon. You know how good I am now with Nellie."

Ma shook her head. "Oh, I don't know. Clifford?"

Pa tipped his head. "I think she could do it. But that means you, Molly, would have to be Ma and Emmy's helper. Can you do that?"

Molly stood up and clapped her hands. "Yes, I will do that." She went over and sat next to Ma and leaned her head against Ma's shoulder and touched the baby's nose.

The day of the picnic, Addy could hardly contain herself. She would drive one of the wagons to and from the port in Detroit Harbor and even Sunset Resort if Pa brought his load there. She couldn't wait to see how Freddy fared with the Bergmans. As much as she loved helping with the boat, this was a first, and her whole body shook as she climbed up on the wagon to fetch the first group arriving on Mr. Dennett's boat. Thankfulness rose within her as she noticed the calmness of the water and the few cumulus clouds drifting slowly across the sky as she arrived at the port, but her new job claimed her focus. And there, tying the lines, was Freddy. She opened her mouth to call to him, but then two girls caught her eye. She stopped and held the reins still, keeping her gaze on the two girls. A third one joined them, and they clamored off the boat and ran to the wagon. Then it dawned on Addy. They had been on the Orphan Train ship with Molly and her.

She sensed a little skittishness in Nellie and climbed off the wagon to stand next to the horse, stroking Nellie's neck, while the few families climbed onto the wagon.

The tall girl with long, dark blonde hair greeted her first. "Didn't we meet on the ship? I'm Gloria. This is my sister, Dulcey. We are with the Arenson family. We were sick for the last picnic but so happy to be at this one. This was our first boat ride since we arrived and so much fun."

"I remember you. Are you . . . I mean, is your family . . . Well, have you been . . . "

Gloria laughed a high-pitched, infectious laugh, and everyone joined in. "I'm sorry. I have a silly laugh, but we've been treated really well and are very happy." She leaned close to Addy and turned her head so only Addy could hear. "But Pauline, there. She came at the same time. She has bruises."

Addy bit her bottom lip. Anger rose up. This should not be. Nellie nickered and nudged her with her nose. *Oh, Nellie, you know me. Pa told me not to be—what was that word? Impetuous.* Addy took a deep breath and nodded. Gloria smiled and turned back to the wagon.

"Addy! We're here." Freddy stood before her, head up and smiling. "I've been working two days a week for Mr. Dennett, and he's teaching me to help with his boat today." He then lowered his voice. "It's better with the family, too."

"I'm glad to hear that."

Mr. and Mrs. Bergman were the last to climb on the wagon. Mrs. Bergman still seemed weak, but her face was different. She looked almost happy—almost. And Addy gulped and tried not to gasp when Mr. Bergman greeted her with a smile.

Freddy helped Mrs. Bergman up onto the wagon, and then Mr. Bergman turned to Addy. "May I assist you getting on the wagon? I understand you are the wagon driver. That's quite impressive, young lady."

Addy could only nod. No words came. She remembered well his refusal of her and Molly and had decided that she didn't like him then. When she met Freddy and recognized his look of abandonment, she moved close to hating Mr. Bergman. One day, she had poured out those feelings to Ma, who just placed her arms around her and said nothing for a few minutes. Ma then told her about forgiveness. She told Addy to consider that the hurt a person endured in life could make them angry and mean or sad and withdrawn. She told Addy that God knew and understood all that, and He offered forgiveness to everyone. And perhaps Addy, after thinking about all that, could forgive others, too. Addy had asked how she knew all that. Ma said Pastor Gunnlerson had helped her learn so much about God. Addy resolved to consider those things and to listen to Pastor Gunnlerson more. She'd found it hard to sit still in church, but after the discussion with Ma, she decided to listen. And indeed, she discovered he spoke about all those things.

So, did Mr. Bergman choose to forgive some people who hurt him or maybe forgive the hard times life had given him? Could a person forgive the difficulties in life? Is that how to handle all the bad that happened? Even when it's your own fault? She'd have to ask Ma. Or maybe Pastor Gunnlerson.

"Addy?"

Her head jerked up. She'd been so lost in thought. Mr. Bergman held out his hand.

Addy took it and climbed up to the wagon seat. "Thank you." Already, the sizzle of anger was seeping out of her.

Gloria leaned forward. "Addy, could Pauline and Dulcey sit with you on your seat?"

Pauline stood up and looked at the frowning couple next to her. "May I?"

"Fine, but don't you cause trouble, girl."

A hint of a smile crossed Pauline's face, but she immediately hung her head as she moved forward. Dulcey nudged Pauline to sit between her and Addy.

Pauline wrung her hands as Addy slapped the reins and directed Nellie on the route to the church. "You're really good with horses. My pa . . . I mean, before . . . well, before the fire when they died." She paused and took a deep breath and glanced behind her. "He taught me all about horses. He was going to get me my own, but then, well, the fire. And now I'm here."

Addy kept her voice low. The rest of the people on the wagon were chatting, so she was sure Pauline's family didn't hear. "Do they let you work with their horses?"

"Oh, no." Pauline glanced back again. "They don't believe me. I do the washing and the cooking. But Rev. Iverson persuaded them to bring me today."

Addy calmed the rising concern for Pauline by enjoying the beauty around her. The blue sky promised a pleasant day. The colors of the trees were almost at their peak. The reds trembled lightly on the branches as a sweet breeze cooled the day only a bit. The intense heat of summer had swept away as the trees turned their glorious goldens and reds.

Just then, a pine snake slithered across the road. Nellie shook her head and her tail and began to prance sideways.

Addy pulled up on the reins, bringing the wagon to an almost standstill, even though Nellie continued to thrash her head. She handed the reins to Pauline. "Hold her as steady as you can."

Pauline's eyes grew big. "But . . . "

Addy was already almost on the ground. She turned and looked Pauline in the eyes. "Do it!" Addy scurried forward to Nellie, grabbing her bridle. Nellie's eyes were wide with panic, and her legs were racing in place. Pauline had a good grip on the reins.

"Nellie, Nellie." Addy pulled on the bridle until Nellie's eyes were even with hers. She held the bridle firmly in one hand and placed the other on Nellie's forehead. "You're okay, girl. You're okay. The snake is gone. You're okay." Nellie's eyes softened, and her whole body shivered. She leaned her head against Addy and nickered. Addy stood a full two minutes stroking her head and neck and talking softly. Pauline sat with the reins in her hand.

Satisfied Nellie was calm and no more snakes were next to the road, Addy climbed up on the wagon. Everyone clapped.

Freddy grinned. "That was great, Addy."

Mr. Bergman doffed his hat. "You have a good ability with horses, young lady. That could have had a tragic end."

Addy felt her face heat up. "Thank you." She was about to take the reins from Pauline but stopped. She turned to face the passengers. "I couldn't have done it without Pauline here. She's pretty good with horses, too." She looked at Pauline's family, and they nodded. Their faces were still stern, but a little less than before. She noted that Mr. Dennett sat next to the couple.

As she retrieved the reins and resumed the trip, she heard Mr. Dennett speak to the man. "Your girl seems to have a knack with horses. I bet you've found that helpful on your farm."

Addy couldn't hear their response but found herself marveling at how what was almost a terrible accident turned out so well for several people. When she'd finally decided to listen to Pastor Gunnlerson, she'd heard him say, "God works in mysterious ways, His wonders to behold." It was a strange saying to her, but he said it was from a recent hymn he'd heard and that the Bible says that God makes "things work together for good." That must be what just happened. Perhaps life would be better for Pauline simply because she attended today and because of the snake. Addy glanced over at Pauline, and she was smiling.

The road held a bit of dust, and Nellie's fearful prancing had drummed it up. No one complained, though. A few waved the dust

away and cleared their throats. Most commented on the beauty of
the colors of the trees.

All the passengers unloaded next to Bethel Church. A few stopped
to thank Addy for handling the horse so well, but most hurried to
see friends and find a spot to place their food. Tables stood next
to the church providing an easy entrance in case of rain. The day
continued to boast blue skies with the occasional cumulus cloud and
just enough breeze to maintain comfort. The temperature in the low
seventies created a perfect day for the picnic. The boys were already
chasing the girls with whatever bug or worm they could find, and the
girls' squeals filled the air. Soon, Pastor Gunnlerson had markers set
up for a game of baseball and races.

Addy remained with Nellie for a few minutes. She realized her
heart was still beating rather fast after the snake incident, and she
assumed Nellie might be in the same condition. After everyone
departed for food and games, she leaned against Nellie.

"You okay, girl? I'm sorry that snake came along." Nellie nudged
her so that she and Addy looked eye to eye. "Are you checking to see
that I'm all right? I am. It was a little scary at first." Nellie nickered
and rubbed her nose against Addy. "Okay, girl. I'll go join the others.
But I'll rub you down a bit first." Addy turned to retrieve the brush
from under the wagon seat, and there stood Carter.

"Addy, Freddy just told me about the snake and how you handled
Nellie." He put a hand on her shoulder. "I'm really proud of you. You're
so good with horses."

Once more, Addy felt heat climb into her face. She wasn't used
to all this praise and didn't know how to respond. "Umm, thanks,

Carter. I didn't really have time to think. And Pauline handled the reins good. I think her family is rough on her." Addy lowered her voice. "I saw bruises, Carter. I think Mr. Dennett knows, but we need to make sure the adults talk to them. And it helped her impress them when I handed her the reins."

Carter patted her back. "It was good. You did good, Addy."

"She did." Addy and Carter whirled around. Jack Figgenschau stood behind them. "I drove my wagon right behind you, Addy, and I saw the whole thing. Everyone is proud of you. But you youngsters should go get some food and play games. That's what you're here for."

Addy looked down. "Thanks, Mr. Figgenschau, but I did it almost without thinking. I need to rub Nellie down for a few minutes."

Carter smiled. "I'll help you, so it'll go faster. Do you have an extra brush?"

"I have one." Mr. Figgenschau walked to his wagon and returned and handed it to Carter. "Just put it back on my wagon when you're done."

"Mr. Figgenschau." He turned back to Addy. "You should know that Pauline, who held the reins for me and is also very good with horses, has bruises. Her family here doesn't let her near the horses. She said her pa, who died in a fire, was about to get her a horse. I think she needs help."

Mr. Figgenschau nodded. "Thank you for your observance, Addy. I'll discuss it with the other adults."

CHAPTER TWENTY

CLIFFORD CHEWED A PIECE OF chicken as Lainey nursed Emmy in the shadow of large tree. Rasmus and Uncle Otis approached them. Each had a plate full of food.

Uncle Otis nodded to Lainey. "May we join you? If inappropriate with the baby nursing, we understand."

Lainey smiled. "It's fine. We're well-covered. Do sit. I'm delighted to see you. Did Aunt Edith come?"

"No, but she sent some food. What a fine event this is. I came at Rasmus' request. We need to discuss something with you."

Clifford set the piece of chicken back on his plate. "Everything all right?" He looked from Uncle Otis to Rasmus and back to Uncle Otis. "What is it? Aunt Edith? Your leg getting worse? Hannah?" Wrinkles formed on his forehead.

"Sit down with us, Clifford." Rasmus sat down on the blanket spread across the grass.

Lainey pursed her lips. "You're worrying me. Do tell us."

Rasmus shook his head. "I've been needing to tell you this. You'd find out soon enough, I'm sure, if I didn't tell you. I asked Otis to come and already let him know. On the day we met, Addy told me about her father and his accident, which left him unable to work."

Clifford nodded. "Yes, she said he was hurt in a work accident. Sounded similar to your accident, Otis."

Rasmus shook his head and took a sip of lemonade. "Not quite." He related the details of the story given to him by Addy that day on the grocery boat. He hung his head. "Clifford, Lainey, she knew the date because it was Molly's first birthday, April 20, 1891."

Clifford sucked in his breath.

Lainey gasped. "Her father was injured rescuing Clifford's ship?"

Clifford rubbed his forehead. "I don't know what to say. How in the world? Does she know it was my ship?"

"No, she doesn't; and I kept this under my hat, so it wouldn't influence you one way or the other when you decided whether or not to take the girls."

Uncle Otis patted Lainey's hand. "I had no idea. Rasmus just told me. I'm rather baffled by it all. I know God didn't cause this, but I believe He's working on the answer." He chewed his bottom lip a few seconds before continuing. "I think, just maybe, it's like your parents saving Carter, and then his parents took you."

Lainey held Emmy to her shoulder and patted her until she burped. "It's so like that, Uncle. My mind is spinning, but will the girls see God's hand to help, or will they see their new father as the cause of their distress?"

"My thoughts exactly." Clifford stretched his neck. "Whew, how do we tell her?"

Rasmus stood. "I think that moment will present itself. Don't try to force it, either of you. Lainey, I did tell your folks—and of course, Hannah—but no one else knows except Otis and you two. Don't fuss about it too much. As strange as it is, I believe God will give you peace and perfect timing. You have a beautiful family. Don't let worry upset that."

Uncle Otis stood as well. "Rasmus is right. You needed to know. I so believe these girls were sent to you. I don't believe you bear the guilt of their father's injury. Now, after this shock—and we're sorry to hand it to you—you need to go enjoy the day."

Rasmus and Uncle Otis walked away and joined in organizing the games. Clifford stared at Lainey and at the ground for a few minutes. He blew out a big breath. "Well, that was a punch to the mid-section. But they're right. It's just too strange, so we really must trust God. Does it make you question our decision to take the girls?"

Lainey smiled. "No, Clifford. Somehow, it strengthens my resolve to be their mother—as God intended. I don't quite understand that, but it makes my love for them more fierce, more intense—if that makes any sense."

Clifford chuckled. "It does make sense, even though it doesn't quite make sense. Well, let's finish our food and join the festivities.

As soon as Carter and Addy approached the food tables, Irene, Doreen, and Flossy ran to join them. Freddy was already eating, so they all plopped beside him on the grass. Homemade cornbread and biscuits covered in apple butter filled their plates, along with chicken and pork chunks, tomato slices, and cherry strudel. Freddy insisted on pulling Flossy's braids, and she slapped his hand and then laughed.

Addy heard a high-pitched laugh and saw Gloria heading their way with Pauline and Dulcey right behind. Pauline gave Addy a tentative smile but then hung her head.

"Pauline, come sit with us. I can't eat all this dessert. Will you share it with me?"

Pauline wrung her hands, then nodded and sat in the spot where Addy made room. Gloria and Dulcey sat as well.

Gloria pulled up some grass and twisted it between her fingers. "Hi. Is everyone here an Otter? This is my sister, Dulcey, and I'm Gloria. We're Otters who live with the Arensons. This is Pauline. She's with the Nundahls."

Carter nodded to Addy. "Pauline helped save the wagon today." He went on to relate the details of the horse and snake incident. Everyone clapped their hands, and Pauline's face turned red; but a smile spread across her face, and she held her head high.

Pastor Gunnlerson blew a whistle summoning the kids to the ballgames and races. Addy grabbed Pauline's wrist. "Let's go. Do you like to race?"

Pauline winced but nodded her head. Addy looked at her forearms and concluded she'd often been gripped very hard and pulled around. She loosened her hold. "I'm sorry. Do your arms hurt?"

Pauline moved her arms behind her and smiled. "I'm okay. Let's join the race. I'm pretty fast."

Addy nodded. "Yes, let's do that. But if you need to talk, I'll listen."

Pauline shook her head. "Let's just race. I'm not supposed to mention anything. This is a nice day. Let's just have fun."

Mid-afternoon brought more clouds, and the consideration of rain raised thoughts of returning home. Everyone knew the dangers of storms on these islands and waters. Addy went to check on Nellie to see if there was any skittishness. Horses sensed storms. Pa said it had to do with air pressure.

She passed Mr. Dennett and Jack talking with the Nundahls, Pauline's family. The tension around them emanated out to Addy. She knew not to get involved, but she slowed her walk to listen. Mr. Nundahl seemed the most agitated.

"I tell you. It's my business. You know as well as I that we take these children as workers. If some want to make them family, fine. But we don't have to."

Addy clenched her fists. It rose up within her to tell him what a wonderful girl Pauline was. But she could see Pa and Ma in her mind's eye telling her to not get involved. She swallowed several times and kept her feet moving, but very slowly.

Mr. Dennett laid his hand on Mr. Nundahl's shoulder.

Mr. Nundahl pushed it off. "I've told you my stand on this."

Mr. Dennett closed his eyes and shook his head, then stared at Mr. Nundahl. "Look, Sven, we see bruises on the girl's arms."

Mrs. Nundahl frowned. "Well, some people just bruise easy. I was helping her get up after she tripped. She's rather clumsy."

Mr. Figgenschau sighed. "Those aren't what she has, and you know it. She's been yanked around. If those bruises are so evident, we wonder if her shoulders, backside, and legs are covered in welts and bruises, too."

Mrs. Nundahl pulled herself up straight. "Well, I never. How could you even speak so? You are a bold man."

Mr. Figgenschau's shoulders slumped. "Look, we've seen this before. We are not being crude here. It's pretty evident. You have a sweet, capable girl. I was in the wagon behind you and saw how Addy and Pauline handled that horse and wagon. Come to find out, before Pauline's folks perished in a fire, she handled horses and was about to get her own."

Mr. Nundahl spit. "You think we can afford a horse for someone who isn't even part of our family?"

Addy turned. She would speak with them. She felt a hand on her shoulder. It was Carter. "Don't, Addy. It won't help."

"But . . ."

"I know. I'll walk you to see Nellie."

"No, just stand here and pretend to talk to me so I can watch and listen."

Carter nodded.

Mr. Dennett extended his hand to Mr. Nundahl, but he wouldn't take it. "Sven, you're a good man, but this will not go well for you if you mistreat the girl. People see. You'll lose business."

Mr. Nundahl's face turned red. "Oh, so now you're the big man and will tell people not to buy my tools?"

"No, this isn't my making, but I can read the sentiment and feel the pulse of the area. People talk. There are many families who have Otters, and if you don't want her as a daughter, fine, but respect her as a fine worker and a good human being. Tell me, do you yank around your customers?"

"How dare you!"

"Think about it, Sven. You wouldn't do that to your customers, other employees, even your horses. How can you do that to a girl under your care?"

Mrs. Nundahl stretched her neck. "You've got no right to talk to us like this."

Mr. Figgenschau shook his head. "Then, please, tell us. Who will? You must see this is wrong."

Mrs. Nundahl pursed her lips but said nothing.

Mr. Dennett stepped closer. "Please, a lot of community, families, businesses are here today. The bruises are evident but so is her ability to handle a horse. A lot of people have approached her and complimented her on helping Addy. Two young, capable girls. And they've probably seen the bruises. And whether they are caused by you or not, the perception will be that you're hot-headed. Please, we want our kids and communities to go well. Pauline needs to be in school. Are you sending her?"

Mrs. Nundahl looked down. "Well, we have to wait till the bru—" Her eyes went wide.

Mr. Figgenschau finished her sentence. "Till the bruises heal. Well, get her long sleeves if you must. The kids probably have figured it out already, but get her in school and at least treat her like you would a good employee."

Mr. Nundahl looked at his wife and nodded. "I suppose we could do that. It's just that, well, it's just . . . Oh, never mind. I never liked these kind of events, but at least, we came."

Mr. Dennett smiled. "You did, and we're glad of it. The kids liked meeting her, and I think she won a couple races."

Mrs. Nundahl grinned. "Really? I won a lot of races when I was her age. Maybe we should get her some better boots, Sven."

He rolled his eyes. "I suppose. Well. I think everyone is getting ready to leave. Looks like we may have to beat the rain."

A low roll of thunder sounded in the distance. Addy observed the sky. Far to the east, she saw some darkening clouds. She tried to remember all the things Ma and Miss Genevieve taught her about the weather. She couldn't remember if storms from the east were worse or from the northwest. Either way, she needed to make sure Nellie was okay. The breeze was a little stronger and a little cooler. She looked around. Everyone gathered their things and scurried to the wagons.

Freddy ran up. "I just talked to Mr. Hogenson. He runs a hotel in Ephraim and has a big schooner, the *Ebenezer*. He brought some families from Fish Creek, but he said he'd take everyone back to Ephraim along with Mr. Dennett. That way, your pa can go to Ellison Bay and then straight back."

Addy smiled. "Thanks, Freddy. I'll tell Pa."

Soon, the wagons were loaded with tired and happy people, and the horses plodded the dirt roads back to the dock where the boats waited. A few sprinkles of rain fell, but the children were still busy laughing and relating the day's events. A few of the younger ones slept leaning against the adults. Addy kept glancing over her shoulder at the approaching clouds. Still a distance away but moving toward them.

Parents scurried the children onto the waiting boats. Arlo assisted Pa getting the boat cranked up.

Pa grinned at Addy. "You did wonderfully today, girl. Get Nellie back to the barn and rubbed down. Where's your ma and the baby and Molly?"

"They went with Sarah in her surrey. That way, I could carry more people to the boat, and Ma wouldn't have to come here and then go back. And, Pa, Freddy said Mr. Hogenson is taking the ones from Ephraim that you brought, so you can just go to Ellison Bay and back."

Pa smiled. "Yes, he told me. And good plan for your ma going with Sarah. Okay, you get going now. I shouldn't be too long."

"Pa, can I go with you? It might get rough, and I don't mind it."

Arlo came up to Pa. "Everything is set, and everyone for Ellison Bay is on board. You know, I can take your wagon back and rub down

Nellie. I mean, Sarah is there, anyway. I know she'll stay to help Lainey get everything settled."

Pa looked up at the sky. "Okay, Addy, but make sure you pay attention to everything. Like you said, it might get rough. Thank you, Arlo. Let Lainey know that Addy is with me."

CHAPTER TWENTY-ONE

THE SKIES CLOUDED, AND THE wind began to whip. The waves held only a slight chop, but as the *Pearl* turned to the west, the following seas from the east gained a white froth.

Pa glanced behind him as the boat rose and dipped with the waves. "There's an increase in the frequency of these waves. Once we reach the west side of the mainland, we'll be out of the wind."

Addy widened her eyes in question. "What about when we come back, Pa?"

Pa smiled. "That could be rough. We may have to pull into Gills Rock."

"Pa, you know I don't mind rough waves."

"I know, but we don't want to be rambunctious in our bravery."

Addy dropped her head. "Okay."

Rounding the northwestern bluff of the mainland, they found themselves in calm waters. Sighs of relief were heard around the deck of the boat. The clouds marched from east to west and grew thicker.

"Pa, are these stratus clouds, the thick, gray blanket? Ma says they bring steady rain but not storms."

"Your ma knows how to read the weather. She's probably looking at it right now. Uncle Otis taught her all that when he was still the lighthouse keeper on Pilot. I think they may be that; but there were cumulus clouds earlier, so these might be a combination, and we may still encounter a storm. Keep your eyes on the lookout."

As everyone unloaded at the Ellison Bay dock, Grandpa Ruckert turned to Pa. "Son, you want to stay the night? I'm not sure those east winds have let up."

"Thanks, but I sense we should just get going. I'll be meeting those waves rather than dealing with following seas, and my *Pearl* is seaworthy."

Grandpa put his hand on Addy's shoulder. "You'll be all right?"

Addy smiled and hugged him. "Grandpa, I kind of like rough seas."

Grandpa rolled his eyes and shook his head. "Well, don't be foolhardy, you two. I'm glad, at least, that everyone else is on this side of the bluff. Wait, what about Rasmus?"

"You know, if it's bad, he'll stay with Uncle Otis in Newport Town or with Julius and Marla on Pilot. He knows what to do. He's probably more exposed to the waves than we'll be on our way back."

"Pa, did Mr. Dennett's boat go by? The *Ebenezer* left before us, but I don't remember seeing Mr. Dennett's boat."

Pa rubbed his chin. "You know, I didn't see it either. I think they were waiting for a few families when we left. Maybe they decided to stay." Pa checked his engine and gasoline level.

"Son, do you have enough gasoline? You know, we have it available in Ellison Bay now, thanks to Hogenson and Dennett. What a blessing those two are to the progress of this area."

"I have enough. Thanks. I did worry and wonder if I'd have enough access when Emil Lind so generously refitted the *Pearl* to run on gasoline. But right away, he paved the way to get supplies up to Ephraim; then Dennett and Hogenson made it even more available.

But enough talking. Good to see you, Pa. Thanks for getting people here today." He handed Addy a life jacket as he donned his.

They made good time heading north. Addy stood at the rail, studying the bluff line and waving to anyone on shore. "Pa, who is Emil Lind?"

"He and his wife were close friends of your ma's first parents. He helped finance the resort and this boat. They are two incredibly generous friends from Chicago."

Rounding the bluff into waves full of froth required Addy to hang on tight. Heading into three-foot waves caused them to ride upward and slam down in the trough between. Pa angled the boat, so the drop was not quite so severe.

"Addy, get right by me and hang on."

"Okay, Pa, but I want to watch for Mr. Dennett's boat."

"I have a feeling they stayed on Washington. Better to be safe."

Addy nodded. The wind whipped her hair, and the dark clouds grew darker. As Pa had warned, the clouds were not just stratus, but part cumulonimbus, the storm clouds. Did she hear a low rumble of thunder in the distance? Sounds were drowned out by the increasing roar of the wind. Waves slapped the bow of the boat and sent an occasional small flood of water to where she and Pa stood.

A bell sounded. A bell? Addy shook her head and cupped her ears. What in the world did she hear? "Pa, did you—"

"Look!" Pa nodded to the left.

Addy tightened her grip on the boat as she rose up on tiptoes and leaned as far out as she safely could. There in the distance bobbed Mr. Dennett's boat. Addy found it hard to determine what didn't seem right.

Pa took a deep breath. "Okay, they look like they may be in trouble. I think I heard their sounding bell, and they look tossed around. Addy, when I turn a little more toward them, we may get some waves broadside. It will rock us wild. I want you on the floor and holding on. Now."

Addy obeyed. Pa didn't turn fully sideways of the waves, but the rocking of the boat caused Addy to slide back and forth. Addy held to the base of a seat.

Addy could hear passengers on Mr. Dennett's boat yelling. Snippets came to their ears. "Fre . . . over . . . waves . . . can't . . . "

Then a sound from a different direction arrived. "Help me!"

Addy forgot her order to stay on the floor and hang on. She popped up and looked to the right of the boat. Nothing. Then something. Someone. Arms flailing and then sinking. "Pa! Pa! Someone's in the water." A face with pleading eyes once more rose above the wave. "Pa, it's Freddy. It's Freddy."

"Addy, can you get me the line with the ring on it? And put the rope ladder over the side. I'll throw it out to him, and I may need you to take the wheel while I pull him in."

"Yes, Pa." Addy dutifully found the ring and checked the security of the knots tied to it. "Shall I tie where the dock lines are usually attached?"

"Yes, do it quickly and make sure it's tied securely."

Addy handed the ring to Pa and took the wheel. On the second throw, Freddy grasped the ring but could not get it over his head. "Just hang on, Freddy; I'll pull you in." Pa pulled the line hand-over-hand, bringing Freddy within five feet of the boat. As he reached to take Pa's hand, he lost his grip on the ring, and a wave washed over his head. Almost immediately, he was again fifteen feet from the boat.

"Let me take the wheel, Addy. I'm going to get between the waves and Freddy. Then I want you to toss the ring to him. I'll need to hold the boat steady."

"Okay, Pa." The boat deck was slippery from all the waves that had splashed and the rain that now pummeled them. Addy slipped as she moved to the side of the boat but grabbed the rail and steadied herself as Pa brought the boat around. Freddy's face spelled panic and weakness. His eyes pleaded with Addy. The boat rocked wildly, and Addy's first toss landed far from Freddy. She pulled it back in and said a silent prayer for accuracy. The ring slapped Freddy's arm, and he tried to grab it. The boat was only a few feet away, but Freddy seemed unable to hold on. His eyes were glazed. "Freddy! Grab it!"

Addy lost all awareness of anything but the determination to help her friend. She threw her leg over the side of the boat and found the ladder rung with her foot. Her other leg followed, and she lowered herself into the water. With one hand, she clung to the ladder and with the other reached for Freddy. She got his hand, but he didn't grip hers. The boat tipped, and she let go of the ladder.

"Pa!" Addy wasn't sure he heard her, but she kept her eyes on Freddy. She looped her arm through the ring that floated nearby and wrapped her other arm around Freddy's neck. Only then could she look up. Pa was at the rail and pulled the ring to the ladder. Addy let go of the ring and pushed Freddy's hands to the ladder. Freddy grabbed the ladder but just hung there. Pa reached over and pulled on Freddy's arms. Addy tried to push Freddy up but found that motion sent her underwater.

She surfaced, coughing and sputtering. She had already started drifting away from the boat. Panic threatened as she smelled fear surrounding her. But she summoned all the strength within her and swam to the boat. She saw Freddy's legs disappear over the side and onto the boat. Pa's face appeared. His eyes were wide when he saw Addy. He pulled in the ring and sent it to her. She grasped it, and Pa drew her back to the ladder. Her arms wobbled as did her legs as she climbed. She felt Pa's arms around her and then found herself on the floor next to Freddy gasping and coughing. Exhaustion coursed through her body.

Freddy pulled himself to a seated position. "Addy, you okay? You saved me. Mr. Ruckert, thank you. If you hadn't come . . . "

Addy sat up. Pa stood at the wheel. "Hang on, you two. The rain is making it hard to see, but thankfully, the waves have lessened."

Addy looked around. He was right. The boat was not rocking as much. She barely noticed the rain, for she was soaked. She let her gaze rest on Freddy. She smiled. "You look like a drowned rat."

He grinned. "You do, too. I've been wanting to go swimming again, but not quite like this."

"What happened? How did you end up in the water?"

"Mr. Dennett was about to turn a little more south, and he'd asked me to make sure everyone was seated and hanging on and that all their items were secured because it was getting rough. I'd just turned to go back to where he steered the boat when a wave hit us broadside, and I tumbled right over the railing. Everyone screamed, and he tried to bring the boat around to fetch me, but his rudder got stuck in his sharp turn. The waves started dragging me further away, and then they saw you and rang the alarm bell."

Addy shook some of the wet out of her hair and rubbed her arms as the chill in the air assaulted her. "Why did you leave the harbor so late?"

Freddy frowned. "Pauline. She ran into the woods when the men were arguing about her. The triplets went to find her and then got lost. Her family and the girls were the last to arrive at the docks. Pastor Gunnlerson brought them in his wagon. When everyone realized they weren't at the dock yet, Mr. Dennett offered to wait, since he had room. Her family was really steamed."

Addy heard cheering and clapping. Mr. Dennett's boat was about twenty feet away. The triplets lined the railing and cried, wiping their eyes with handkerchiefs. Addy and Freddy stood. The waters held only a steady chop now, and the skies had lightened a bit. She knew sunset was not far away, even though the clouds blocked the view of the sun. Gyda Bergman dabbed her eyes as well. Mr. Bergman had his arm around his wife and gripped her shoulder. Everyone on the boat was wet from the rain, but Mr. Bergman looked as soaked as Freddy.

Pa maneuvered close to the other boat, and a couple of the men helped tie the boats together placing padding between, so damage to the boats didn't occur from bumping.

Mr. Bergman held out a hand to Freddy. "You all right, son? We were so worried about you."

Freddy reached out to take his hand, but when Mr. Bergman said "son," his head jerked up. Mr. Bergman smiled. Freddy scrambled onto Mr. Dennett's boat and fell into Mr. Bergman's embrace. Mrs. Bergman patted the boy's back and wrapped a blanket around him. Everyone watched with mouths open. Addy marveled again that an almost-tragedy had perhaps been a blessing. That phrase. "God works in mysterious ways, His wonders to behold."

Then the attention turned to Addy. Mr. Bergman released Freddy and walked to the rail. "Miss Addy, you are one of the bravest young ladies we've ever met. Although we didn't start out well with you, it seems you are right where you should be." He glanced over his shoulder at Freddy. "And perhaps, Freddy is where he should be, too." Everyone clapped.

Pa wrapped a blanket around Addy. "Thank you, Charles. We're delighted she's ours. But she sure is full of surprises."

Everyone laughed; then a small movement caught Addy's eyes. Mrs. Nundahl reached over and took Pauline's hand. Mr. Nundahl jerked his head around when he saw it. Would he rebuke his wife? He seemed to think better of it. He brought his chin up and nodded. He gave his wife a quick smile. Addy breathed a sigh of relief. Perhaps life for Pauline would now improve.

"Mr. Dennett, you seemed dead in the water. Are you okay now? Do you need me to tow you back to Washington?"

"Thanks, Clifford, but we're good now. I jerked the wheel to come around trying to rescue Freddy, and the rudder jammed. I killed the engine, and Charles jumped in to free it up. Lots of excitement here, but thankfully, he knew just what to do."

Pa nodded to Mr. Bergman, while Addy stood with wide eyes. Mr. Bergman gave a slight nod back to Pa. Addy had noticed that the men often did that. Just the slightest nod said a lot.

The sun peeked through the clouds as it descended close to the horizon, indicating that daylight would continue for less than an hour. The darkening skies would make navigating more perilous than daylight traveling. The storm stalked the western side of the Bay of Green Bay now, leaving calmer seas and milder winds in its wake.

Mr. Dennett cleared his throat. "We have little daylight left and one to two hours to travel. With calmer seas, we should be okay.

And since we'll be protected on the west side of the mainland if that east wind picks up again, we can make good time." He glanced at the Bergmans. "We may need to spend the night at the Hogensons' hotel in Ephraim if there's a question getting from Ephraim to Chambers. And I'll pay that bill. Freddy could use some pampering, and Charles sure helped me out of a jam. He deserves some thanks." He looked at Mrs. Bergman. "So, no fretting on the cost, Gyda. All will be well. My workers know to check your animals if we are delayed." He nodded to Pa and Addy and began to ply his way through the waters toward Ephraim.

Addy plopped on a seat. "Wow, Pa, what a day. Did you notice that the Nundahls actually looked less angry?"

"I did. God displayed His handiwork today. And I think we'll hear of a big turn-around with Freddy and the Bergmans."

"Freddy told me both he and Mr. Bergman were working for Mr. Dennett part-time, and everyone was happier." Addy wrung her hands. "You know, Pa, I . . . well, I . . . I had to go in after Freddy. He was floundering. He could've drowned."

Pa stretched his neck. "I know, Addy. And you did save him. And then I had to save you." He raised his eyebrows and looked down at her.

Addy hung her head. "I know, Pa. Thank you."

"Come here, girl."

Addy ran to lean against him, and he wrapped his arms around her. "We love you, but we do have to rein in some of these impetuous ways of yours. Somehow, you need to learn what's brave and what's foolish."

Addy just nodded her head and tried to absorb his strength and love. She needed to do better, but she had to do what was necessary.

She'd had to save Mrs. Figgenschau, and she'd had to save Freddy. She didn't plan to do dangerous things or speak out of turn, but, well, it just happened.

Soon they were in dry clothes and sipping soup and eating warm apple pie with Ma and Molly. Emmy was asleep and Grandma Hilga was in her bedroom. Ma alternately groaned, laughed, and smiled as the day's events were related. She rubbed her hand over her mouth, looked at her husband, and shook her head. "Thank God everyone is okay. Addy is going to have to help me write some of these stories."

"That sounds like school. I don't know."

Ma grinned. "Oh, I think we need to do this. A bit of reflection on your impetuous ways might be good."

"Pa said I needed to learn what's brave and what's foolish." She looked from her father to her mother and back.

"And writing might be a good way."

Grandma Hilga walked into the dining room with a mischievous smile on her face. "Miss Lainey, look what was delivered while you were gone. Arlo brought it early today and asked me to hide it in my room until everyone was home."

Lainey splayed her hands. "Whatever could it be?"

Addy jumped up. "Ma, could it be your dresses?"

"Oh my. I forgot. Help me open this up."

Two dresses lay on the table. Addy and Molly touched the fabric, oohing and aahing the whole time. Lainey also ran her fingers over the buttons and the neckline. "I don't know what to say." She scrunched her face. "I hope they fit." She turned to Clifford. "Thank you for this."

Clifford bent to kiss her forehead. "Go try them on. We all want to see."

Molly put her finger to her lips. "Just don't wake up Emmy, Ma."

Soon Lainey emerged from the bedroom. "This is perfect for an everyday dress." The cotton fabric boasted vertical stripes of sky blue and powder blue. The scoop neckline was high but gentle. Covered buttons flowed down the front of the bodice. "And with these buttons in the front, nursing will be easy." She ran her hands over the three-quarter straight sleeves. At the waist, the bodice sported a short, flared edging. The dress skirt gathered slightly at the waist and fell softly to her ankles.

Mrs. Figgenschau smiled. "Lainey, that sky blue matches your eyes, and the powder blue keeps the stripes from appearing dull. The colors blend so nicely. It's really a lovely dress."

"Ma, you're so pretty. I want to look and dress just like you when I grow up." Molly hugged herself.

Addy grinned. "I never cared much for dresses, but that sure is nice, Ma."

Lainey held out her arms for the girls. "We'll have to see about getting some new dresses for you two."

Clifford took another bite of apple pie. "Try the other one on, sweetheart."

Everyone stood and clapped when Lainey walked out with the next dress. She twirled and laughed. "Oh my, I feel like a princess."

Clifford took her hands and kissed her. "You look like a queen."

The girls giggled.

Mrs. Figgenschau felt the fabric. "The bodice is taffeta. It's stunning. The emerald green accentuates your hair."

"I love the color and the pleated bodice, again with buttons down the front. Look at these puffy sleeves." Lainey twirled again. "This chiffon skirt is so soft. What a wonderful gift."

Just then the baby whimpered, and the whimper soon escalated to a wail.

Lainey laughed. "Well, I guess the fashion show is done. I'll get into my night clothes and tend to this little one. Clifford, can you play with her a few minutes until I'm ready to feed her?"

CHAPTER TWENTY-TWO

WINTER ARRIVED EARLY THAT YEAR and lasted much longer than Addy expected. But it wasn't as awful as she thought it might be. The thought of not being on a boat or seeing anyone from the mainland did not sit well with her. But then in January, with the ice frozen solid, people actually put sleigh planks on their wagons, and the horses pulled them over the ice.

Addy leaned out over the side of the wagon sleigh to observe the blue of the ice. She could see swirls of white under the surface that wound in and out of turquoises and deep blues. She felt dizzy in amazement. She tapped Molly. "Look, you can see almost to the bottom of the ice. It's so pretty."

Molly looked over and pulled back. "Is that water down there? Can we sink into it?"

Pa reached back and grabbed her hand. "Don't worry. The ice is thick. And see those extra planks? If we come to a crack, we can place them across the crack and then just continue on."

Molly swooned. Her face went white. "Cracks in the ice. Planks. But . . . but . . . "

Ma swatted Pa. "Clifford, you're scaring her. Molly, we do bring the planks, but if we see any problem, we'll go back. They are for emergency only."

Addy put her arm around her sister. "Don't worry, Molly. The ice is very thick and solid. Lots of people are traveling, and Pa knows where to travel to keep us safe. Right, Pa? You know, I read Ma's story about you crossing the ice from Rock Island to Washington."

Ma widened her eyes. "Oh, let's talk about that another time."

Molly squinted her eyes. "What?"

Ma's eyes bored into Addy's, and she shook her head. Addy grinned. "Well, Molly, it was a day much like this . . . "

Ma bit her lip and shook her head.

Addy stretched her neck. "Well, you know it all turned out okay because here Pa is, and he's not afraid to travel on the ice."

Molly whined. "Addy, tell me."

"Well, Pa was smitten with Ma."

Molly giggled and clapped her hands.

"So, he wasn't paying attention."

Pa looked over at his wife and back at Addy and shook his head. "I paid attention."

Ma laughed.

"Well, a squall blew up—a blizzard—and it swirled all over the place, so Pa didn't know which way to go 'cause the wind changed. Now, to the north was open water."

Molly's mouth formed an *O*, and alarm filled her eyes.

"Well, the cow stopped and wouldn't go forward."

"A cow was pulling the sleigh?" Molly turned her head and squinted.

"No, the horse was, and the cow was behind; but she knew and stopped."

Pa, Ma, and Molly all said together. "Smart cow."

"Pa got out and tried to get the horse to go and then discovered it was the cow. Then he heard the crack and water slapping the ice."

Molly wrapped her arms around herself and shivered.

Addy stretched out her words. "He very carefully turned the other way."

Molly took a deep breath. "So, he got across the ice."

Ma turned. "He might not have, but Mr. Hanson and my pa went looking for him and found him. It was scary. That's why we pray a lot."

Molly looked at each one. "I'm so glad people come to help. Carter and David helped when Addy fell. And Addy went and found Mrs. Figgenschau. And she jumped in to save Freddy."

Addy stretched her neck. "Well, I didn't jump in. I went down the ladder. Well, then I had to let go to save him."

Pa groaned. "I was trying to get the boat between Freddy and the waves, so he could get to the boat more easily. Then I turned around, and Addy was gone. My heart rose into my mouth, and . . ."

"Your heart was in your mouth?" Molly narrowed her eyes. "But how could you breathe?"

Pa laughed. "It's an expression to say how scared every part of me was. Well, here we are in Gills Rock." Pa slapped the reins, and Nellie crossed onto the snow-covered mainland. They paused at the top of the hill that faced the bay. Pa climbed down and gave a handful of food to Nellie and rubbed down her sides and flanks. The girls huddled next to Ma. Emmy had slept bundled close to Ma across the ice but stirred when the movement stopped. Emmy yawned, and her eyes fluttered. Addy could not think of anything so cute.

Ma pulled the blanket a little closer around Emmy and gently bounced her. "Clifford, it's best she sleeps the whole way. I don't really want to nurse her in this cold."

Pa's shoulders came up, and a sheepish grin spread across his face. "Oh goodness, didn't think of that. Nellie, you should be good till we get to the store." He climbed back up on the wagon and lightly slapped the reins. The snow cover on the rutted road made traveling much smoother with the sleigh planks than with the wheels in summer weather. There were a few icy patches where the wagon lurched a bit one side to the other, but they gave it little heed. In the sunshine, the evergreens sparkled with snow that lay over every needled branch.

"It's so bright. I love the glistening." Molly took a big breath. "Ooh, I can see my breath, too. This is so much fun."

"I can't wait to see Grandma and Grandpa Ruckert at the store. It's been since Thanksgiving that we've seen them. That boat ride was cold." Addy shivered, recalling the windy day they ventured to Ellison Bay to have Thanksgiving dinner.

Pa nodded. "Yeah, I was sorry we missed them at Christmas. Too bad the bay wasn't frozen solid by then. Probably just as well with that snowstorm on Christmas Eve."

Molly clapped her hands. "But we're here now, and we get to see the Otters and Grandma and Grandpa. Ma, they'll be surprised at how big Emmy is."

"They will. Grandma is probably standing in the window watching for us now."

Addy laughed. "And before she even says hi to the rest of us, she'll be holding Emmy and telling her how cute she is."

Pa grinned. "You know her well, Addy."

The moment they pulled the wagon in front of the store, Grandma Ruckert ran out with only a shawl wrapped around her. She held it tight, but her eyes were searching for the baby. Without a word, Ma handed Emmy over. Grandma held her close and turned to return to the inside of the store. She paused, looking over her shoulder. "Welcome, everybody. Come in. Come in. But I must talk to this darling one for a few minutes."

Addy shook her head. "Told ya."

They all laughed and tumbled out of the wagon and into the store.

Grandpa stood with his hands on his hips and a huge smile on his face. "You all are a sight for sore eyes. We are so happy you're here, even though I saw that my wife made off with the baby with hardly a greeting to all of you."

Addy hugged her Grandpa. "We knew she would."

"I hope I get to hold her some. Addy, I think you've grown since Thanksgiving."

A baby's wail filled the upstairs. Grandpa laughed. "Shirley, what are you doing to that child?"

Ma started up the stairs. "She's hungry. Let me nurse her, and then Grandpa gets her."

"You're going to make me burp her? You know that can be messy. I might let Grandma take another turn before me."

Footsteps sounded on the basement stairs. Addy turned. Carter's face came into view. Grandpa walked over to help him with the boxes he carried. "I forgot to tell you. Carter is working for me for a while."

Carter smiled. "Hi, everyone."

Addy brushed her hair behind her ears. "Are you off Rock Island for the winter?"

"Yes, the weather didn't work for us to leave the island until the first week of January. We're staying at the Hansons', but Mr. Hanson got me over to Uncle Otis', so I could work here for a month before returning for school."

Molly ran to him and threw her arms around him. "Uncle Carter. I'm so happy you're here. Did you get taller?"

He dropped down to look Molly in the face. "I am taller. Ma says I'm growing like a weed, and my pants are getting shorter."

Addy hung back. "So, you're going to work here for a while?" Why did she feel funny talking to him? What was that little tingle she felt in her back? She turned around to see if the door had been opened and let in the cooler air. And why was Pa grinning as he looked from her to Carter and back? Did he just roll his eyes?

Grandpa placed his hand on the Addy's shoulder. "Let's get upstairs and eat something before we go to the Otter gathering. They'll serve food a little later. Carter?"

"I'm good, Mr. Ruckert. I brought some cheese and nuts with me to hold me over. I want to get everything done, so I can go to the event."

Ma came down the stairs. "Did I hear Carter's voice?"

Carter grinned. "You did, Sis. How are you?"

Ma embraced her brother. "Oh, it's so good to see you. How is everyone?"

"They're all at Uncle Otis' right now, and they'll be at the event today."

Addy could hear Ma and Carter continuing in conversation for a few minutes as she went up the stairs.

Ma soon returned to the sitting room upstairs. "Did she fall asleep on you, Grandpa?"

"She did. I can sit with her while you get something to eat. I'm happy."

Clayton Hall, a block from Ruckert's Supply Store, overflowed with voices. Laughing, greeting, and words of direction echoed off the walls of the huge meeting room. Wagons, sleighs, and horses were lined up all around the building.

Ma took Pa's hand. "It's been a long time."

He laughed. "And I remember it like it was yesterday."

Grandma Ruckert shook her head. "What a grand time that was." She giggled. "And funny."

Addy stopped. "Is this where you found out your teacher was Pa's cousin?"

Molly brought her shoulders up and closed her eyes. "And you fell in love? Addy read me your story."

"Okay, all you girls. I'm going to talk to the men." Pa stalked over to where several men stood.

Addy turned to her mother. "He's not mad, is he?"

Ma patted her shoulder. "He loves the story, but some days, it's just too much girl talk. Remember, at our house, he's outnumbered four to one."

Molly squealed. "There're the triplets. C'mon, Addy."

The first hour, everyone seemed content to visit and hear about everyone's Christmas and what news winter had brought to the various towns in the area.

Addy saw Pauline talking to Freddy and approached them. Pauline hugged Addy. "It's so good to see you, Addy."

Freddy patted Addy's back. "We're still telling the story of you rescuing me."

Addy shuffled her feet. "Thanks, but you both look good. You look happy."

Pauline lowered her voice and pulled up her sleeve. "Look, all my bruises have healed, and I haven't gotten any more since we were on Washington."

Addy blew out a big breath. "Gosh, that's great. I heard that argument that day."

"I did, too; and I ran away, which made the boat leave late, and then Freddy fell in."

Freddy laughed. "Scary day, but since then, our families have changed. They're even talking about us taking their name."

Addy tilted her head. "Do you want to?"

They both nodded. Pauline shrugged her shoulders. "It seems a good thing to do. I mean, we'll never forget our first parents, but if we can have a family now . . . Well, I like it."

"Me, too." Freddy slipped his hand into Pauline's. "And we kinda like each other, too. Did you know there's going to be a dance after we eat?"

"There you are." Addy turned as Carter walked up beside her and laid his arm around her shoulders. "Hi, Freddy, Pauline. How are you two? You both look good." He grinned. "So glad my niece here was able to rescue you in the water. That must've been scary."

Addy felt her face heat up. Pauline and Freddy looked to her and then back to Carter. Freddy stuck out his hand. "Thanks, Carter. We are doing well. But are you really her uncle?"

"Well, I'm her ma's brother, so yes."

"That's interesting. Well, Addy sure is a good friend."

Carter smiled. "She's a keeper, all right. Oh, there are a few people I need to see. I'm sure I'll talk to you again later."

Addy shook her head, and shivers ran down her body. What was that? She looked with questioning eyes at Pauline.

"He likes you, Addy."

Freddy nodded. "He sure does, but he's your uncle. Wait, you're an Otter, so you're not related. That would work."

Addy pulled back. "What would work?"

Pauline leaned in and whispered. "Marriage."

"That's ridiculous. I'm only twelve. Why would you . . . I mean, who thinks like that at our age?"

Freddy took Pauline's hand again. "Well, maybe in a couple years."

Addy and Molly joined in the merriment of a myriad of games. Flossy won the spelling bee. Addy could not imagine knowing that many words, let alone being able to spell them. Pa encouraged her to join in, but she declined. And she was glad of it, as each word of the first round of words were misspelled in her mind. However, the egg in the spoon race fit her enjoyment.

Placing the end of the spoon in her mouth, she stood still while the egg was placed in the bowl of the spoon. *Don't breathe. Look straight ahead.* She heard everyone cheering as she took the lead. Groans of disappointment from the other contestants rose while she commanded herself not to pay attention. Beads of perspiration rolled down her forehead into her eyes, and she had to blink. The egg wobbled. Then her chest constricted. She couldn't hold her breath much longer. Because of the sweat in her eyes, the finish line looked blurry, and now she needed to clear her throat. She'd almost arrived when the sneeze rose in her throat and her nose itched. Just a few more feet. She had to take a breath. Gritting her teeth on the spoon, she tried to do most of the breath through her nose, but the sneeze wouldn't let her. A small breath came out, but then it whooshed; and the spoon vibrated against her teeth, and the egg tumbled off. Doreen passed her, arms out to balance herself and making little sounds through her teeth, probably trying to breathe. Doreen crossed the finish line to clapping and cheering. But then she spit the spoon out of her mouth, and the egg flew and smacked her twin as she ran up to hug her winning sister. Fortunately, the eggs were hard-boiled, so it didn't make a mess but it left a red mark on Irene's cheek. Still, the laughter didn't subside for several minutes.

A few other games held everyone's attention until the food was served. Sandwiches, stews, and casseroles covered the table. Addy and Molly joined Pauline and Freddy while they ate. Addy heard a wail and knew Emmy must be hungry. She saw Ma take the baby to a corner to nurse. A welling up within at the love of this family brought tears to her eyes. She looked down so no one would see. When she looked up, Pauline was gazing at her.

Pauline smiled. "Someday, I'll have a good family like yours." Her voice was barely a whisper, but Addy understood and nodded. Whether with the Nundahls or with Freddy, a good life was ahead for Pauline.

Addy startled when the music filled Clayton Hall. Whirling around in her seat, she saw a group of musicians in the far corner. Soon people were dancing. She couldn't remember ever seeing anything like this. She laughed and clapped her hands. Then she realized people were clapping in time to the music. She joined in and felt her grin overtake her whole being.

Freddy took Pauline's hand, and her face reddened as she nodded and stood. It was so much fun to watch as they went out to the dance floor. Freddy didn't seem to know just where to place his hands, and they both looked so stiff. Addy giggled.

Molly tapped her arm. "Let's go get Emmy, so Ma and Pa can dance."

"Good idea, Sissy."

Ma pursed her lips and raised her eyebrows. "I think I know what this means. I haven't seen your pa for a while."

"I'll hold Emmy. Molly, you take Ma and find Pa so they can dance."

Ma's laugh was infectious. She wore the striped dress, and Addy thought she looked beautiful, even though Ma thought the dress wasn't that fancy. Addy giggled as Molly took Ma's hand. Emmy snuggled, and Addy ran her fingers over her face. "This is a good life, Emmy. I'm really happy." A little pang of guilt rose up. "Oh, baby, sometimes I really miss my first parents, and I'm not sure if they're even alive. I think my papa is. I'd like to know. But I'm happy here. I hope you never have to lose your parents like Molly and I did or like our ma did." She bent and kissed Emmy's forehead and sighed deeply.

Molly ran up to her. "Look, Addy, they're dancing."

Addy's face hurt from smiling so much. Molly leaned against her. "I think they really love each other, don't you?"

"Yes, Molly, I do."

Molly took a turn holding Emmy before Ma and Pa joined them. They were holding hands. Pa lifted the baby up high, and her squeal made them all laugh.

Addy turned at a tap on her shoulder. Carter stood there. "Come on, Addy. Dance with me."

Addy jerked back and felt her face redden. "What? Me? Uh, I don't know how to dance."

Carter grinned. "It's easy. I'll show you." He looked at his sister. "You don't mind, do you, Lainey?"

She pulled her lips between her teeth and tilted her head. "Just don't run off with her."

Addy's stomach did flip-flops, and goosebumps appeared on her arm. And no words came. Whatever did Ma mean? She looked at Pa. His face was straight with a hint of a smile, but she felt she could almost hear him chuckling. She narrowed her eyes at Pa, but still no words came.

Carter tugged her hand. "It's okay, Addy. Besides, after I saved you on the rock slab, I should get a dance."

Addy couldn't believe how many emotions could roil around within her at the same moment. She was strong and impulsive and cared deeply for other people, but these emotions were different. Confusion, happiness, not fear but nervousness, embarrassment. And then she couldn't breathe. Would she faint? And what about the shivers in her back? Maybe she was sick. She glanced back at her parents. Ma had her hand over her mouth but nodded at her. Dad just sat beaming. So confusing.

Addy finally found her feet moving with Carter. His hand somehow was burning her back, but she was breathing. She looked around, and nobody seemed to pay attention. Lots of people were dancing. Pauline and Freddy. Irene and Doreen danced with each other. Flossy was with one of Jack Figgenschau's boys. Addy couldn't remember which one was Roy and which was Forrest. She glanced up at Carter.

He smiled down at her. "You're doing fine, Addy. You don't need to be nervous."

"I'm really sorry if I didn't thank you for helping me when I fell."

"Oh, don't worry about that. I just wanted to dance with you. I'm glad you're part of the family."

With that comment, Addy let out a big breath that blew the hair out her face. He's family. It's not like with Pauline and Freddy. Just friends. Just family. That's good. She felt the tension leave her body and was amazed at how much easier it was to dance when relaxed. Although, she'd really rather be running a race or rubbing down a horse or working on a boat. But it was okay.

CHAPTER TWENTY-THREE

WINTER FADED AS THE TEMPERATURES warmed to tolerable and the snow disappeared in patches. Daylight lingered just a bit longer, and Addy's heart soared for spring and summer. Winter hadn't really been bad, but she longed to be out of school and out of doors. Miss Genevieve made school fun—well, as fun as school could be when you didn't really want to be there.

Miss Genevieve had even held a Valentine's party. Miss Rose came with her new baby—a girl named Clara. Miss Rose and Ma sat with their babies, laughing and reminiscing. Addy loved to hear them tell the story of the Valentine's Dance when she spurned Pa and was so confused. And she wasn't that much older than Addy was now. Addy had plenty of time before she felt smitten, as Ma and Miss Rose called it. Although, when Carter asked her to dance at that event, those shivers found her back, and Ma and Pa had the most peculiar smiles. Too confusing. Surely, she wasn't smitten with Carter nor he with her. She was way too young. At school, he sat and learned with the older kids, but outside, he included her in the games. Occasionally, when Miss Genevieve had all the students working on science projects, Carter partnered with her. But that was because she was good at science. Wasn't it?

At home, Pa was around more in the winter. He chopped wood for the fire to keep the house warm and the oven cooking. He built snowmen with Addy and Molly and even had an occasional snow-ball fight with them. He played board games with them at night and often read a story to them. Life at home was warm and filled with laughter. Addy was content.

Occasionally, she found herself waking up at night crying. She'd dreamed about her parents, and the ache of not knowing for sure if her mother died, the agony that she wasn't there for her mama if she did die, and the confusion of where her father might be overwhelmed her. He'd lost all his girls. And somehow, she had the deep sensation that he, too, was lost. She loved how this pa—Mr. Captain, as she still liked to call him sometimes—referred to Ma, Emmy, Molly, and her as his girls. Her first papa did that, too, on occasion, if she remembered correctly. Her memories of that life were fading, and that made her sad.

One night when she awoke crying, Ma came in. She said she'd just nursed Emmy. Sitting on the edge of the bed and holding Addy's hand, she said nothing.

Addy sniffled. "I'm sorry, but I miss them sometimes."

Ma wrapped her arms around Addy. "I miss my parents still. You may always miss them, Addy. I know it hurts; but it's normal, and it's okay."

"You're not mad or anything?"

"Never. We understand, Addy."

One morning not long after, as the sun broke through the clouds and promised the warmest day yet, Addy found her parents at the breakfast table deep in discussion. She hesitated. She knew some conversations were private, and parents had to do such things.

Pa looked up and waved his hand for her to join them. "This concerns you, Addy. We need to ask you something."

Panic rose in her throat. What had she done? Everything had been so good—or, at least, she thought so.

Ma grabbed her hand. "Oh, Addy, don't worry. We want your opinion on something."

The pent-up air whooshed out of her, and she sat down. Ma poured her glass of milk and dished some eggs on her plate. "Go ahead and eat."

"Can you tell me first? Or ask me?"

Pa chuckled. "Addy, we've been thinking about your worries about your parents."

Addy pulled her shoulders up and squinted. "Okay."

Pa reached over and patted her hand. "Relax, girl. What we are wondering is if, perhaps—and only if you want to—we should make a trip back to Harrisville and see if we can find your pa."

Addy froze. No words would come out. It seemed impossible. Could she discover what happened? Did she want to know? Did they really mean . . .

"Addy? Did you hear your pa? We thought you might want to do this, but you don't have to."

Addy blinked. "I, uh, I, well, yes, I think I would. But are you sure? How long does that take? Would you really want to take the baby? I mean, you have the resort and the ferry. How would you have time?"

She looked up. Both Pa and Ma were smiling. Pa shook his head. "We've discussed all that. We think late May would work. We won't open the resort until early June. Actually, we decided that a while ago because of the baby, and so you and Molly would be out of school and able to help. And the ferry business will be fine till then."

Ma took a sip of coffee. "Emmy and I will stay here. Sarah and her kids will stay with us, so Arlo can assist your pa on the boat."

"I can help on the boat."

"And you will, but it's a two-day journey one way, and it'll be better to have two adults along."

"Molly?"

Pa smiled. "Yes, Molly will go, too."

Clifford glanced over at Addy. She stood with her face pressed against the window of little pilot cabin. "Addy, it's really rough out there. Maybe you should take a seat. You and Molly could even go lay down. Is she okay?"

"She's taking a nap. She'll sleep through all this. But I like it rough. I mean, it scares me silly at times with those big waves and when the boat plunges between the waves. And I remember when we had to rescue Freddy. But it's a fun scary, not a nervous scary. I just like it."

"Well, Addy, you know why we have to respect the Lakes. Storms can blow up quickly, and a lot of ships have gone down. No one goes out in rough waters for fun. We just sometimes get caught in them."

"Have you ever gone down, Pa?" Addy turned to look at him when he didn't answer. "Did you hear me?"

"I did go down, Addy. Not far from where we're going."

Addy's eyes grew big. "Was it scary? Did people die?"

Clifford glanced over and brought his eyes back to the water. "Yes, it was scary, and my friend, Captain Hank, died. I tried to go after him and hit my head and was washed away. I came to on Thunder Bay Island.

A family found me and took care of me. Once I was awake, I was able to get a boat back home, and it still took a few weeks to fully recover."

Addy's mouth stood open. "Wow, Pa. Did Ma know where you were?"

"We weren't married then, but we were in love. She prayed for me every day. It was almost like God let me hear her voice, and that helped me."

Addy sighed. "That's nice. I remember my papa talking about falling in love with Mama. Do you think we'll find them? I kinda remember hearing about Thunder Bay Island. I think it wasn't far from where we lived."

"Well, Harrisville is not very far from Thunder Bay."

"I still hope they're there. I wonder if maybe Mama might have gotten better and my papa got another job. Do you think they'll still want us?" She paused. Should she have said that? "I mean, we're really happy with you and Ma, but, well, I just need to know. I don't know if Molly can handle it."

"Well, small towns usually know everybody and what they're doing. So, as soon as we get there, we'll ask if they know Walter and Alma Bickel. They'll be able to tell us."

"Ah, Pa, don't tell Molly about your boat wreck. She might get scared."

Clifford nodded. "I won't mention it."

Addy put her face next to the window again. She glanced back to where Arlo sat close to the pistons, keeping his eyes on the waves and the sky. After a few minutes, she hunched her shoulders and slowly turned to face Clifford. "Pa, when did you go down?"

Clifford was silent for a full minute. "It was the spring of 1891."

"That's when my papa got hurt, helping rescue people in a shipwreck. It was Molly's first birthday, April 20."

"Come here, Addy." Clifford gestured for her to come stand next to him. She obeyed, and he placed his arm around her shoulder. "You know Lainey and I love you and Molly?"

Addy nodded and leaned against him.

"Addy, it was working on my shipwreck that caused your father to get injured. I don't know how to tell you how sorry we are."

"It was your fault, Pa?"

"Well, I don't think it was anyone's fault, but unfortunately, that shipwreck cost my friend's life, almost took my life, and caused great problems for your father. And then that made life so hard for you, young lady. I'm really sorry."

A tear sneaked down the girl's face as she looked up. "Me, too. I'm not mad at you. It just makes me sad thinking about it. You got rescued, but my papa couldn't work. Then Mama got sick from working too much, and Molly and I ended up on the Orphan Train." She sniffled and ran her sleeve under her nose. "But then we found you. I want to find my folks, but I don't want to leave you and Ma."

"Oh, we want to keep you. We want to invite your folks to come to Washington Island or the mainland, but if they are well and strong, they may want you back. You are their children."

Addy wrapped her arms around Clifford. "I know. I know. This is hard, but . . . "

"But?"

She stepped back. "You know, my mama told me a Bible story. She really liked it. It was about a lady who had to help the people in the land during some big trouble. She was afraid to go talk to the king, but someone told her, 'You came to the kingdom for such a time as this.' I think her name was Esther. My mama loved that story.

I almost forgot that when she was getting sick—maybe she knew that Molly and I would have to leave—she told me something. She said, 'Addy, be like Esther; know wherever you are that you are there for such a time as that—that you will be exactly where you're supposed to be and that God is with you.'"

"That's beautiful, Addy. You had a wise mother."

"Does that mean Molly and I are supposed to be with you?"

"It sure sounds like it. What do you think?"

"That I'm important in your family. But what does that mean about my first mama and papa?"

"I guess we have to find that out, and we have to ask God His plan."

Addy stood silent. Guilt rose up in Clifford's throat, and he coughed. His shipwreck had cost Addy and Molly their family. Perhaps not totally, but when he rolled back the time in his mind, Addy's father would not have been injured and would still be able to work. Her mother may have not gotten sick, but she might have. The worry of providing while her husband couldn't work may have brought illness upon her. Addy and Molly might have been happily living with their parents and even have a brother or sister added to the family. The responsibility and guilt weighed heavily. Would it create anger in Addy? What about Molly? She was such a sweet thing. What about when she was older and knew the truth? Would there be a rift? For such a time as this. *For such a time as this?* Right now? This journey? Addy? Molly? *Me?*

"That's real pretty. I didn't know there were so many islands in these lakes."

Clifford refocused and followed Addy's gaze. "That's Mackinac Island. Do you see the fort on the hill? It has been there about a hundred years. The British owned it in the War of Independence. The Americans got it back; then the British got it again; then it came under the ownership of Americans once more after the War of 1812. It just recently closed. I think they're going to make it a visiting place for tourists."

"Have you been there?"

"We've made deliveries to the island, but I haven't spent any time there. How about you? Have you visited there?"

Addy's laughter filled the cabin where they stood. "Pa, I haven't visited anywhere. Well, except on the Orphan Train." She grimaced. "And we didn't visit. We stopped at a few places, and the kids who had no assignments were paraded around for local folks to decide if they wanted them. Reminded me of the farmers going to auction to buy cows. Papa had taken me to watch that a couple times."

Clifford put a hand on her shoulder. "I'm sorry, Addy. I'm glad, though, that you and Molly came to us."

Addy took a deep breath. "Me, too. I don't know what might've happened to us. But then, I was pretty sure I could get a job and take care of Molly." She grinned up at him.

"You've got plenty of time to get a job. I like having you as my first mate." He took a step back. "In fact, it's time you took the wheel for a while. The winds have calmed now. I want you to go no closer to land than we are now. But I want you to go directly toward that island. I think we'll stay overnight there. Do you see the outline of the Grand Hotel on this side? I want you to aim the boat between the hotel and the fort. Can you calculate that, figure it out?"

"Yes, Pa. But you'll be right here, right?" She raised her eyebrows as she glanced his way.

"I'm going below to fetch us something to eat and check on Molly. So, you're on your own for five or ten minutes. Can you do that?"

Addy straightened and threw her shoulders back. "Aye, aye, Captain."

Clifford stood back and watched for a full minute to confirm his confidence in Addy's ability. "Addy, don't forget Arlo's in the stern. He can help, too, if you need it." Then he climbed the narrow ladder into the small hold that held the galley and a small place for bedding down.

Molly was sitting and rubbing her eyes. A big smile spread across her face when she saw Clifford. "Hi, Pa."

Clifford grinned. "Molly, how'd you sleep?"

"I like this little bed. But I'm hungry. Is that okay?"

He tussled her hair. "It sure is, young lady. I'm hungry, too. Want to help me?"

A few minutes later, Clifford helped Molly climb the ladder to the main deck, then handed her a plate with sandwiches and cookies. He scrambled up behind her and set the food on a small table that folded up from the side wall of the boat.

Addy glanced back at them. "My arms feel funny, Pa."

"Oh, it's easy to get uncomfortable holding the wheel steady for a long time. You get used to it, but it takes some time." Clifford stood behind her and grasped the wheel. "You did a great job keeping her steady. Grab a sandwich and sit for a while."

A short time later, the *Pearl* sat moored to a pier on the southern side of Mackinac Island. Scents of food mixed with the smells of horse droppings and engine smoke. One scent stood out. What was it?

Addy squinted as she stepped off the boat with Molly. "Chocolate?"

Arlo laughed. "This place is famous for its fudge. I plan to get some for Sarah."

Molly tugged on Pa's arm. "You better buy some for Ma, too."

"Oh, I will. I already have strict orders. And maybe we'll eat a little bit ourselves."

Addy started toward the little village. "Yes, yes."

Several ships unloaded passengers, and men stood by surreys calling people's names and the names of hotels. Women in beautiful shirtwaists and feathered hats walked arm-in-arm with men in handsome suit coats. Addy couldn't take her eyes off the colors, the lace, and the delicate embroidery of the outfits and the coiffed hairdos.

"Wow, people are pretty fancy here."

Pa grinned. "Indeed. Many tourists visit here from Detroit and Chicago."

People walking and carriages pulled by stately horses crammed the narrow street. As they stepped around small piles of manure, Addy noticed the street sweepers trying to keep the road clear. She assumed those with aprons were the maids or the cooks. Men with uniforms stood at the doors of the hotels, opening them for the well-dressed visitors. Porters unloaded and carried luggage into and out of the hotels. How could people have that many clothes?

They stopped to buy fudge in a cluttered, tiny shop. Pa gave her and Molly each a piece when they walked back outside.

"Mmmm." Addy thought her eyes would roll right back into her head as she looked skyward. "This is sooo good. Wait, what is that up there? Is that the fort?"

Imposing white walls guarded the top of a hill at the end of the street. Addy stared. "Did they fight battles there?"

"They had cannons to blow up boats."

Molly's eyes widened. "Do they do that now?"

Clifford shook his head. "No, Molly. They are no longer at war. Don't you worry."

Molly released a big sigh and let her shoulders loosen. "That fudge was so good, but my stomach feels a little funny."

Pa took her hand. "Let's get some solid food in you."

They stopped at an outdoor café and ordered pasties, hand-held pastries filled with beef, onions, and potatoes.

Ma had insisted they stow extra blankets, but the night was mild. The girls bedded together in the little bed in the tiny cabin. Pa and Arlo fell asleep on the main deck, despite the sounds of those calling to each other on the docks and boat employees enjoying their time off.

The cawing of the gulls greeting the sunrise woke the little group on the *Pearl*. Addy peeked out at the brightening morning to see porters from the steamships running back and forth loading food, luggage, and passengers. The clunk of carts as their wheels thumped over the wooden slats on the dock made sure no one remained asleep, and engine smoke overtook the freshness of the small waves rolling into shore.

Arlo located a supply of gasoline and refilled the boat tank. Pa cranked the handle to get the pistons moving. Addy climbed onto the dock to untie the lines and then jumped back on the *Pearl* while Arlo held on to a piling before he shoved the boat away from the dock. Soon, they were plying through the waters, dodging the fishing boats and an early steamship leaving a big wake.

"Hang on. We can't avoid this wake." Pa looked around at the girls. Molly and Addy sat down and hung to the side railing. Arlo wedged himself next to Pa, making sure the rhythm of the pistons continued. The *Pearl* rose and dropped over the wake wave with a whoosh. Molly closed her eyes and groaned. By the time they reached the far side of the wake, the wave had reduced in size and caused little concern.

They encountered only gentle breezes and a slight chop as they traveled down Lake Huron on the eastern side of Michigan. Pa let the girls take turns with the wheel, standing nearby, ever alert to any issues. When Thunder Bay Island came into view, Pa pointed it out to Addy.

"Pa, does it make you feel sad when you see that?"

Pa closed one eye and tilted his head as he steered the *Pearl* in a wide berth around the island. "There are many reefs along here, so it's wise to travel a good distance from shore. No, I don't think I feel sad. It's a weird little shiver that I feel in my back. It would be nice someday to see the family who helped me. I did thank them, and we sent them a letter of thanks as well and a little money to help compensate for all they did for me. But I'm so happy I made it home. Well, I do feel very sad that Hank lost his life. I think of him often. He was a good friend. And now, I feel so sad that your dad was injured trying to rescue our crew."

Addy moved close and whispered. "You get shivers? So, is that a fearful feeling or a little bit sad feeling? I mean . . . well . . . " Addy looked around. Molly gazed at the water, and Arlo calculated the depth of the water. "I mean . . . Pa, I get shivers when I'm around Carter. Does that mean I'm afraid of him or sad? I don't think I feel afraid or sad, but I do feel weird. I mean, Carter is the best. He's so nice. I just don't understand this."

Pa grinned and placed his arm around her shoulder. "Well, young lady, you are almost thirteen. Maybe it's a boy/girl thing."

Addy scrunched her face. "What? I know I'm a girl, and he's a boy, and we're friends. You don't think . . . She looked up and raised her eyebrows. "That I'm, well, that maybe I'm, uh, sweet on him?"

"Maybe."

Addy's eyes looked in every direction. "But he's not. I mean, he's just nice, well, really nice." Her eyes widened. "No, Pa, he's not . . . " She coughed and lowered her voice. "Sweet on me." Addy stretched her neck and kept her eyes wide. "Pa?"

"I think maybe he is."

"Aahhh." Addy bent over and shook her head. "No, Pa. That can't be. I just like having friends, and he's one of my favorites. That's just . . ." Addy straightened and closed her eyes. "I can't think that way."

Pa grinned and lifted her chin, so she faced him. "Don't you worry. These feelings come and go as you get older. I'm glad you don't want to think that way. Any boy interested in you is going to have to get my approval."

"Pa, no one is interested in me. Well, maybe Carter. But that's it, and I don't want any more, for a long, long time."

"That's a good attitude. Look, there's Harrisville."

CHAPTER TWENTY-FOUR

ADDY SIGHED AS PA PULLED alongside the dock. A few fishing boats were also tying up after a day on the pristine waters of Lake Huron. Pa nodded to the fishermen but focused on making sure the boat was secured. Addy hopped onto the dock and tied off the bow and stern line. Pa added another line, and she studied it and him.

He smiled. "It's a spring line that helps keep the boat from bumping the dock. The north winds are picking up, and this will keep the boat and the dock from being damaged.

One of the fishermen walked by and paused. "Welcome. You new here?"

Pa smiled. "Ah, yes, we are." He winked at Addy. The fisherman didn't notice.

"Well, if you don't have people here, there's a small hotel on the main street, a few blocks to the south. Once I unload our catch and get it on the wagon, I can give you a ride if you like."

Pa reached out to shake his hand. The strong smell of fish wafted over Addy and she coughed. Pa chuckled. "That's nice of you, but we're ready for a walk. By the way, do you know a Walter Bickel?"

"Name sounds familiar but can't say as I've made his acquaintance. Well, enjoy your stay."

Pa paused. "Do you need a hand unloading? I've worked fishing boats."

"That's right nice, but I can't take on any more help at this time. If you're looking for work, you might try the railroad."

"I'm not . . . I . . . Thank you, sir." Pa took both girls by the hand and walked up the hill to the road. Arlo walked alongside. Pa noted the train station a short distance ahead, but he turned south per the man's instructions. "Does it look familiar, Addy?"

An overwhelming sadness settled on Addy's heart. "It does, Pa. My first papa and mama used to bring Molly and me to watch the train come in. For some reason, they called it the Turtle Line, so Molly and I always thought we would see turtles. Maybe they thought it was slow." She smiled. "Papa used to tease me about looking for turtles. But he explained it was mostly timber that they carried and some kind of stone. I think it was linn stone."

Pa tilted his head. "Do you think it was limestone?"

Addy looked up. "Yes, limestone. They carried passengers, too. It was fun seeing people get on and off. Well, until we were the passengers going to meet the Orphan Train." She glanced over to her sister. "Molly, you okay?"

A tear tracked down Molly's cheek. She sniffled. "I remember looking for turtles with Mama and Papa. What are we going to do, Addy? Do we stay with them now?" She stopped and burst into tears.

Pa picked her up and held her. "Molly, we just want to find them. They may want you back if they can care for you now."

"But I don't want you to leave us, either." Molly's sobs picked up steam. Pa just held her. "I won't leave you, Molly. I will be here for you. Let's get something to eat. We'll get a room at the hotel, and then we'll ask around about your folks. Addy, do you remember where you lived?" He set Molly back on the side of the road.

"Mmm-hmm, it's right over there." Addy pointed to a small house covered with ivy and peeling paint. It sat between two other small houses on the side street. None of the houses looked well-kept. Grass was overgrown. Children played out front, while some adults stood talking.

"Do you recognize anyone?"

"I think I might know a couple of the kids, but not the adults."

The adults glanced their way but had no reaction. They then walked into the houses with the children at their heels.

Addy took a deep breath. "They all went into our house. That must mean Ma and Pa don't live there anymore."

Molly slipped her hand into Addy's. "Maybe they got another place."

Addy wiped her eye with the back of her hand. "That's probably what happened. Pa, we're hungry."

Pa nodded, and they turned onto Main Street. Just a short distance along that street stood the Harrisville Hotel. It advertised rooms and meals. Pa checked in for one night with two rooms. He and Arlo would take one room, and the girls would be in the next. They realized they left their bags on the boat, and Arlo said he'd return to fetch them after eating.

They sat at a square table in the corner by the windows that faced the street. Wagons, pulled by horses, and two vehicles without horses passed. Molly's eyes got big. "Look at that, Pa. What are those?"

"They're called motor carriages. Pretty amazing, huh?"

"Can we get one?"

"Well, some say the day is coming when everyone will have one of those. But it'll be a while for us."

Addy clapped her hands. "Catherine said that her brother Sam went to work on building ships in Sturgeon Bay, but now he's in Detroit to build motor carriages. Maybe he can make us one."

Pa chuckled. "That would be nice, now, wouldn't it? Detroit is in southern Michigan, and maybe that's why some of those are here already."

After a meal of beef stew, Clifford approached the hotel manager. "We're looking for Walter Bickel. Do you know where we might find him?"

"Didn't know him well. He had a small place in town. I think his wife died."

Addy put her hand over her mouth. Molly leaned against her and closed her eyes.

The man observed the girls, then coughed. He studied them for a few seconds. "Are these . . . You girls look like . . . I'm sorry. Are you the Bickel girls? I'm so sorry."

Pa drew each girl in. "They are. Now, they are with my wife and me. But we wanted to find out . . . Well, tell the Bickels that their girls are well cared for. We wondered about their mother. You say she, ah, passed?"

The manager hung his head. "There's a cemetery about a mile out. Not exactly sure where the grave is, but it's there. So sorry. And I haven't seen Walter in weeks." The man turned away.

"Wait, one more question. Do you know if there were any relatives around?"

"Wouldn't know. Lots of people are related to lots of people. Some aren't related to anyone. Just don't know. Sorry."

Pa held out his hand. "Thank you, sir. You've been most helpful." The manager extended his hand to shake Pa's. He smiled at the girls and returned to his office.

As they turned to leave, an elderly man beckoned with his hand for Pa and the girls to join him. They walked over to his table. "Please, sit with me." Pa and the girls obeyed.

Arlo remained standing. "I'll go get our bags from the boat."

Pa nodded then turned to the man. "I'm Clifford Ruckert, and this is . . . "

"Wait. Wait." The man grinned, and his eyes twinkled. "Is it Adeline, Amolia?"

Addy's mouth dropped open. "Mr. Harris! You were the only one who always called us by our proper names." She grabbed Pa's hand. "Pa, he lived next door, and he used to run the train depot before we were born; but he would go with us to watch the people get on and off."

Mr. Harris nodded. "And sometimes, we'd see them load some timber or take off some limestone."

Molly stood and moved right next to Mr. Harris. "I remember you. You brought laundry for Mama to do, and you would read to me sometimes."

Mr. Harris placed a hand on Molly's shoulder. "That I did. I felt so bad when your father got injured. I tried to get him a job at the train depot. My son ran it. The only openings they had were for wranglers—people to load and unload—but he couldn't do that with his injury. I got a lot of people to bring their laundry to your ma. She was gifted in getting clothes clean and looking almost new. It was so sad when she got sick."

Addy stretched her neck, then faced Mr. Harris. "When did Ma . . . you know . . . when did she, um, go?"

"Not long after you girls left. Not sure you remember, but I went with your pa to the train depot when you left for the Orphan Train.

After the train left, he just fell apart. He sobbed so loud, and I just had to hold him, so he didn't collapse on the street."

Addy wiped away the tears rolling down her cheeks and handed Molly a napkin from the table. Molly leaned once more against her sister.

Mr. Harris laid his hand on Addy's. "I almost caught the next train to go after you. It broke their hearts to see you go. Mine, too." He turned to Pa. "The girls look cared for. You look like a fine man. But are you bringing them back . . . I mean, are you wanting to give them back?"

Pa shook his head. "Not at all, Mr. Harris. My wife and I fell in love with them almost from the first moment we saw them. But they need to know about their parents—if they're well and here and to give them peace of mind that we'll care for their daughters with all our love. My wife lost her parents and almost ended up on the Orphan Train. We knew we'd have to consider the possibility that if their folks could now care for them and wanted them back . . . "

Mr. Harris stared at Pa and almost imperceptibly shook his head. "As difficult as it was, they believed it was best for the girls. I think that remains true."

"Is Mr. Bickel, Walter, still in Harrisville? Wait. You're Mr. Harris. Is Harrisville named after you?"

Mr. Harris smiled. "My father. We bought the land from the Davissons." He chuckled. "This might have been Davisville. I was the first postmaster here. But I'm sorry to say, Walter left. He didn't tell me where or why he was going. Maybe just to find a job. After Alma passed, he was a broken man. His girls and his wife were gone. Too many memories. You know, in time, memories become precious, but right after loss, memories only hurt. He didn't give it time enough.

"He owned his little house over on Church Street, and he said he'd sell it to provide some funds to live on for a while. Before he sold, I would visit and sit with him often. I saw where he kept his money. I slipped some of my money in there. I didn't have any need. We'd heard some awful stories of what could happen to children on the Orphan Train. I've always wondered if perhaps he went to find the girls and make sure they were okay. He never said that, but I saw a determination and a sadness, a hopelessness and an anger in his eyes. Then one day, he just left. Shortly after, I found out he'd sold the house, and another family had moved in."

Addy tapped Pa's arm. "Can we go to the cemetery? I need to see the gravestone."

"Let's do that now." Pa stood. "Mr. Harris, you have been most helpful. I thank you. You have given us some answers and some hope. We thank you. If our friend, Arlo, returns, please inform him where we went."

Molly threw her arms around Mr. Harris's neck. "If Papa comes back here, will you tell him where we are and that we love our new ma and pa? Maybe he would come visit."

"I'm sure he would do that, Amolia. He loved you mightily. I'm so glad I got to find out that you are okay."

Addy walked over and shook Mr. Harris' hand. She mumbled, "Thank you." She hung her head and walked to the door and waited for Pa and Molly.

Mr. Harris took Pa's hand again. "They're good girls. I'm sure you know that. Would you be so kind as to occasionally send a letter and let me know how they are, what they're doing? If Walter ever returns, I can tell him. Even if I'm gone, my son will get the letters and pass them on if Walter is here. My name is Levi Harris. The town is Harrisville, Michigan. Wait, did you tell me where you are?"

"We live on Washington Island at the tip of the Door Peninsula in northeastern Wisconsin."

"My goodness. That's a distance. Did you come on the train?"

"No, I'm a ship captain. We came on my boat, the *Pearl*."

"I will pray for good seas on your return. But you should go to the cemetery now while the daylight is still good. It's just a mile out on the left in a little wooded area. She's on a hill near the back. Bless you. So glad I was here today."

"We are, too. Thank you again."

Pa and the girls walked, holding hands, up Main Street. After ascending a small hill, they found a few houses and then a countryside of woods, fields, farms, and a few hills. They spotted the tiny cemetery tucked into a patch of tall trees after about twenty minutes. Without a word, they walked down a grassy lane between gravestones.

"He said she was on a hill toward the back. You girls okay?"

Both nodded and started up the hill. Molly pointed. "Is that it?"

The gravestone was small, standing only a few inches off the ground, but the name stood out in large letters: "Alma Bickel, wonderful wife and mother, 1867-1897." Addy and Molly stood and stared. Molly threw herself on the ground and wept. Addy knelt and ran her fingers over the letters. She turned and looked up at Pa. "I love Ma—Mrs. Captain—but I miss this mama so much." Her voice broke, and she doubled over and sobbed. Pa knelt and rubbed the girl's back. Molly rose and embraced her new pa and continued to weep.

Soon, the weeping stopped. Pa tapped Molly's nose. "Tell me what you remember about your mother."

"She was pretty. She had long hair, and she would let me brush it. Sometimes, she would sing." Molly turned and sat leaning against Clifford and sighed. "She was a good mama. Is she in Heaven, do you think?"

Pa put his arm around her. "I'm sure she is, healthy and strong."

Addy's eyes pierced Pa's. "Why couldn't she be healthy and strong here? Why do we have to wait till Heaven? It doesn't seem fair. I mean, we're really happy with you, but why did Papa have to get injured? Why did Mama have to get sick and die?"

"I sure don't know, Addy. I wish I did. But what was that Bible verse she told you? 'For such a time as this'? We can grieve the past, but we must look and go forward and trust that God will comfort us and guide us. And I know these bad things aren't His plan, but He helps us through and brings us into good things."

Molly leaned against Clifford. "Like you and Ma—our new ma."

"Yes, we are so blessed that you came into our lives. And the only way we can live our lives to the fullest is to trust that right here, right now, He's with us and will take care of us and guide us into all His plans. I think if everyone did that, we'd see a lot more of His protection around those we love. I know that the reason I survived the shipwreck was because Lainey and others prayed for me."

"But why did you have the shipwreck at all, and why did your friend die and our papa get injured?" Addy's eyes pleaded for answers.

Pa sighed. "I don't know, Addy. I wish I had answers for you. I do know we face a lot of rough areas—hardship—in this life, but there's a verse in Isaiah that says when we pass through the waters, they won't overflow us. I guess we each just need to pray and trust. All God's promises in the Bible are for everyone. He tells us to not be afraid, and in Psalms, He says His angels protect us. Maybe we just need to believe it more."

Molly's eyes grew big. "Angels? Ooh. Ma had a picture of an angel. Are there lots of them?"

Pa tapped her nose. "I think everyone has an angel who's assigned to help them."

Addy shook her head. "But . . . "

Pa nodded. "I know, Addy; some things don't seem right. But we need to go."

The sun rose in brilliance with skies promising to shine blue, and the seas were calm as the small crew left on Clifford's boat the next morning. Molly and Addy stood gazing back at shore as the *Pearl* cruised out into Lake Michigan and then north. Arlo had preceded them to the boat, doublechecked the engine, obtained enough gasoline, and made sure the *Pearl* was travel-hardy so they could be on their way at daylight.

Pa observed the shoreline and the maps. "I have to make sure I avoid that shoal that extends out a mile-and-a-half just north of here."

"Is that where you went down?" Addy looked over her shoulder at him.

"We got past that one, but then the winds blew us into another one a little further north."

Molly turned. "I had a dream last night. There was an angel, just like in that picture Mama had."

Addy sighed. "I wish I had that picture."

Pa glanced back at the girls. "Maybe we can find a picture similar. I'm sure there are more."

Molly continued. "Mama was in the dream, too. She told me she was happy and healthy in Heaven."

Addy and Pa turned. "Really?"

Molly smiled. "She looked good, Addy. She was pretty again. She said that she was happy that we were with our new ma and pa. She told me to be happy and to tell you she was proud of how you took care of me."

Addy's eyes filled with tears. "She did?"

"And she said that God would always watch out for us, just like Pa told us yesterday at the cemetery. And she said He would give angels to help us, too."

Arlo stepped up. "Let me take the wheel here, Clifford. I think your girls need you right now."

Pa submitted the wheel to Arlo and sat down in the bow. Both girls piled on top of him. Addy cried, and Molly just leaned. Pa wrapped his arms around them. "That's good, Molly. That's good. It'll be okay, Addy. God is with us. His angels will help keep us safe." He sat silent with his girls for a few minutes.

When Addy's sobs subsided, he pulled his handkerchief out and wiped her eyes and cheeks. "Dear Lord, right now, we thank You for Your presence. We thank You for keeping us safe, for guiding us not only today but also throughout our lives. Please live strong in my girls here and in our little Emmy, too. And we ask that Your angels take care of Walter, wherever he is. Please give answers as You see fit concerning him. Thank you that we met Mr. Harris and learned so much. We trust You to lead us and Walter in ways that honor You."

Pa looked up. "That's Thunder Bay Island in the distance. Let me take the wheel, Arlo. I want to stay far away from any shoals that dwell in this lake. I'm going to follow that cargo ship there. They know these waters the best."

Molly pulled on Pa's arm. "Should we stop now and say thank you to the family who took care of you there?"

Pa chuckled. "That would be nice, but with these calm seas, I'm hoping we might be able to get home by this evening. Arlo was able to find enough fuel to keep us going without stopping."

"What about eating? Do we have enough food?"

Arlo grinned. "I purchased more than enough yesterday while you visited with Mr. Harris."

CHAPTER TWENTY-FIVE

A MAN ENTERED NEWPORT TOWN walking with a limp. No cane, just a limp. Otis barely noticed him as he sat on his porch having a cup of coffee before walking to the lumber company to work on the books. It was his daily routine. One he loved. Sure, sometimes he missed being the lighthouse keeper, but God had provided well for them. And they hadn't had to send Lainey to the Orphan Train. At times, he regretted giving her up to the Engelsons on Rock Island, but it had been best for Lainey. It was a happy family. Sure, he wished he saw more of her, and every time she spent time with them, he loved her more.

Edith still lived with a bit of guilt that she had suggested sending their niece to the Orphan Train, but thankfully, it hadn't happened. Edith was under so much stress and heartache at the time. She didn't know how they could survive financially; plus, she was still grieving the loss of their little Mandy—both she and Otis still grieved. Oh, it was less and less, but that loss was still resident in their hearts. It probably always would be.

But joy of joy, Lainey now had that little girl. She'd even given her the middle name of Mandy. Emma Mandy. She took a chance of surprising Edith with the name, hoping it didn't bring her more pain. Edith had wept and laughed. Such a surprise and what a blessing. And that little girl sure looked like Mandy. Holding her brought so much peace. They'd made more trips to Washington Island since she was born than they had in the whole last few years. Otis chuckled. Life was good.

The man limped past the house. Otis had been so lost in thought, he'd paid him little attention. But now, he studied him. The man looked full of grief that he tried to hide. Otis knew how that was. It took him a while to accept his fate of not being able to continue as a lightkeeper and walking with a cane. At least the emotional and physical pain were now gone, for the most part. Otis sensed the aloneness of the man. He'd faced that same demon in past years.

"Hello."

The man glanced Otis' way and nodded. He attempted a smile but kept his walk going.

"Please, come sit a bit. I have coffee. And we may still have some breakfast we can share."

His face was drawn. Pain, hunger, sadness? His salt-and-pepper hair needed a cut. His clothes looked like they might need a wash as well. "Thank you, sir. I'm okay."

Otis tucked his chin and peered at the man over his glasses. "Oh, I can see that. We're a friendly lot here and not too nosy. Come sit a bit."

The man paused. He turned and limped toward Otis. "Thank you, sir. Coffee and just a bit of breakfast would be most kind."

Otis stood and turned to call Edith. She was standing inside the screen door.

"I heard, Otis. I'll get the coffee and then heat up the bacon and cook a few more eggs. Won't take but a minute or two."

"Thank you, dear." Otis turned back as the man ascended the steps by placing one foot, then hauling up the other before going to the next step.

"I apologize for my gimpiness. I was injured quite a while back in a work accident."

Otis grinned and reached for his cane. "Same for me. How are you doing? You don't walk with a cane?"

"Well, I did have one; but somewhere on this journey, it was lost, perhaps stolen. But I'm managing."

"Such a coincidence, my friend. I have an extra one. My wife—"

Edith came through the door, coffee in one hand and a cane in the other. "We don't need this one, sir. We're happy to share our blessings. Please have a seat. Here's your coffee. Breakfast will be out in a few minutes."

The man's eyes welled up. "Thank you, ma'am. You're so kind." He gingerly sat in the chair next to Otis and took a sip of coffee. He then ran his hands over the cane. "This is a right fine piece of craftmanship. Are you certain you don't need it?"

"We don't need it at all. I think God planned it for you. By the way, I'm Otis, and my wife there is Edith."

"My name is Walter. I've come from . . . Well, I've come a long way." He looked away, then hung his head before meeting Otis' eyes.

Otis smiled. "No need to explain. Just know you're welcome. And you'll find most people here a friendly sort."

"Do you think there are any jobs to be found? I mean, for someone like me without full physical strength?"

Edith came out the door with a plate heaping with scrambled eggs, bacon, and biscuits slathered in butter.

"Oh my, ma'am, this is wonderful. Thank you so much. Could I work in your garden or scrub your porch or something to repay your kindness?"

"Oh no, you just sit and enjoy. Have a conversation with my husband. He loves to visit." She turned and smiled at Otis before returning to the house.

Walter took a bite and closed his eyes. "Oh, so good. You have a fine wife, Otis. I sure wish my Alma was still on this earth."

"I'm so sorry for your loss, Walter. Not sure what I'd do without Edith. We've had our share of rocky times, but the good Lord has brought us through."

"I wish I'd known how well the Lord can provide before I lost her. I think things would have been a lot different."

"Did you have children?"

Walter took a deep breath and looked away from Otis. Then he took a bite of bacon and sighed. "Yes, but they're gone now."

Otis reached out and placed his hand on Walter's shoulder. "I'm so sorry. We lost a little girl as well. There's no heartache as great as that, I don't think."

Walter stared at Otis. "Oh, I'm so sorry. I didn't mean to make you dwell on that. I mean, well, as far as I know, mine are . . . were . . . well . . ."

Otis tilted his head and squinted his eyes. "They—?"

Walter stood. "You know, I just really need to find a job. Do you think there is anything here?"

"Walter, please sit and finish your breakfast. I'm sorry. I won't pry. Don't worry. But if you're good with books, numbers, and accounting, there may be a spot in the lumber company where I work. We'll walk there together and see if they can use you."

Walter remained standing and staring at Otis. He sat back down and studied his hands. "Okay, I'll try that. Maybe this place will work. Nothing else has, and I'm almost out of money. Thank you again for your kindness." He picked up his plate and finished his breakfast. Once done, he retrieved his coffee cup and took a few sips.

Otis and Walter walked together to the lumber company, both assisting themselves with a cane. A slight breeze rose from the lake and blew gently across the men. The smells of horses, fresh wood, and fuel competed with the sweetness of the breeze.

"It's a fine cane, Otis. Perhaps if I can find a job, I can repay you its worth."

"That's not necessary. I can use only one at a time. I'm glad it can be put to good use. But here we are."

The lumber company occupied the largest clapboard building of Newport Town. Several people entered along with the two men. Otis greeted each one by name. "These are salesmen, supervisors, accountants, dock workers, steamer engineers, lumbermen, furniture-makers, and wagon drivers. The company employs or houses a great variety of workers. That's why I'm hopeful there'll be a spot for you."

Walter grinned. "That's encouraging. I like working with my hands. I wonder if furniture-makers would take me on. I could drive a wagon, but if I had to load and unload, that might be a problem with my limp."

"I apologize, but we have to go to the second floor. My leg no longer has pain, but I take a little longer on the stairs. Do you have pain?"

"On occasion, but I can do the stairs, slowly, as well."

Otis grabbed the railing and placed his good leg on the step. He then brought his cane and other leg up to join the first. He slowly ascended this way.

Walter followed in the same pattern and chuckled. "We make quite a pair. Hope no one else needs to get up right now."

"Oh, they wait or scoot around."

They rounded the corner at the top of the stairs. Several rooms with windows greeted them. Otis loved that he could look right through the offices to windows that looked out on Lake Michigan. It was almost as good as being on the gallery of the lighthouse. A stout man with thinning hair and big eyes strode out of the first office.

"Otis, good morning. Have you brought me another employee?" The man shook Otis' hand, then extended it to Walter.

"George, I may have. Allow me to introduce Walter, a new friend in need of a job. As you can see, he, like me, has a gimpy leg but has many other talents that you might find useful. Walter, this is George, the general supervisor for this whole operation."

The two men shook hands. "Tell me, Walter, how are you at working schedules? The man who's been keeping track of ships arriving and leaving, cargo for the ships, schedules of when wagons will arrive, when the shipments will arrive at the necessary destination, and when and where the deliveries are to go has a family emergency in Green Bay. We need someone right now. He's here until this afternoon and can walk someone through the procedures. Walter, could you fill in? He will probably return, but it would be yours for a few weeks. Maybe by then, there will be another opening."

Walter gulped. "I . . . I have a sharp mind. I have not done this before, but would love to learn. I do learn quickly. I've worked in a variety of jobs."

"Congratulations, Walter. You are here at the right time. Follow me. Thanks, Otis. Have a good day."

The sun slid slowly on the horizon into the depths of the water. The last of the oranges and purples lingered on the clouds. Addy smiled up at Pa. "You timed that good, Pa. You sure are a good captain." She jumped out onto the dock and secured the lines. "My legs feel wobbly. Why is that?"

Pa set the bags on the dock and lifted Molly out of the boat. "You haven't gotten your land legs yet; you're still walking with sea legs."

Molly took a step and staggered. She giggled. "Oh, this is funny. Are you and Arlo going to wobble, too?"

"I think so." Pa stepped off the boat and walked lopsided. He grabbed Molly and swung her side to side. Molly's squeals filled the air; and soon, Arlo's children, Sarah, and Ma, carrying Emmy, were running across the yard.

"Pa, you're back!"

Arlo scooted around Pa and Molly and scooped his children in his arms. "Yes, we are." He reached his arm out to Sarah and drew her in for a hug.

Ma stood with a big smile on her face. Pa released Molly, who ran and threw her arms around Ma's waist. "We missed you, Ma." She turned. "Right, Addy?"

Addy hung back with her head down. Pa turned and went back and took Addy's hand. He bent down and whispered in her ear. "'For such a time as this,' Addy. God knows where your first papa is, and one day, we'll find him. Don't you worry. Be all God made you to be in 'such a time as this.'"

Addy nodded and wiped a tear from her eye. She walked, hand-in-hand, with Pa toward the resort. Arlo and his family had already gone inside. When Addy reached Ma, she looked up. Ma had a sweet expression on her face. Emmy put her arms out. Addy grinned and took Emmy in her arms. "I missed you, Emmy, and you, Ma. We didn't find . . . Well, we found Mama's gravestone, and Papa left. No one knows where he went."

Ma laid her hand on Addy's shoulder. "God knows where he is, Addy, and will help you find him."

Addy took a deep breath. "That's what Pa said, too."

"Are you hungry?"

Addy grinned. "Starved."

"Well, let's get something to eat. I'm so glad you made it home safely."

Molly grabbed Ma's hand. "And Mama told me in a dream that she's happy we're with you and that God has angels to help us."

Ma bent down, so she could face Molly. "What a wonderful dream, Molly. I believe it."

Molly widened her eyes. "And we went by that Thunder Island, where Pa went down. And did you know, that's the same time our first papa got hurt?"

Ma looked back at Clifford.

He nodded. "I told them."

Addy turned. "It's okay, Ma. I mean, it was hard, but it's okay. We're going to trust God now."

School wrapped up in the two weeks after the return from Michigan. Miss Rose returned those two weeks and helped with the final exams. During the final week, the students threw a party to welcome Miss Rose back and thank Miss Genevieve for all her good work. Miss Genevieve informed them at that time that she'd been hired by Appleport School near Sister Bay on the mainland to teach the following year.

"Miss Genevieve?" Addy stood near the door to the school.

"Yes, Addy? Why aren't you out playing or racing with the rest of the students? You're my outdoor girl."

Addy smiled. "I like being your outdoor girl. But I wanted to thank you."

Miss Genevieve placed a hand on Addy's shoulder. "Well, I enjoyed teaching you, Addy. You really are a good student and a very smart girl."

Addy pressed her lips together and tipped her head. "The reason for that is you, Miss Genevieve. I mean, I love Miss Rose—and she's my ma's best friend. But you made me a good student. I didn't really want to go to school. It's always been a little boring for me. But you helped me really learn in a way that I enjoyed. I'm going to miss you."

Miss Genevieve hugged Addy. "I will miss you, as well. But you don't need me to continue enjoying your education. Miss Rose is going to include a lot more outdoor and hands-on science learning. She's taken notes on that aspect of my teaching, and I've taken notes on the many wonderful methods she has. You are going to be fine."

"Thank you."

"Did you find your parents, Addy?"

"No. I mean, well, my mama died, and we saw her gravesite. And my papa left town after she died, and no one knows where he went."

"Oh, Addy, I'm so sorry."

Addy looked up and allowed a slight smile to spread across her face. "But I think maybe I've actually found my parents—the Ruckerts. I think I'm realizing this was meant to be. I may always miss my first parents. Ma—this ma—says I will. That's because she lost her parents at the same age as me. She got new parents and was and is very happy but says she still misses her first parents. So, she's the right one to be my ma now, and, well, this pa. Well, he's the best."

"Addy, I know your birthday is in a few days. You'll be thirteen. You are a wise young woman, and I know you will do great things in your life. I'll be back to visit now and then. If you're on the mainland, I hope you'll visit me."

Addy grinned. "I'll try. Thank you." She felt a blurriness in her eyes and knew she might cry. And the heat crept up her neck. Her face would soon be red. She turned and ran to join the other girls in the races and wiped her eyes with the back of her hand as she ran.

It surprised Addy that she was actually a little sad on the last day of school. That had never happened before. Molly hugged all her friends and skipped most of the way home, relating her favorite experiences of the school year to Addy. Addy nodded and laughed at her stories. She knew Miss Genevieve would be the one she'd miss the most. But now, she could help Ma with Emmy and the resort, and Pa promised she could help him on the *Pearl*. Summer would be good. She shook off the melancholy and skipped with Molly.

As much as Addy enjoyed her friends and the Otter gatherings, she chose to simply have cake the night before her birthday with Ma and Pa, Emmy, and Molly and then watch the sunset. She felt a need to soak in this family and appreciate them. Plus, she wanted to help Pa go get the guests the next day. She also knew the summer season created a lot of necessary work for the islanders. She didn't need a big party. There would be an Otter gathering in late June, and all the islanders would have games and a parade and fireworks on the Fourth of July.

So many things now made her content. It was a new feeling. Maybe she'd come to terms with the loss of her first parents. Mama was gone. She still grieved, but all along Addy had sensed deep inside that her mama had died. She didn't know how; she just knew. Maybe her mama somehow told her that. That must be it. Her mama knew, and so did Addy. Her missing papa was another matter. Maybe he found another wife and had a child now. Ouch. Addy pulled her shoulders up. Why did that make her cringe? It didn't seem right. It actually hurt a little. But why wouldn't he marry again? It probably would be a good thing. She didn't want him alone. Would she ever know? *God, I think I'd like to know.*

On their way to get the resort guests, Addy shared her thoughts with Pa. "What do you think, Pa?"

"Addy, I think you're growing up. Part of me wants you to be a little girl, so I can be a good pa; but I love who you are, and I think you will be and are a lovely, young woman."

Addy grinned and felt some heat in her face. She leaned against Pa. He put his arm around her, and they enjoyed the ripples of the blue water reflecting the clear, blue sky. To their left stood the rocky bluffs of the mainland interspersed with sandy coves and villages. She could hear the slight whoosh of the waves as they kissed the shoreline. Addy knew she could never move far from the water. Being on the water was who she was, and it was where she needed to be.

This group of guests stayed only a few days, and the next group was not scheduled until two days later.

After dinner the last day of the guests' visit, Pa turned to Ma. "Lainey, come with Addy and me on this return trip. Bring Emmy and Molly, and we'll swing around to Newport Town on the way back from Ephraim. It will be the longest day of the year." He paused and planted a kiss on Ma's forehead. "It's also our anniversary."

Molly clapped her hands. "Anniversary? How long have you been married?"

Pa winked. "Well, let's see, it's more than three, but it goes so fast. Let me think." He held his chin in his hand and stared off in space, appearing to try to remember.

Ma swatted his arm. "You know how long. It's been five years."

Pa jumped backward. "That's right. Five years. How could I forget?"

Molly put her hands on her hips. "Ma, I think he's teasing. He winked at me."

Pa held up a finger to his mouth. "Shh, Molly, don't tell."

Ma laughed. "He's quite a teaser, isn't he? But I think that would be a wonderful idea. And, we'll still have a day to get ready for the next set of guests."

CHAPTER TWENTY-SIX

"WHAT A NICE STRETCH OF weather we've had." Ma turned to the girls. "June is sometimes cool and rainy; but this year, it's so pleasantly warm with not too much rain." Ma held Emmy on her hip and rocked back and forth with one hand on the rail. A slight breeze sent her hair into her face. She just shook her head to get it out. Emmy giggled as Ma's hair tickled her face.

"The water's been great." Pa shifted from the wheel to glance over the side. "And look how clear it is on a day like this."

Addy and Molly leaned over the rail and oohed and aahed as fish passed below the boat. Molly turned and tugged his sleeve. "Pa, could we go fishing sometime? I'd like to try that."

"That's a great idea, Molly. We'll plan on it. Okay, there's Newport Town. I hope Uncle Otis and Aunt Edith are home and don't mind us dropping in."

"It is early for him to be off work; but Aunt Edith is probably home, and we'll still have enough daylight to get home even if we see him only after work."

Pa brought the boat alongside the dock, and Addy secured the lines. She held out her hand to help Ma. Ma handed Emmy to Molly and climbed off. She turned and took Emmy, and then Pa lifted Molly to the dock and joined his girls. As they neared the end of the dock, Addy stopped. Molly bumped into her.

Molly crossed her arms. "Addy, you need to keep going."

Addy didn't move or look around. "Shhh. Molly, look."

Molly stood next to her sister. "What?"

Addy grabbed her hand. "Look, Sissy. Look at that man."

A man had walked out of the building that was the main hub of the dock. He walked away from them. He had a cane and a limp.

Addy gulped. "Molly, do you see him?"

Molly nodded. "Addy, is it . . . "

"I . . . I, uh . . . I don't know, but he looks like . . . "

Molly whispered. "He does, Addy. He does."

The man paused. Had he heard them? Did he have a sense? He turned slowly.

Addy caught her breath. Would it be? It couldn't be, could it? His turn took an eternity.

Addy stared. He stared. He studied Addy. Then Molly. His hand went over his mouth. His shoulders slumped. "Addy? Molly?"

Addy covered her mouth with her hands. "Papa? Is it you?"

Molly blubbered. "It is, Addy. It is!"

They ran, almost blinded by the tears that coursed down their cheeks. The man let go of the cane, fell to his knees, and spread his arms. Addy and Molly ran into those arms. The only sounds were sobs and deep, exhaling sighs.

"I can't believe it. I'd almost given up finding you." The man shook his head and hugged the girls.

Molly touched his face. "We went looking for you. All the way to Harrisville. We saw Mama's grave."

"You what? How did you get to Harrisville? I've been looking for you ever since your mama passed."

Addy straightened and wiped her face with the back of her hand. "Pa took us. Well, our new . . . Well, he took us in." She looked back at Pa and Ma. "Umm, we've been calling him Pa. I hope that's okay. But he took us in his boat to help us find you. Wait, you've been looking for us?"

Her first papa smiled. He grasped his cane and stood. He wrapped an arm around Addy and turned to Pa. "I owe you a great debt of gratitude. I've been searching for months and had given up. Thank you for taking them in. They look wonderful and well cared for." He freed his arm from Addy and extended his hand to Pa. He nodded to Ma. "Ma'am, thank you as well."

He looked Pa in the eyes. "But, sir . . . "

"Clifford Ruckert."

"Mr. Ruckert, I'm Walter Bickel. How did you happen to go to Harrisville?"

"I'm a boat captain. I run a ferry from Ephraim to Washington Island to our resort. We—my wife Lainey and I—wanted the girls to have answers, so we traveled by boat to look for you. I'm so sorry for the loss of your wife."

Ma smiled. "I see the resemblance. Addy has your eyes. I think it's your smile that Molly has."

Mr. Bickel touched Molly's head. "My wife and I always thought that. You are very perceptive. I'm blessed to know they found their way to you. I feared so much that they may have ended up in dire circumstances."

Addy turned to him. "Papa, some kids do have bad families, but we have gatherings now to help all the Otters. That's what we call all the kids who came on the Orphan Train, and the adults talk to the families who might be hurting the kids. And it's really helped. But how did you get here?"

"I walked a lot. Some people gave me a ride. I took the train a few times. When I got to Milwaukee, I heard a steamer came up this way with Orphan Tr—What did you call them? Otters? And along the way, I've just gotten what little work I could with this gimpy leg."

Addy looked back at Pa. He closed his eyes.

Her first papa continued. "And then I just kept traveling and asking. No one seemed to know, or they sent me where I didn't find you. I limped into town here a few weeks ago; and I met a man who also had a limp, and he got me a job."

Molly took his hand and looked up into his face. "Was it Uncle Otis? He has a limp."

"Well, his name is Otis. I was going to walk over there now. He got off work early and invited me to visit and have dinner. His wife is very gracious and a good cook."

Molly grinned. "That's Auntie Edith."

Ma stepped forward. "Mr. Bickel, we are on our way there as well. They are my aunt and uncle. I lived with them when my parents passed."

Mr. Bickel nodded. "Then you have an inherent understanding of what my girls have been through."

"I do. However, I can't imagine what you have been through. Perhaps we can talk about all of this with Uncle Otis and Aunt Edith. Did they know you were looking for the girls?"

"No. I didn't tell them. It was beginning to seem hopeless, so I was just working on what I needed to do."

Uncle Otis stepped out on the porch as his family approached. "What a surprise. And a pleasant one at that. Edith and I were just mentioning that this is your anniversary, the longest day of the year." He chuckled, then tipped his head. "I see you've met our new friend Walter." Uncle Otis squinted. "But what am I missing here? Do you already know Wal—" He took a deep breath. "Are you? Is he? Have we found your father?" Uncle Otis sat down on the wicker chair with a thump. "Well, I'll be."

Walter hesitated. "Yes, Otis. I'm their father, and you, their uncle. I do believe I may be causing more problems with my presence, and if you'd rather . . . "

Pa clapped Walter on the shoulder. "No, this is good. Come up and sit. Catch up with your girls."

For some reason, Pa looked a little pale. Addy hoped he wasn't getting sick. She remembered the paleness her first mama had when she took ill. But maybe it was the surprise of finding their father. It was the reason they went to Harrisville, but so unexpected here. Pa and Ma with Emmy went inside, and Addy could hear them talking with Aunt Edith but couldn't decipher the words.

Papa! Her first pa. She didn't know whether to laugh or cry. Molly already sat on his lap. Papa looked pretty good. He had that same expression that her new pa had. Pale. Unsure. Whatever would she call them? She had two fathers! It was confusing. Papa looked at her, and she went close so he could wrap an arm around her. Familiar scents that she couldn't quite describe caused memories to float through her mind of happy times with her parents, and a rope tightened around her heart. She was still tied to this man. What would they do?

Molly spoke what Addy pondered. "Papa, will you take us away? Did you come to get us?"

Addy looked up. Aunt Edith stood with the door partway open, and Ma with Emmy on her hip and Pa right behind her. All had wide eyes and pressed lips. Even Uncle Otis.

"Perhaps tea and cookies while we talk—or before we talk." Aunt Edith set a plate of cookies on the table and poured tea for everyone. A strange smile sat on her face, and her head twitched a little. Ma, Pa, and Aunt Edith sat down. A tenseness seemed to settle on everyone. It was like the first day of school when everyone had to be on their best behavior but didn't really know what to do. Except Molly.

"You know what, Papa? When you got hurt, it was the same time as our new pa was in a boat wreck."

Uncle Otis sputtered his tea. "Excuse me. Wrong pipe. Molly, maybe we should wait on that story."

Pa stood. "No, Walter should know." Pa's stern face made Addy's stomach do a flip. She looked up at him with her eyebrows raised. His face softened, and he sat down. "Walter, as I said, I'm a boat captain; and on my first voyage on Lake Huron, as a first mate, our boat struck a shoal in a gale. We were just north of Harrisville."

Addy's father set his cup down and shook his head. "You were on the *Horowitz*? I helped rescue the crew. I'm so sorry you lost your captain." He scratched his head. "But I don't remember you. Oh, wait, were you the man who was lost and then later washed up on Thunder Bay Island?"

"That was me."

"What a coincidence. And now you have my girls."

"Walter." Pa closed his eyes for a moment. "I understand it was in your attempt to rescue my boat and me and my crew that you were injured."

"Well, yes, but . . . " His eyes held Pa's. "Clifford, that is not your fault. Life has many ups and downs. The wreck wasn't your fault. My injury wasn't your fault, either."

Pa rubbed the back of his neck. "However, had we not wrecked, you would not have been injured. You lost your job, which may have contributed to your wife's illness, and then you lost your girls. I'm so sorry."

Pa sat with his head in his hands. Addy's father set Molly on her feet and pushed on the arms of the chair in order to stand. He took a step to Pa and touched his shoulder. "Clifford, I have no animus toward you or to the circumstances. I've found that a life of forgiveness is better than a life of regret, so even though I cast no blame on you, I forgive you. I'm just delighted to find the girls. And without any jealousy, I think you've given them a better life than I could."

Addy looked around. There were tears dripping down everyone's cheeks.

Her father sat back down, and Molly climbed back in his lap. "So, Papa, what are you going to do now? Do you want to live with us? We have a really nice place on Washington Island. It's a resort, so there's lots of room. That would be okay, wouldn't it, Ma? Or are you going to keep working with Uncle Otis? You'd still be close. How would that be? Would we move here?" She scrunched her face and looked up and waved her hands. "What do you think?"

Aunt Edith stood up. "Maybe some more tea. I should get dinner started. Otis, could you help me?"

Ma shifted Emmy on her lap. "Aunt Edith, wait. Perhaps we should all discuss this." She reached over and took her husband's hand. "We do have room at the resort, and, Walter, you are most welcome."

Pa smiled. "That's true, Walter; you are truly welcome. But you're working here, so maybe . . . "

Addy's father interrupted. "This job here is temporary, as all my recent jobs have been. So, I'll soon have no means to support myself, let alone the girls. It is perhaps enough that I've found them and that I know they're in good hands."

Addy gulped. "No. You can't leave. We just found you. We looked and looked, and now you're here." She turned to Pa. "You can give him a job, can't you?" Tears coursed down her face, and she ran down the porch steps and around to the barn. She buried her face in Fresnel's neck. The horse nickered and laid his head on her shoulder. She paused and grabbed a carrot from a pail outside his stall. "Here you go, boy. Let me get one for Pilot, too."

Both horses gobbled the carrots, then looked at Addy. She went inside Fresnel's stall and grabbed a brush to rub him down. The rubbing motion soothed her insides, but the tears still flowed. "Fresnel, I have two pas now, and I can't choose. I want both of them. I don't know what to do. For a while, Molly and I had no one; and now, we have two. And we have a new ma. She's the best, Fresnel." Addy took a deep breath and leaned her head against the horse.

"Addy?"

Aunt Edith and Molly stood in the doorway. "May we come in?"

Addy sniffed and nodded. Aunt Edith handed her a handkerchief. After blowing her nose, Addy leaned on the stall gate. "Is he just going to leave, Aunt Edith? We just found him. Are Pa and Ma okay? Do they think we don't love them anymore?"

Aunt Edith cupped Addy's chin. "I don't know all the answers, Addy. You are blessed to find him, but it may take a few days to sort out all the plans. But I think you can be sure that you aren't going to lose anyone."

"You really think that?"

"You know, when we let Lainey, your new ma, go to be the Engelson's daughter, it broke our hearts, but it was the best thing for her. She thrived on Rock Island. And we still got to see her—maybe not as often as we liked—but she is still, and always will be, our niece, and we'll always be close."

Molly pulled on Aunt Edith's hand. "And, Auntie Edith, you lost a daughter, too."

She pressed her lips together, then smiled. "We did. Loss hurts, but God helps us heal."

Addy opened the gate and stepped out. "So, what should we do?"

"Let's go in the back door, and you girls can help me with dinner, while your folks and Uncle Otis discuss it all."

Clifford sat with his elbows on his knees and his chin in his hands. "Walter, if you'd like, we can find work for you on the Island."

"I can't do much with this gimpy leg of mine. I would be a burden."

Lainey smiled. "Can you do dishes? Can you start a campfire? Can you help your girls with homework?"

Clifford held up a hand. "Now wait, I might be able to use him on the boat. Did you know Addy is a natural on the water? She can even steer the boat. I'm hoping to teach her how to dock the boat this summer. She's amazing, and I would guess she inherited that from you."

Otis grinned. "Walter is good at scheduling. That's been his job here. He organized the shipments and drivers and just about everything over at the dock. Wouldn't that help with the resort and the ferry?"

Clifford stood. "Well, I think it's settled. We sure could use help with that. Not sure we can pay as much as they did here, but you'd have a room and all the food you want. And your girls would have their father close."

Walter chewed his bottom lip and looked to the side. "Well, for a while."

Clifford tilted his head. "What do you mean? You'd come for only a while? Listen, I love the girls fiercely, but you—"

"No, that's not it." Walter shook his head.

Otis leaned forward and placed his hand on Walter's arm. "What is it, then?"

"I'm not well. I spit up blood a couple times after my wife died. Thought maybe I had a bad tooth, so I went to see the doc." Walter looked around.

Otis smiled. "The girls are inside with Edith. She'll keep them busy. Please continue."

"Well, it wasn't a tooth." He met Clifford's gaze. "And it wasn't a result of my injury. Doc said it was probably in me a long time. It's some disease that's easy to miss and doesn't get bad till there's not much you can do. Different than my wife. Hers was pretty fast." He hung his head. His voice wobbled. "So, anyway, I don't have a lot of time. When I found that out, I decided I might as well go look for the girls, make sure they were okay. If they weren't, I don't know what I'd do; but just seeing them for this short while, I know that God provided well for them. I'm so thankful."

Lainey sighed. "I'm so sorry to hear this. But you can't leave. Please come and have what time there is with your girls. And maybe there's a remedy. We have a doctor on the island, and there are more here on the mainland. And then Mrs. Figgenschau can heal just about anything with her herbs."

Walter looked up and grinned. "Mrs. Who?"

"Figgenschau. A dear friend. Addy and Molly have become very close to her."

"I don't think there's a remedy for this. It would be nice to be with the girls, but would it be harder in the long run? And if I get too sick . . . Well, as I said, I don't want to be a burden. Maybe I shouldn't have come."

Clifford shook his head. "No, they longed to know, and we're all glad to have found you. You know, they sat at your wife's grave and told stories about her. And they grieved. Grieving is hard work, but it helps one move on. Now they've found you. And they need you for as long as you're here."

Walter's gaze went from one to the other. "Should I tell them of my illness?"

Otis stood up. "I think not now. In time. Let's rejoice in this reunion. When does your job here end?"

"Actually, it ended today. The man returned a week early, so they paid me and let me go today."

Clifford clapped Walter's shoulder. "Then you'll return with us to the island after dinner. So, let's celebrate this reunion." He turned and embraced Lainey. "And let's celebrate our anniversary with this wonderful family."

CHAPTER TWENTY-SEVEN

AND SO, ADDY AND HER family returned to Washington Island. She continued to call her new father Pa and her first father, Papa. Molly agreed, and soon life took on a wonderful routine. Pa occasionally brought Papa with him on the boat, but mostly, he enjoyed working around the resort. He helped fix broken boards, paint the cottages, schedule guests, do dishes, and take little walks with Molly. He and Addy often sat together to watch the sunset. Every time, he would say, "You know, Addy, my favorite color is sunset."

Addy loved telling him all her activities, concerns, and dreams. Life felt full. Her favorite times were the sunsets with Papa and the times with Pa on the boat. She told him the same things she told Papa, and it satisfied something deep within.

Papa joined them in the Otter gatherings. He shared with some of the Otter families his experience in sending the girls to the Orphan Train. He impressed upon them that these were not unwanted children who didn't deserve good care but that they were loved and let go because of circumstances beyond the parents' control. He surprised them all when he offered to pitch the ballgame one time. He leaned on his cane with one hand and threw with the other. The kids loved it and clamored for him to pitch every time.

When the winter winds started, Papa offered to drive the wagon to and from school. It became another special time with the girls.

Around Thanksgiving, he took the girls aside and explained the situation of his illness to them. Molly cried, and Addy pleaded.

"But, Papa, have you seen a doctor? Doctors can help. And Mrs. Figgenschau has all her remedies that can cure anything."

Papa reached out and grabbed Addy's hand. "I've been to the doctor here, and Mrs. Figgenschau has given me her concoctions. They've helped immensely, but this is advancing. I can feel it."

Addy pulled her hand away. "You should've told us. You knew all this time."

Papa hung his head. "I thought about it, and I didn't want anything to darken our time together. I've also spent some time with Pastor Gunnlerson, and I've made my peace with God. I know I'll join your mama in Heaven. That should be a comfort to you."

"Papa!" Molly threw herself across his lap and sobbed.

He rubbed her back. "Girls, I love you. I always have. And if I can love you from Heaven, I will. But this time has meant so much to me. And Clifford and Lainey are the perfect parents for you. I won't ever have to worry about you."

Addy rested her head in her hands and rocked it back and forth. Tears dripped on her lap, and she didn't try to stop them. "I love you, too, Papa. I don't want you to leave."

"I don't want to either." He kept squeezing his eyes shut and opening them again. "But I'll always be in your hearts."

The days moved slowly after the revelation of Papa's illness. The skies were grayer, and the once-sparkling snow seemed to have no sparkle. Even Emmy's laugh and toddling ways didn't cheer Addy. Molly didn't say much. Instead, she hugged and held everyone close.

Addy, on the other hand, went from sadness to anger. Still, she knew that somehow, she'd come through it. Ma was her rock. She'd already lost her parents. Ma didn't press or scold, but she'd sit with Addy and hold her hand. She'd listen, and she'd pray. Addy wanted to be angry at God, but she knew He was the one who would get her through.

Around Christmas, she felt the anger seep away, and deep settledness arrive. She told Papa about it, and he took her in his arms. He felt weaker. His arms were not as strong, and his face seemed shrunken in. Still, she felt his love.

Uncle Otis and Aunt Edith came for Christmas. The ice had hardened early, so they came on their sleigh. They sat with Papa alone for a while. Addy wondered if they were saying goodbye. Both Aunt Edith and Uncle Otis had tears in their eyes.

After Christmas dinner, they played board games and ate pie. They told stories of past Christmases and watched Emmy run from one to the other. Ma had made a soap solution so that they could blow bubbles. Emmy chased them and squealed at every bubble she saw. Her giggles brought laughter from everyone.

Papa cleared his throat. "I have a gift for each of my girls." He glanced around. "I wish I had one for each of you, as you have all been so marvelous to me."

Ma shook her head. "You have given us the gift of your presence, and we are so thankful for that."

A tear tracked down Papa's cheek, and he swiped at it with the back of his hand. He held out two packages wrapped in brown paper to the girls. Addy smiled and tore the paper off. There was her mother's Bible. "Oh, Papa, this is the best gift ever—except for you." She stood and threw her arms around his neck. "Thank you, Papa. I love you."

Molly took her time removing the wrapping on her gift. When she looked at it, she began to sob. "It's . . . it's . . . what I wanted . . . so much." She held it up. It was a small painting of an angel standing guard over children. "It was Mama's, and I . . . I . . . needed it. Thank you, Papa." She, too, hugged him and cried.

The next morning, Addy walked in to check on her papa. He lay so still. Too still. She found it hard to breathe. Hard to put one foot in front of the other. But she did. She knew. She sat on the bed and took his hand. It was still warm. He must've just left. He would be greeting Mama now. Tears rolled down her cheeks and dripped onto her papa's hand. The sun peeked through the curtains. She found thankfulness welling up in her. She didn't quite understand. But she and Molly would survive. They had found their papa. Well, he had found them. They saw Mama's gravesite. They had time with Papa. They had parents now who would care for them, who already loved them totally. Life would be okay. No, it would be good, really good. And Papa would always be in their hearts and their memories.

Addy chose to celebrate rather than grieve her papa's life at the funeral. Amazed that she wasn't as sad as she expected, she shared a few stories of life with her papa. Molly sang a song. Only recently had they discovered what a beautiful voice she had. Despite the snow and cold, they managed to dig a grave in the small cemetery near the church. Uncle Otis and Aunt Edith had remained so they could attend. Ma's parents had only the week before closed up the lighthouse on Rock Island. So they, and all the Hansons were there, as well as Arlo and Sarah and their children.

Thankfulness for their presence filled Addy. She stood at the gravesite, shivering in the cold, after everyone returned to the church for a meal.

"Goodbye, Papa. I'm so glad you're here. I can visit this place often. Thank you for finding us. And don't worry. I think we'll be fine. And you know, I will always watch over Molly. Always."

Addy felt an arm around her shoulders. She startled and looked up. Carter wrapped both arms around her, and she buried her face in his chest. She wept and wept. When she pulled back, her eyes stung from the tears. "Oh, Carter, I've gotten your coat all wet and slobbery."

He grinned and pulled out a handkerchief for her. "It's okay, Addy. I hope you don't mind, but I heard what you said to him. And I know you'll always watch out for Molly." He took her hand. "And I want you to know, I'll always look out for you."

This time, the tingle that went down her back was warm. "I know you will, Carter."

The two walked back to the church, hand-in-hand.

The End

For more information about

Judy DuCharme
and
Addy of the Door Islands
please visit:

www.judithducharme.com
www.facebook.com/judy.ducharme.18
@packerjudy

For more information about
AMBASSADOR INTERNATIONAL
please visit:

www.ambassador-international.com
@AmbassadorIntl
www.facebook.com/AmbassadorIntl

If you enjoyed this book, please consider leaving us a review on
Amazon, Goodreads, or our website.

More from Judy DuCharme and Ambassador International

Tassie, named for a lost religious relic, has her sights set on her career and love, and she doesn't have time for silly children's stories. Dismissing the blood moons as circumstance, her unbelief threatens to keep her from her destiny. When Tassie finds herself in the center of worldwide turmoil and a terrorist plot, can she accept her family history and fulfill her place in the future of Israel? Or will the country of her heritage finally fall to its many enemies?

For Lainey, life on Pilot Island is more trouble than it's worth. Auntie Edith is always fussing at her, and Uncle Otis spends his time manning the lighthouse. Each day, Lainey stares out at the Great Lakes, praying this will be the day that brings her parents home to her from their travels. Will she ever come to love the islands and its treacherous waters, which seem to only bring a lot of shipwrecks and heartache? Will she ever be able to go home?

I Want a Water Buffalo for Christmas tells the journey of LeGory, a young water buffalo, who brings life to a family in dire need. Several circumstances fall into place to create the life-giving wonder of providing for those less fortunate.